KILLER
WEEKEND

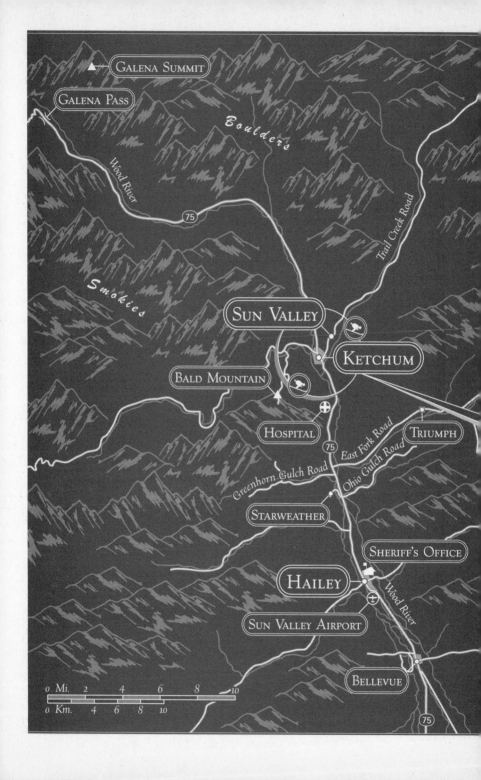

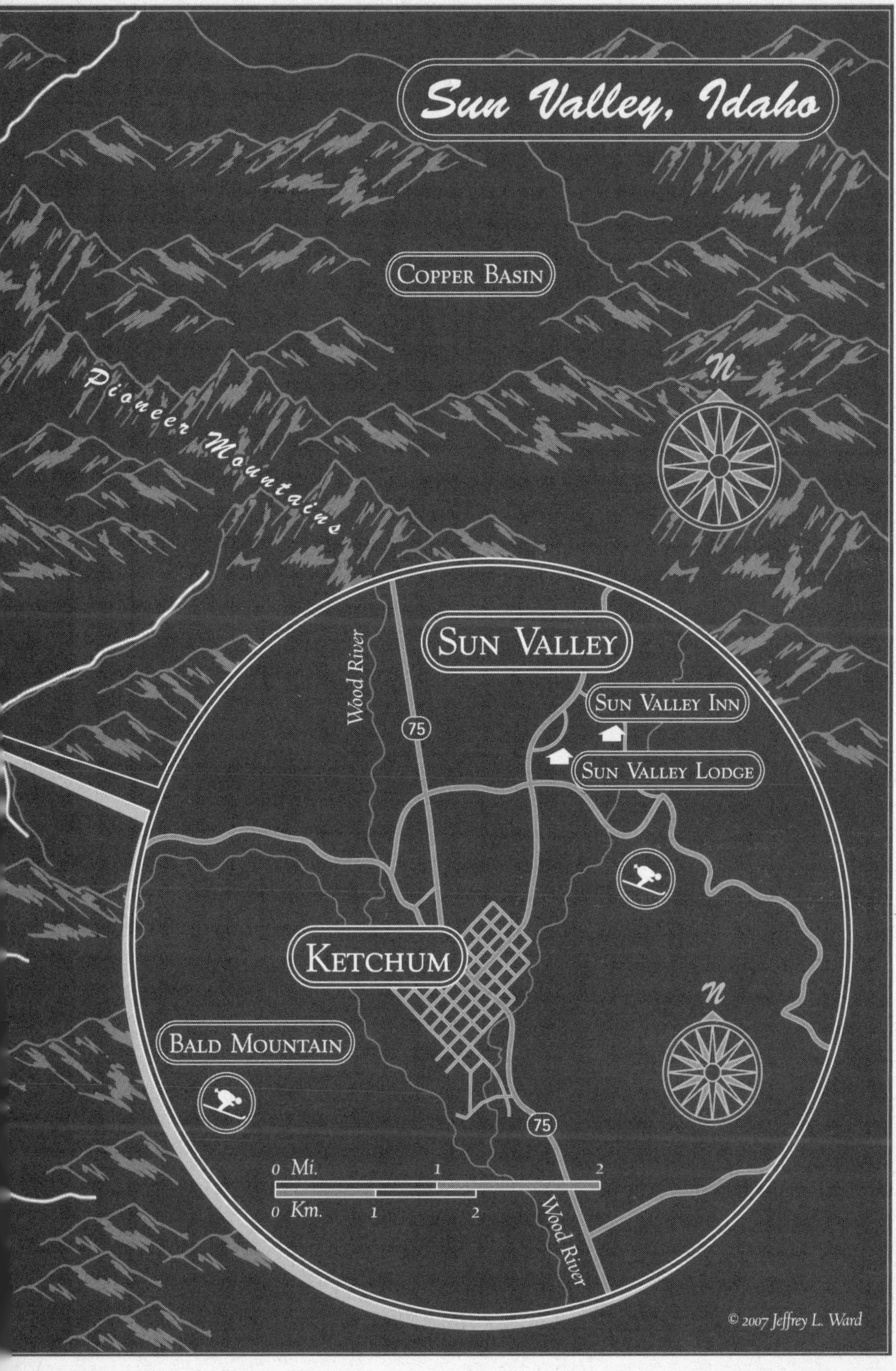

Sun Valley, Idaho
Copper Basin
Pioneer Mountains
N
Sun Valley
Wood River
75
Sun Valley Inn
Sun Valley Lodge
Ketchum
Bald Mountain
N
75
0 Mi. 1 2
0 Km. 1 2
Wood River
© 2007 Jeffrey L. Ward

OTHER BOOKS
BY RIDLEY PEARSON

Peter and the Shadow Thieves
(with Dave Barry)

The Kingdom Keepers

Cut and Run

The Body of David Hayes

Peter and the Starcatchers
(with Dave Barry)

The Art of Deception

The Diary of Ellen Rimbauer
(writing as Joyce Reardon)

Beyond Recognition

Probable Cause

KILLER
WEEK

END

Ridley Pearson

DOUBLEDAY LARGE PRINT HOME LIBRARY EDITION

G. P. PUTNAM'S SONS   NEW YORK

This Large Print Edition, prepared especially for Doubleday Large Print Home Library, contains the complete, unabridged text of the original Publisher's Edition.

G. P. PUTNAM'S SONS
Publishers Since 1838
Published by the Penguin Group
Penguin Group (USA) Inc., 375 Hudson Street, New York, New York 10014, USA • Penguin Group (Canada), 90 Eglinton Avenue East, Suite 700, Toronto, Ontario M4P 2Y3, Canada (a division of Pearson Penguin Canada Inc.) • Penguin Books Ltd, 80 Strand, London WC2R 0RL, England • Penguin Ireland, 25 St Stephen's Green, Dublin 2, Ireland (a division of Penguin Books Ltd) • Penguin Group (Australia), 250 Camberwell Road, Camberwell, Victoria 3124, Australia (a division of Pearson Australia Group Pty Ltd) • Penguin Books India Pvt Ltd, 11 Community Centre, Panchsheel Park, New Delhi–110 017, India • Penguin Group (NZ), 67 Apollo Drive, Mairangi Bay, Auckland 1311, New Zealand (a division of Pearson New Zealand Ltd) • Penguin Books (South Africa) (Pty) Ltd, 24 Sturdee Avenue, Rosebank, Johannesburg 2196, South Africa

Penguin Books Ltd, Registered Offices:
80 Strand, London WC2R 0RL, England

Published simultaneously in Canada

ISBN 978-0-7394-8637-5

Printed in the United States of America

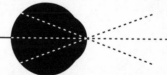

This Large Print Book carries the
Seal of Approval of N.A.V.H.

For Marcelle

(and our love of Idaho)

PROLOGUE

As she stood in her small closet undressing for bed, Elizabeth Shaler was annoyed to find some mud left behind by a running shoe that she now put away. About the size of a dollar bill, the mud covered the carpet and spanned the crack of the trapdoor that led down into the three-foot-high crawl space beneath the house. Liz pulled on a cool cotton nightgown. At her feet, cracks appeared in the mud, then widened and spread. These cracks had nothing to do with where she stood, but were instead the result of upward pressure from beneath the trapdoor.

Liz, just shy of six feet tall and athletically fit, placed her dirty laundry into the wicker hamper and tidied up. Her hanging clothes were organized by color and type, her shoes neatly ordered on the shelves. Had she glanced down she might have noticed the widening cracks in the mud, might have noticed the hatch coming open.

She looked around the bedroom for the biography she was currently reading, only to realize she'd left it in the kitchen.

As she headed down a narrow hallway lined with her family's photographic history, behind her the crawl space hatch popped open an inch. From within the darkness there appeared the top of a knitted ski mask, followed by a pair of skittish eyes.

The kitchen and the adjoining living room afforded Liz a spectacular view of the horizon dominated by Sun Valley's rugged mountain skyline, still aglow at 10:10 P.M. She loved this place, her second home, so far from New York and the political life she'd chosen.

She poured herself a glass of water, grabbed the book from the counter, and headed back down the hallway, both hands occupied.

Patrolman Walt Fleming groaned.

Earlier in the summer the town had adopted a free bike campaign. Thirty bright yellow bikes had been spread around town as community property, with the understanding no one would steal them. They were used by anyone wanting to pedal from one place to the next. But the instructions on the bikes clearly stated they were to be well cared for and left in any of the many bike stands around town, a policy prone to abuse. Walt—on a bike himself, one of four officers assigned to "pedal patrol"—spotted one of the bikes dumped into some bushes a half block up the hill from the community library.

He inspected it for flats or damage and, finding none, decided to walk it down the hill to a bike stand in front of the library. He was on his way downhill—walking awkwardly between the two bikes—when he spotted a crawl space screen vent ajar on a house foundation. He might not have noticed, but the framed wooden screen was bent and splintered on one corner—suggesting it had been pried open. Worse, he knew this house: It was on the KPD watch list, the residence of Elizabeth Shaler, New

York's young attorney general, a woman whose politics and guts he admired. The Shaler family had been coming to Sun Valley for fifty years. Her parents were featured in photographs with Ernest Hemingway on the walls of the Sun Valley Lodge.

He continued walking a few more yards—the *click, click, click* of the bike gears the only sound on the street. But the appearance of that screen nagged at him. A rookie cop, he was always looking for trouble. Right or wrong, he connected the jimmied screen to the ditched bike, and he decided that together they gave him reason enough to investigate. He laid the bikes down on the curb and worked his way back—quietly—to take a closer look.

Her hands occupied, Liz bumped the bedroom door shut with a throw of her hip. She headed straight for the end table with the glass of water and the book.

The overhead light went off.

She smelled something—*someone*—sour. And she turned around defensively.

But as she did, a hand clapped over her

mouth. Before she had a chance to react, her arm was twisted up behind her back and she was driven down to her knees.

It happened fast: One second the glass of water was tumbling to the carpet, where it shattered against the end table; the next, her hands were clamped behind her and her wrists and mouth were bound with duct tape. The intruder dragged her painfully by the hair to a chair in front of the vanity and sat her down. More duct tape secured her to the padded chair. Tears streamed down her face.

The only light in the room was street light seeping in through the blinds, and a rose-colored hue from the digital clock by the bed. He wore a ski mask and a black T-shirt, but the blue hiking shorts seemed out of place. This was no Ted Bundy. He had a small scar on his left knee. He smelled sharply of sweat. She faced the mirror. He moved nervously behind her.

"You stand for all the wrong things," he said, his voice taut. "And you'll pay for that." He sounded like he was trying to talk himself into this.

Nonetheless, he owned her, and this bothered her more than anything—this sense of control he enjoyed.

"You take companies apart with no thought for the people who actually work there. Come out here—you and all the obscenely rich—and leave the rest of us behind to scrap and fight for a job that's long gone. What do you care? There's always a few weeks in Sun Valley to look forward to. I saw the article in *Vanity Fair*: I know all about you."

He'd tagged himself: She'd only broken up a few monolith white-collar companies; he was a reader of *Vanity Fair*. He was in over his head. Her attorney instincts kicked in: If only she could get the tape off her mouth and reason with him.

A knife blade glinted. "Riddle me this: How far does a woman politician make it without a face?" He cut her then, a hot, thin line of blood running across the back of her neck. She felt it sting. Suddenly he was for real, and this changed everything.

"At the end of this you will look like the monster you are," he said.

She turned away from the reflection in the mirror, determined he not see her fear.

As she did, a movement to her right won her attention: The doorknob turned.

The intruder was fully focused on the mirror, moving from side to side behind her, brandishing the knife, prattling on: "Now where should we start? Huh?" He cut a strap off the nightgown, exposing her left breast.

"What's a woman without her tits?" he asked her reflection. He amused himself with his own answer: "Richard Simmons." He cackled loudly, sounding like an old crow.

Shaking now from terror, she knew better than to look at the door, but couldn't help herself. Someone else was in the house. An accomplice?

Shifting in the mirror from her left to right, he caught her looking. He raised the knife in that direction, his face contorting behind curiosity.

She saw the door coming open. Judging by his expression, this was no one he expected. She threw her weight back in the low chair and went over, colliding with him. Tying him up.

She screamed behind the duct tape. The bedroom door flew open. A figure—a uniform—closed the short distance and threw himself into the intruder. The two stumbled across the room in lockstep and smacked into the wall. She heard a *whoosh* of expelled air; the crack of bone. The *swish* of the knife blade. A wet, visceral grunt.

She struggled against the tape to get free. The men separated, the knife handle protruding from the belly of the one in the uniform. He staggered backward and a flash of light appeared from his side. The loud clap of the gun's report deafened her.

The intruder, thrown back by the bullet's impact, wailed and spun and fell to the floor, writhing in pain. A bitter smell filled the room. "You shot me. You fucking shot me!" the intruder whined, squirming in pain. "Fuck. Fuck, fuck, fuck!"

The cop staggered toward him, the gun extended. The intruder froze. The cop viciously stomped on the gut wound, and the intruder passed out.

The cop bent over him and she heard the metallic click of handcuffs.

"Are you all right?" he asked her, his voice guttural and wet.

She groaned through the tape, tried to nod.

"Officer wounded," he said, speaking into

a radio clipped to his shirt. He recited her street address and a series of codes. He then took two steps toward her and fell first to his knees before collapsing forward, his head on her bare chest, their faces only inches apart.

"Your Honor . . . ," he said. And then he passed out.

EIGHT YEARS LATER

PRESENT DAY

THURSDAY

One

Six men, all wearing white hard hats and orange ear protectors, huddled in one corner of what was to become a themed fast food restaurant, That's a Wrap, that would sport vinyl wallpaper of Monroe, Bogart, Julia Roberts, Tom Hanks, and Harrison Ford. Not twenty feet away, on the far side of a temporary wall, passengers hurried down a long hallway that connected Salt Lake airport's concourses C and D.

The entrance to the work site was through a thick sheet of black plastic. Sheetrock dust covered the floor along with scraps of aluminum conduit, pieces of electrical wire, and a half dozen used paper cups from the Starbucks down on concourse D.

There was debate among the workers

about how to install a length of ventilation duct; the architect had neglected to note the location of the sprinkler system.

"There's no way, Billy, that you're going to get around that pipe," the foreman said at last. "And you sure as shit can't go through it."

Billy disagreed. To illustrate his suggestion, he dragged two sawhorses to below the spot in question, threw two lengths of aluminum studs across them, and climbed up, while the foreman shouted out for him to use a stepladder because he didn't want to lose his workman's comp record.

But by then there was no stopping Billy. He punched a section of ceiling panel up and into the space above, and slid it to one side.

Shining a flashlight, he poked his head up inside.

"What the fuck?" he said. He withdrew his head and addressed his fellow workers. "Is this one of those haze-the-rookie things? Because if it is, it sucks."

When no one answered, Billy jumped down and used a broom handle to knock the additional ceiling panels out of the way. The fourth panel wouldn't budge. Neither would the fifth, or the sixth. He tried another, and it lifted partially. Billy carefully slid it to the left.

Now he and the others could see up into the false ceiling.

"What is that?" one of the men said. "A suit bag?"

It was a six-foot length of bulging, heavy black plastic, zippered shut.

The foreman took a tentative step forward.

"That ain't no suit bag," said the smallest of the six workers, a man with a goatee and a tattoo of three X's on his neck. He spoke softly, which was not his way. "That's a body bag. And there's something in it."

Two

Walt Fleming pulled the white Grand Chero-kee marked "Blaine County Sheriff" to the curb in front of Elizabeth Shaler's home. As he sat behind the wheel, staring up at the house, Walt realized he was rubbing the scar through the shirt of his blue uniform, a firm reminder of that evening eight years earlier. It still pulsed hot from time to time, for no reason at all. It did so now. He felt oddly nostalgic for a moment, reliving the event that had propelled him to the front page and secured his bid for county sheriff, an election he'd won by a landslide.

Now a household name, Liz Shaler had recently returned to her Sun Valley home—albeit a second home—allegedly to announce her candidacy for president. Walt's job, along with the people inside, was to keep her alive. He radioed dispatch that he was leaving SD-1, his Cherokee, and heading inside.

A black Porsche Cayenne parked behind the Cherokee, and out from the passenger seat stepped Patrick Cutter, with his George Hamilton golfer's tan and porcelain white smile. Walt acknowledged Dick O'Brien, Cutter's security chief, visible through the windshield. O'Brien, stocky, and with an Irishman's nose, offered Walt a mock salute. Two dark-suited minions, a man and a young woman, both of whom, judging by their black clothing, knew nothing about dressing for the arid Idaho summer, attempted to follow Cutter but were quickly turned back by their boss. They returned to the idling car a little sheepishly.

Liz Shaler's 1950s ranch home would have fit inside Patrick Cutter's six-bay garage. Walt wondered how that made Cutter feel as he bounded up the walkway like a kid arriving home from school.

The Secret Service agent held the door for Walt. "Looks like Dryer called in the varsity," Walt said to Patrick Cutter.

"There's been a credible threat," Cutter announced. It struck Walt as both odd and unfortunate that Patrick Cutter, no matter how many billions he was worth, should have such intelligence ahead of local law enforcement. With the Cutter Communications Conference—C³—less than twenty-four hours away, the proper chain of command would have been Dryer, Walt, and *then* O'Brien, who would tell Cutter; not the other way around.

Cutter could read a man's face. "Don't worry, Walt, no one's pulling an end run on you. Dick O'Brien received the intel ahead of even Dryer."

"That's not possible," Walt blurted out, without thinking.

"That's the way it is," Cutter said. "We do *a lot* of business with the military. Believe me. Those are our satellites they're using, for Christ sakes." He winked: a mannerism Walt found intentionally offensive.

They stood half in the house. A man with bad acne scars approached from the open kitchen. He was dressed like a preppie, wearing a white shirt, no tie, a blue blazer, blue jeans, and loafers. He offered his hand to Walt while still too far away for them to shake.

"Adam Dryer," he said.

"At last," Walt said. The man tried a little too hard with the handshake.

"You guys have not met?" an astonished Patrick Cutter asked.

"Not face-to-face," Dryer said, still shaking Walt's hand. "But if e-mail were any judge, we're practically married."

"Mr. Cutter mentioned a credible threat," Walt said, getting free of the man's eager hand.

"Did he?" Dryer asked, looking at Cutter disappointedly. "Have you met the AG?" Dryer stepped out of Walt's line of sight.

Elizabeth Shaler was on the phone in the kitchen. Her eyes lit up at the sight of Walt, and she waved enthusiastically, then pointed to the phone and scrunched up her face into complaint. She wore a sleeveless white shirt with a simple string of pearls. The countertop blocked sight of the rest of her, but she hadn't added a pound. If anything, he thought she looked a little too thin and not a day older than when the two of them had been in this house together under much different circumstances.

"I guess you have," Dryer said, seeing Shaler's reaction. He sounded almost jealous.

"It's a small town," Walt said.

"Or was," Cutter added, trying too hard to be friendly, "until people like me moved in. Right, Sheriff?"

"Everybody, take a deep breath," Walt said. "Everything's fine. I want to hear about this threat. But first, I think I'm being summoned."

In fact, Liz Shaler was waving him over to her and pointing down the hallway. She placed the phone down, gave Walt an affectionate hug, and said to Dryer, "I'm going to steal him for a minute."

As she led him by the hand, Walt felt a pain in his gut just beneath the scar. Liz Shaler sensed this somehow and inquired, "Too familiar?"

"I'm fine."

"It's been too long," she said, closing the door of a small study behind him. "Oh my God, how good it is to see you!"

She devoted her full attention to him. If it was an act, she was profoundly gifted.

"And you, Mrs. Shaler."

"Liz. Please. Are you kidding me? It's Walt, not Sheriff. Is that okay?"

"I prefer it."

"Really good to see you. So much has happened," she said. "Where to begin?"

Walt felt she owed him none of this and was about to say so, but her energy silenced him.

"I appreciated your note," she said. "About Charlie."

"It was a tragedy. I wasn't even sure you'd see my note. That it would get through to you."

"It did. You never met him, did you?"

"No, ma'am."

"But your note was very kind, as if you had. It meant a great deal to me. And stop it with the ma'am!"

Walt fought back a smile. He said, "We stay in here too long and Dryer's going to have me vetted."

"You would have liked him—Charlie. And he, you. He knew all about you—about your saving me."

"Hardly."

"Of course you did," she said. "Do you suppose Adam Dryer doesn't know?"

"I would doubt it."

"Isn't that strange? And should I tell him?"

"Your decision entirely," he said.

"You'd rather I didn't," she said. "I can see

it in your eyes. Gosh, it's good to see you. Isn't it strange how something like that connects two people? I feel like . . . Well, I'm gushing. Forgive me."

"It's an honor to be part of your security detail."

"Oh . . . please. I loathe the Secret Service. Not the men themselves—they're just doing a job—but being watched and accounted for twenty-four/seven. It's absolutely oppressive."

"We're going to have a tight net around you this weekend. I hope you're still speaking to me Monday."

She grabbed both his hands in hers. "Monday, and the Monday after that, and every Monday forever, Walt. I can tell you're nonchalant about this, but I've never forgotten that night, and I never will."

"May there never be another one," Walt said.

"Amen to that."

A knock on the door.

"Probably another fund-raising call," she said.

"So the rumors are true?" he asked.

She bit back a smile. Her eyes were positively luminous. She smelled like a garden of lilacs. "I have absolutely no idea what you're talking about."

She pulled open the door. There were five people jammed into the hallway, all vying for her attention.

"Not exactly the same as running for county sheriff," he said over her shoulder, unsure if she'd heard him or not.

He glanced up the hallway toward the bedroom. He remembered hearing the glass break, could still feel the grip of his weapon cool in his right hand as he slipped it from the holster. Could still feel the hot jolt as the knife entered him. He'd shot three men in the line of duty since that first time—had killed one of them. But nothing came close to this memory. And though he hadn't admitted it to her, he, too, felt a kindred bond with this woman unlike anything he had with anyone.

She had heard him, for she turned over her shoulder and spoke to him, as if able to block out the five voices all speaking at once. "You didn't tell me about the divorce, and I'm going to honor that. But when you're ready, I'd like to hear about it. If you're okay with that."

They moved as a group then, back down

the hall until she let out an ear-piercing whistle without touching her lips. Walt had once had a baseball coach who could whistle like that. Her entourage shut up, and she was tall enough that when she rose onto her tiptoes she lifted above them. "I have a security meeting with Sheriff Fleming, Agent Dryer, and Patrick Cutter right now. It's confidential, and none of you are invited. After that, I'm going fly-fishing for the afternoon. And after *that* I'm yours again. I ask you to respect my schedule, and for the time being to leave the house and take a break. Jenna, that means you, too. Okay . . . so go. Go!"

The group of handlers dispersed immediately. A moment later it was just the Secret Service detail of four agents, including Dryer, and Patrick Cutter, and Walt. He noticed for the first time that some press was encamped across the street in front of the library, their dark lenses aimed like rifle scopes.

"Let's get to it," Dryer said, clapping and rubbing his hands together.

One of Dryer's men lowered and twisted the living room blinds shut, then left through the front door. Walt noticed another of the detail stood outside the kitchen door. The four of them took seats on a couch and a pair of art deco overstuffed chairs that had been a part of the house since the 1950s. A rectangular glass coffee table, covered in magazines and newspapers, sat as an island between them.

As the four-way conversation began, Walt took a quick assessment: Dryer was efficient and down to business, as he'd learned to expect of the government man; Cutter seemed slightly aloof and impatient, a man with his eyes on the bigger picture; Walt's job seemed to be to play the paranoid local cop, but he resisted playing to the stereotype; for her part, Liz Shaler found it in her powers to give each person her full attention while scribbling out the occasional note to herself. Walt envisioned the discussion as a transcript written from the recording made by the digital pen that Patrick Cutter placed in the center of the coffee table with everyone's permission.

FLEMING: So, a credible threat.

DRYER: A telecommunications intercept. Most likely the NSA, although we got it from the Bureau.

CUTTER: Dick never tells me who we get this stuff from. But it's obviously for real.

DRYER: Very real.

FLEMING: Do we have a transcript?

DRYER: It's coming, which probably means we'll get it Tuesday or Wednesday, after the conference and Ms. Shaler's talk, Sunday morning, are long behind us. Government work.

FLEMING: But credible.

DRYER: Mentions "AG" and a price of five hundred thousand dollars.

SHALER: My stock has gone up. The first man to try to kill me was a volunteer.

CUTTER: Dick feels it's of concern, certainly, but it was apparently stated vaguely enough that it could be for any date, now or well into the future.

FLEMING: I take it means we make adjustments. Have we considered canceling the talk?

CUTTER: Let's not get carried away.

FLEMING: You'll excuse me, sir, but any of us getting carried away is what we're trying to prevent.

DRYER: Any talk of cancellation is premature. We've received twelve threats in the past three weeks. This is by far the most credible, but we need more intel.

CUTTER: It's the end piece of the conference. I will honor and respect whatever decision you make, Liz, but you know the stakes.

SHALER: No one's canceling anything. Walt is just looking after me. I appreciate it, and I'm going to listen to him and give it some thought.

DRYER: It comes back onto you, Sheriff. We all report to you.

CUTTER: But not the decision making! Liz can make up her own mind about appearing or not.

FLEMING: I agree with Special Agent in Charge Dryer: We need as much intel as possible. Has the threat been assigned?

DRYER: It didn't come from OC. That's what we got from the Bureau. Not mob. A third party, someone unknown to them, is behind the buy. That could be good news, could be bad. But at least it's not some crime family, because that would scream duck and cover, as far as I'm concerned.

FLEMING: And maybe still does.

DRYER: For now we stick with the plan: My guys cover her in transit and in situ. Your boys clear the routes, handle crowd containment, traffic flow, and advise us on back-door routing. If there's any investigation to take place, that's going to have to come from you, Sheriff. It's not what we do, and I don't have the staff. I've asked the Bureau to stay on top of this, but you never know. They're overworked and underpaid, just like the rest of us. Most of the rest of us.

CUTTER: I can offer any of Dick's team. He has a couple dozen men on the ground, as far as I know. Most, if not all, are ex-Bureau or military. No one with less than twelve years. A bunch of investigations among them.

FLEMING: I'll get with O'Brien then. Thank you.

SHALER: I want you all to know that this isn't the first time and won't be the last, I'm sure. I feel very safe in your care. I'd like to be kept up on what we know, and I'd be the most comfortable if Sheriff Fleming acted as go-between. So I trust, Agent Dryer, that every effort will be made to keep the sheriff in the loop at all times.

FLEMING: Sure thing.

What the transcript would never reveal, Walt realized, were the nuances of glances and telegraphed body language that accompanied the discussion. Patrick Cutter believed he had the most to lose. He worked himself up throughout the meeting, growing steadily more agitated. Special Agent in Charge Dryer maintained a dispassionate calm, but failed to make eye contact with Walt even once, confirming how uncomfortable he was with Walt's theoretical control of the conference's security, and his relationship with Liz Shaler; Dryer was a take-charge man, and he saw Walt as standing in his way. Liz Shaler had stood up for Walt, perhaps a little too much, focusing her attention nearly entirely on him over the ten-minute discussion, embracing Walt as her ally, and perhaps even using this support as a threat to Patrick Cutter and Agent Dryer. Walt came away better informed but oddly less confident of his own position. There were games at play, both subtle and overt. The unspoken but clearly apparent alliance between Cutter and Dryer was what he feared most—they meant to have Liz Shaler to themselves, and now saw Walt's participation as an impediment.

A commotion at the front door grabbed their attention, and it was a mark of their high nerves that both Dryer and Walt reached for their weapons.

Three

The guard at the front door announced, "The guide's here."

Dryer responded, "Show her in."

At five feet eleven, Fiona Kenshaw stood an inch taller than Walt. She wore her brown hair up in a ponytail pulled through a ball cap that read "Kiss My Bass." She wore a purple T-shirt pulled snuggly over her firm frame, and a pair of hiking shorts with multiple pockets.

"Small world, Sheriff."

Dryer offered Walt a look that said, "You know her, too?"

"Fiona works for the department part-time as our crime-scene photographer," Walt explained.

"Our waiter at dinner last night," Liz Shaler

said, "let it slip that she had a master's in marine biology from Scripps. Ski-bummed three years ago and never left. Only in Sun Valley."

A man followed her through the front door—unannounced, Walt noted—drawing everyone's attention, including Fiona's. It was Danny Cutter, Patrick's wayward younger brother. A radiantly handsome man in his early forties who bore little physical resemblance to his older brother, Danny owned a room the moment he entered—a quality other men envied and women found irresistible. Danny had parlayed this into personal gain for most of his life. Danny blew past Fiona to Liz, whom he kissed affectionately and hugged. He shook hands all around, including with Walt, apparently bearing no grudge over his arrest two years earlier, an event that had been a major setback to his business career. Despite the fact that Walt had the man's photograph and fingerprints on file at the office—a drug possession—he couldn't help but like Danny.

Liz leaned toward Walt. "Look, I know Danny had some problems, but they're behind him now." Walt found her sympathetic

tone illuminating. It wasn't easy to stay upset with Danny Cutter for very long.

Danny approached Fiona with the ele-
gance of a bullfighter. He shook her hand,
and unabashedly sized her up. Walt half expected Fiona to curtsy.

Walt caught Dryer's eye. "Danny wasn't
announced by your guy. Why not?"

"Mr. Cutter's known to us," Dryer ex-
plained. "He's a personal friend of AG
Shaler's. Listen, we're aware of his priors,
Sheriff, if that's your concern—"

"My concern is that whoever's coming after her needs access. If you're not screening
every single person—myself included—"

"Danny Cutter?" Dryer asked incredu-
lously.

"He's vulnerable. He's a convicted felon
on probation. And he has access—open access." Walt's phone rang, sparing him more
of a reply. He slipped through the door and
took the call outside.

It was Nancy, his assistant.

"Transportation Security Administration
director from Salt Lake City airport is holding for you. Can I put him through?"

"What's it about?" Walt asked.

"Said it's urgent, or I wouldn't have bothered you."

"Urgent?" The front door guard overheard this. Walt headed to the Cherokee for privacy. He slid behind the wheel.

"And don't forget your father," Nancy said.

"Who could forget my father?" he mumbled. "Okay," he said into the phone as he started the engine for the sake of the air-conditioning. "Put him through."

"Listen, we don't know exactly what we've got, only that in this new era of sharing intelligence"—there was no doubting his sarcasm—"it's my responsibility to pass along this kind of thing in a timely fashion." Nate Capshaw spoke slowly, as if imagining each word before uttering it. Or maybe, Walt thought, he was considering his choice of words for the sake of legality, carefully weighing how it might read on a court transcript sometime down the road. This won Walt's attention.

"And much appreciated," Walt said.

"Workers here found a body this morning just over seventy minutes ago."

Walt's internal alarm sounded: Why call the Blaine County sheriff about a body at the Salt Lake airport? "It was inside a body bag that was in turn hidden inside the suspended ceiling of a commercial space under construction between our C and D concourses." Capshaw was reporting a murder that showed great premeditation.

Walt's rapid breathing was amplified by the cell phone.

"Still warm," Capshaw said.

His hands were sweating on the wheel. "So why me?"

"Our video surveillance was down on that concourse because of the work going on. But one of my guys—listen, this is a long shot—but he followed a guy on a hunch. Thought maybe he recognized him from a past life. Used to be a state cop in Rhode Island. This is about the same time as whoever's in that body bag was being done, right? My guy loses the suspect in E—the E concourse. Frickin' madhouse, E, with all these regional jets. But this guy in the body bag . . . This was a pro job. No question about that. No ID on him. Labels cut out of the clothing. Face cut up. Fingertips removed. Some teeth pulled. A real fucking mess—excuse the French. This guy was meant to be a John Doe, and he's going to stay that way. And the thing of it is . . . all the cameras we got in E—working cameras, I'm talking about—and we never get a decent look at his face. Are you kidding me? This guy's fucking Baryshnikov the way he moves. Keeps his back to the cameras the whole time. Then we lose him in the men's room."

"But why me?" Walt asked again.

"Seven flights departed from E in the minutes after we lost him. I'm calling all seven destinations, starting with you. Because the first flight to depart was headed up there to Sun Valley. You've got that shindig up there this weekend, right? Offers a guy like this some fairly big targets."

"Sounds like he got his target," Walt said. "Call the FBI field office. Ask them to check with Washington. I think they're going to be interested in your John Doe."

"The flight arrives there in fifteen minutes," Capshaw said.

"Jesus, why didn't you say that five minutes ago?" Walt flipped on the flashers, sped away from the curb. He ran the red light at the intersection of Sun Valley Road and Highway 75 and headed south.

"Give me whatever description you've

got," Walt said, waiting to launch the siren until the phone call concluded.

It was twenty minutes to the airport, on a good day.

Four

Seven minutes later—eight minutes before wheels down—BCS dispatch had rallied three of its eight cruisers. Two had sealed Friedman Airport. The third, driven by deputy Tom Brandon, pulled up to the terminal only seconds behind Walt.

"We've got six minutes," Walt told Brandon, a big-boned, thick man in his later twenties. A pair of aviator glasses hid his dark eyes. Tommy Brandon had been ski patrol on the mountain for six years before applying to the Sheriff's Office. His star had risen quickly, and with it, Walt's reliance on him. "Suspect is average to tall, dark hair, black T-shirt, jeans or black jeans."

"Sheriff?" Other deputies often addressed Walt informally by his first name. Brandon never had, and Walt appreciated it. "That description fits half of the guys in this valley."

"It's all we've got."

"And Pete?"

Pete Wood ran security at the small airport. His guys were trained to unzip bags and stare at X-ray machines.

"I briefed him on the way in. His guys will keep their distance. This guy killed a man in Salt Lake," Walt said. "Keep alert, Tommy. Sounds like he's pretty good with a knife."

"At least he's coming off a plane, he should be clean."

"Should be," Walt said ominously. "If he's got checked luggage, he could have a piece in there. So if and when we get a twenty, we keep him away from baggage claim. We do not want a hostage situation."

"Got it."

The Friedman terminal looked bland—like a one-story brown shoebox—when compared with its extraordinary backdrop: a string of foothills rising a thousand feet off the valley floor. This midsection of the valley, the town of Hailey, eleven miles south of Ketchum/Sun Valley, qualified as the transition point between high desert to the south and alpine to the north, leaving the south-facing slopes of the foothills barren, covered in nothing but knee-high wax weed and sagebrush. The north slopes, holding snow longer in the springtime, and the moisture it contained, were covered in evergreen.

The sound of a plane on approach caused both men to turn and look up.

"Showtime," Walt said.

Brandon raised his voice above the roar of the turboprop. "What about shoes?"

"Shoes?" Walt nearly had to shout.

"Suspects change their hair, their face, but just as often leave on the same pair of shoes. Do we have a photo?"

"No photo. Shoes," Walt said, sounding impressed.

"You aren't careful, Sheriff, I'll run against you in the next primary."

Walt studied his deputy for the crack of a smile or any sign that he was kidding. But Brandon maintained a poker face.

From the other side of the small terminal came the sudden winding down of the turboprops. The plane had landed.

Five

The forward door of the Brasilia EMB-120 was lowered, and as the gate-checked hand luggage was wheeled around on a trolley, Walt watched from inside the glass of Gate 2, a well-lit space shared with three car rental agencies along the back wall. Baggage claim was accessed by three garage doors.

The trolley was stacked with roller bags, fly rod tubes, duffel bags, and a wicker gift basket. Passengers descended the steep stairs, picked over the trolley's contents, and headed toward the terminal.

"Waiting for someone?"

Walt turned and recognized the woman behind the Hertz counter from a fund-raiser the week before.

"Yes, as a matter of fact."

"Has the divorce gone through? I haven't seen it in the paper. Sorry to hear about that." She didn't sound so sorry.

"Yeah." Walt briefly took his eyes off the line of arriving passengers. "Julie, right? The wildlife dinner?"

"I did the door. Wearing the elk antlers? How humiliating was that? I had to endure endless comments about my 'nice rack.' "

Walt avoided checking out her rack by returning his attention to the arrival. The first few passengers were retirement age; then came two families with young kids; then several men who looked like the Cutter conference prototypes, CEOs dressing down in blue blazers, button-down shirts, and khaki pants. A silver-haired golfer and his wife wearing matching St. Andrews sun visors followed the four executives.

"I'm bothering you," Julie said.

"Busy at the moment," Walt said.

"On the job? Seriously? What's up?"

"Just a meet-and-greet. Maybe we could do this later," he suggested, still not taking his eyes off the arriving passengers.

"Sure," she said. Walt didn't like letting her

icy tone go uncorrected, but he had no choice.

He checked over with Brandon, who shrugged: still no suspect.

The arriving passengers began to mill about, blocking his view of the plane. Walt moved closer to the arrivals door in order to get a better view. A snarl had formed around the baggage trolley. Two female baggage handlers were arguing with a guy, his back to Walt.

He caught Brandon's eye once more and signaled that he was headed outside. The dry, hot air slapped him in the face. He hurried toward the commotion, holding his weapon in the holster as he jogged.

A baggage handler spoke up. "You cannot go back there, sir!"

Walt felt a surge of adrenaline. *Someone's trying to breach security.* He couldn't make out what the man said but it made the woman even angrier.

Walt involuntarily unsnapped his holster.

"What's going on here?" he asked, grabbing the man by the shoulders and spinning him around.

He wore wraparound sunglasses and carried a white cane in his right hand.

He pulled away, stumbled, and nearly fell over a loose bag. Walt steadied him, apologizing and introducing himself in alternating strokes.

The man was blind.

"What's the problem here?" he asked finally.

The passenger composed himself. "I asked to see my dog. He's a service dog. I shouldn't be made to wait."

"I've explained to him, Sheriff," the woman said, "that no one besides us can go back there, sir."

"Your dog's back there?"

He nodded vigorously. "They required me to kennel him and to check him like baggage. They made me sign a release because of the July heat. I just want to make sure he's okay."

"We can do that," Walt said. "But we're going to have to do it inside at baggage claim. She's just doing her job: No one's allowed back there."

Walt glanced over his shoulder, wondering how many passengers he'd missed during this encounter. He hoped Brandon had gotten a good look.

"You're the sheriff? Seriously?" The blind

man sounded amused. A wry smile overcame him.

"Blaine County sheriff. Yes. Let's take this
inside. Okay?"

"Rafe Nagler." He switched hands with the
cane and stuck his right hand out into
space. Walt took hold and they shook
hands. "I'm here for the Cutter conference.
There's supposed to be someone here to
pick me up."

"We'll get it sorted out. Can I offer
you . . . ?" Walt took him by the elbow.

The blind man allowed himself to be led.
"Thank you, Sheriff."

"I'm sorry for the confusion," he said.
"Your first time here?"

"Yes. I've heard wonderful things. Did you
know there's a ski program for the visually
impaired?"

"Not this time of year," Walt said.

"No." Nagler smiled. "Maybe not. But kayaking, and rock climbing."

"Kayaking? Seriously?"

Nagler leaned his head back and laughed,
showing his teeth. "I'm bullshitting you," he
said. "But the rock climbing's for real."

Walt grinned but of course the man

couldn't see it. Then he faked a laugh, which sounded stupid.

"I've never attended the Cutter conference, but it's said to be the single most important such meeting in the country."

"Patrick Cutter knows how to throw a party," Walt confirmed.

"The *Journal* called it the most influential three days to the communications business," Nagler said.

"Sounds right."

"Called Patrick Cutter a kingmaker. Disney bought ABC as a result of this conference. Brighton Distilleries acquired a film studio and changed its entire business plan."

"And you are?"

"A dreary professor invited to bore the executives for an hour on Saturday."

"I doubt that."

Walt pulled open and held the door, the air-conditioning catching in his throat, a welcome relief. He eagerly scanned the interior. Brandon was nowhere to be seen.

"Do you see Ricky's kennel?" Nagler asked.

"Oversized items are delivered at the far end."

"I'm good now, Sheriff, thank you." Nagler

extended his cane and gently broke Walt's grip.

He negotiated his way through a minefield of pulled luggage and impatient passengers.

Walt rose to his toes and saw Brandon standing alone. No suspect. Anxiety flooded him. This was the perfect place to identify and arrest a possible hit man arriving to kill Shaler. Right here and now. The contrarian in him wanted to believe that the murder victim in Salt Lake City had been the intended target, that the job was over and done. That the feds had gotten it wrong. That he and O'Brien and Dryer had nothing more to worry about. This was how Cutter would spin it. Possibly Dryer along with him.

Time worked against him. Baggage arrived, sliding down the short, stainless steel chute with a jarring bang. Like cows at a feeding trough, the passengers approached and nudged one another aside.

The crowded space became more chaotic with passengers wielding bags. The terminal's automatic doors clapped open and shut. Walt spun a full circle, his frustration mounting. Another few minutes and the terminal would be all but empty.

He signaled Brandon and caught his attention. The two men stepped outside in
concert, each through a different door. Together they inspected the parking lot for
anyone who'd managed to slip past unno-
ticed.

Brandon stood by the taxi stand and
hotel/van pickup. He leaned his head into
several of the vehicles, scanning the board-
ing passengers.

Over Walt's radio came Brandon's voice.
"I've got zilch."

"Ditto," Walt replied.

"Hang on . . . we've got a situation inside," Brandon announced.

Walt turned and hurried back into the terminal.

Six

A wall of onlookers blocked Walt's view. He crossed the room and forced his way through the small crowd that had gathered. At the same time, Brandon reached the center of the huddle.

It was Nagler, the blind man again, kneeling on the floor in front of a cream-colored kennel. He was crying, or cursing, patting the floor violently, feeling for his cane. Catching it with his right hand, he lifted it roughly as if to whip the confused baggage handler. Walt jumped forward and grabbed the man's forearm and peeled the cane from his fingers.

"Hold it!" Walt said sternly.

"Sheriff?" Nagler's face was flushed and splotchy. The sunglasses had slipped down his nose, giving Walt a fleeting glimpse of a milky eye with no iris, no pupil. Only a sickening, yellow-white bulb.

"There's been a tragic accident," the baggage handler said.

"Bullshit!" Nagler said. "They killed my dog. They killed Ricky!"

"The heat," the handler said. She fingered a large neon orange tag attached to the kennel's metal grate door. "The release spells it all out."

"You think I *read* your stupid release?" Nagler shouted. "Is it in Braille? Give me a break! They said it was a formality, an insurance thing. That it was a short flight—an hour—and that people flew their pets all the time."

"It's true, they do," the baggage handler said. "But it's the middle of the day, sir. And a hot one at that. And—"

"My dog is dead," he wailed. "Do you have any idea—"

"There's nothing more to be gained here," Walt said. "We're sorry for your loss. Let's get you to where you're going. Get you settled."

"Settled? I'm not leaving Ricky."

"We'll get him to the local vet. You can decide how you want to . . . handle things from there. Didn't you say someone was meeting you?"

"That would be me." A twenty-something woman with a fresh face and freckles stepped out of the small crowd. "Karen Platt. I'm a greeter for C^3. I'm Mr. Nagler's greeter. His driver." She turned toward Nagler. "I am, like, so sorry about the dog. Ohmygod, I can't imagine . . ."

Nagler came to his feet. Walt placed the cane back into the man's hand.

"Promise me you won't hit anyone with that," Walt said.

"Ricky and I . . . ," Nagler said but was unable to finish. He threw his head back, looked to the ceiling, and took a deep breath. "You have no idea."

"We'll see if we can't do something. Maybe we can find a dog for the weekend."

"It doesn't work like that. Ricky and I have been together six years."

"Maybe we can do something."

"Did you check any luggage, sir?" Brandon spoke up, his low voice drawing Nagler's attention. Ever the practical one; always thinking ahead.

Nagler fumbled in his back pocket and

pulled out a ticket sleeve. Stapled to the inside of the sleeve was a bag tag. He handed
it in Brandon's direction. Brandon took it
and passed it to Nagler's driver. She went
down the line of the few remaining bags
and, checking baggage strips, pulled out a
hard-shelled Samsonite.

"No one read me the release," Nagler muttered. He swung his cane out in front of him,
but without the energy that had fed his ini-
tial anger. "Where's the car? Ricky could
have gotten me out of here just fine." He
tested the area with the cane and made his
way slowly, Karen Platt dragging his suitcase.

Brandon shut the wire door and hoisted
the dog kennel like it was a loaf of bread.
"Tough break," he said to Walt.

Walt glanced around, having almost forgotten about their suspect. He felt the
weight of defeat.

Elton John's "Goodbye Yellow Brick
Road" leaked out of speakers in the ceiling.

Shit, he thought: He'd have that tune
stuck in his head the rest of the day.

Seven

Rafe Nagler pulled himself out of the Volvo, his white cane at his side. A voice summoned in a thick Eastern European accent. The man sounded big. He grabbed Nagler firmly by the arm.

"Welcome to the Sun Valley Lodge."

"Thank you." Nagler swung his cane. The bellman took him by the arm. "Lodge or inn?" he asked, as he was led up some stairs. "I thought the conference is at the Sun Valley Inn."

"Actually, we offer the two hotels: the lodge, which is where you are now—more upscale and geared for entertainment; and the inn, just across the pond, that provides additional rooms and houses our conference and banquet facilities."

Karen Platt, his driver, called out that she'd take care of his bag. She sounded both anxious and nervous, as she had been for the twenty-minute ride from the airport, and the half hour spent at the vet making arrangements for Ricky's cremation.

"Would you describe the lobby to me, please, with twelve o'clock straight ahead?" Nagler said to the bellman as they entered the hotel.

"Of course. It's a big room, almost two rooms connected by a hallway running nine o'clock to three o'clock. It's large. Grand. There's an alcove immediately to our right—registration desk. Concierge is ahead—one o'clock—at a large desk, mahogany or cherry with a leather top. There are some columns between here and there. Square; wood-paneled. Eleven o'clock, two more columns. Double doors at twelve o'clock far at the end of the lobby that lead outside to the patio. Down the hallway I mentioned are some wonderful photographs, historic photographs of the lodge and its famous guests: Marilyn Monroe, Bobby Kennedy, Jimmy Stewart, some presidents. Perhaps I can describe some of them to you during your stay."

"I'd like that," Nagler said.

"The Duchin Lounge is at eleven o'clock, near the doors to the patio," he continued. "There are two couches and several chairs between where we are and the Duchin Lounge. A coffee table. The entrance to Gretchen's, breakfast and lunch, is behind the concierge."

"At one o'clock," Nagler said.

"Yes, sir. Very good."

Nagler turned right. "Registration?"

"You're a quick learner."

"You work with what you're given. That scraping sound beyond the patio doors?"

"The outdoor skating rink."

"An outdoor skating rink in July?"

"Exactly! Unbelievable, eh? We are famous for our weekend ice shows. Very important skaters."

The desk receptionist had a French accent and handled his reservation with aplomb. She retrieved a leather tote bag for him loaded with gifts from the C^3. She noted mention of his service dog.

"There's been an accident," Nagler said, his voice tight. "Ricky's not with us."

The receptionist and the bellman both offered their condolences.

Nagler and the bellman rode the elevator to the third floor, discussing the hotel's history and construction.

They arrived at the room and the bellman admitted him. Nagler pulled a bill from his left pants pocket and handed it to the man. Left pocket: tens. Right pocket: ones.

"Listen," Nagler said, after following the bellman's quick description of the room's layout. "Ricky, my dog, was my eyes. I've grown quite dependent on him. It's not that I can't negotiate with my cane—of course I can—but I'm out of practice. If you could pass word around to the staff . . ." He offered another three tens into the air and they were accepted.

"It will be our pleasure to make your stay as enjoyable and comfortable as possible. I'll pass the word."

Nagler's bag arrived. The bellman placed it on a stand and offered to unpack it. Nagler declined.

As the bellman retreated toward the door, Nagler stopped him, saying, "There's a movie theater, isn't there?"

"The Opera House. Yes."

"Does it run a matinee, by any chance?"

"*Sun Valley Serenade* shows every day at five."

"Sonja Henie and John Payne with Glenn Miller. Excellent."

"Can I escort you over?"

"Yes, please."

"Around four forty-five?"

"That would be perfect."

"See you then. The name is Karl, sir."

"Thank you, Karl, for everything."

"My pleasure, sir. I'll see you later this afternoon." The door clicked shut. Nagler was alone. He locked the door and threw the security lock; he then felt his way into the bathroom, closed the door, and locked this as well. He located the sink, closed the drain, and washed and dried his hands. He removed the mirrored sunglasses and, with his left index finger, held his eyebrow firm as he pulled down his lower lid with the other hand, exposing his eye—a bloodshot, yellowish orb. Then he pinched the surface of his eyeball and removed the contact lens.

And he could see again.

Eight

Danny Cutter made two mistakes: The first was to look it in the eye; the second was to turn and run from it.

He'd been struggling at the time to catch up. He'd hooked into a snag off the western bank of the narrow Big Wood River. At first he'd thought it was a submerged branch, because he'd felt a little give as he tugged on the fly rod; but then, with no more give left in it, he was thinking rock: that the Adam's fly, intended to float, had nonetheless dipped below the surface and was currently tangled in some green moss adhered to a rock. Far in the recesses of his angler's mind lurked the distant possibility that he was actually onto a fish—a lunker—and that it had "sat down" and was awaiting his next move; so he moved toward it. But a moment later, he was certain he'd snagged.

He wanted to catch up with Fiona, the guide, and Liz Shaler, now about thirty yards downstream, for two very different reasons. Liz was an important friend; Fiona was hot. Never mind that a pair of Secret Service agents, one on each side of the river, crept through the thick underbrush and shadowed the attorney general as best as possible. Never mind the ease with which they'd eavesdrop on any conversation, given the amazing quiet of the river. He could work around that.

Fiona had led them across a private bridge to a secluded estate hidden deep within the Starweather subdivision. They were mid-valley, about five miles north of Hailey.

The river turned slightly east about a half mile down. The water was knee deep and moving swiftly, the bottom rocky, uneven, and slippery. It was framed within walls of towering cottonwood trees on either side, broken by stands of aspen, tangles of chokecherry, and the colorful shock of golden willow.

Slowly, the group in front of him moved

in unison downriver. He stepped carefully toward his snagged fly.

Reaching it, he slipped his hand underwater and followed the taut line. He pricked his finger on the sharp hook and happened to glance up.

A cougar. Less than ten yards away.

For an instant he was stunned—awed—by the sight. Then something more primordial kicked in as he realized he was *too* close.

The cat was poised, ready to pounce. To strike.

This wasn't a Discovery Channel moment: She was hunting, and he was *meat*.

He turned and ran, splashing forward, slipping on the mossy stones, sucking the waders heavily out of the water.

Down the river, the sound drew the attention of the others, who turned hopefully, expecting to see Danny Cutter in control of some massive trout. Instead they saw him stumbling frantically across the river, aimed slightly downriver to allow the current to help his movement. His running was awkward and urgent.

"Bees," Fiona Kenshaw said. "He got into—" But she cut herself off as the cougar burst offshore into the river as if running on the surface, her paws weightless, her flight graceful and undisturbed.

"Good God!"

Danny heard the charge behind him. It sounded like a bull elephant.

In desperation, he glanced over his shoulder, turning slightly upstream. With this motion, his rod moved like a whip. With the cougar one pounce away from striking, the graphite tip of the nine-foot rod sharply struck the cat on the nose.

The animal dropped its head and went head over heels—a half flip that threw a shower of water at Danny and knocked him down into the river.

The cougar took off in the opposite direction without an ounce of lost momentum. It hit the shore in full stride, blurred into the tawny grasses, and vanished, living up to its nickname: *ghost of the Rockies*.

Cutter lost his rod as his waders filled. Fishermen drowned in less water, unable to regain balance, victimized by the panic and the weight of water-filled waders. Danny aimed his feet and legs downstream. He used the current to help him stand. Chilled to shivering, he staggered toward the river's edge and collapsed onto terra firma, winded and dazed.

Somehow—miraculously—he'd escaped a cougar attack. He was alive. Unhurt. He took it as an omen, an arbitrary warning of the preciousness of life. And he swore to God it would not go unheeded.

Nine

Walt's office door swung open, followed by a strong wind that turned out to be his sister-in-law, Myra. She, of the nervous constitution and skeletal frame.

Her voice could crack glass. "What if you showed Kevin one of those horrible shots of a car all smashed up by a drunken teenager? Maybe that would shock him into thinking straight. Maybe he'd forget about those canyon parties. Or maybe you could lock him up for an afternoon, you know, right here in your jail, and show him what that's like if you're busted for drugs. He's your nephew after all."

"I'll take care of it, Myra, I'll speak to him," Walt said without turning from his computer. "You can go now."

"Am I interrupting?"

He knew that voice. He angled to see Fiona just behind Myra, who blocked the door. Fiona wore the small tight T-shirt and hiking shorts he'd seen her in earlier, though her hair looked worse for wear and her face was shiny with sunscreen.

"I called you," Walt reminded. "How could you be interrupting? Myra? Anything else? Good. Then get out of the doorway and let her in."

Myra was none too subtle about looking Fiona up and down and then glancing back to Walt judgmentally.

"Myra!" Walt chastised.

But Myra couldn't help herself. "I like what you've done with the uniforms," she told him. Then she added, "You'd better call Kevin."

"Out!"

She huffed off.

Fiona entered, slack-jawed.

"My brother's widow," Walt explained, "has installed me as a surrogate father—sometimes an awkward fit."

"I had a stepmother I hated," she said, sliding into a captain's chair that faced his desk in the impossibly small office. She kept her legs extended. Long legs, made longer by the shorts, but cut off by the desk, which was something Walt regretted.

"Thanks for saving me," he said.

"Anytime."

"I called because—"

"You need help with some photos. You explained over the phone."

"It's been a long day."

"Danny Cutter was nearly killed by a cougar."

"You want to run that by me again?"

She explained her witnessing the attack from thirty yards downriver.

"We packed up and came back early, and Danny headed off to lunch with his brother. Men. You can't really just pick back up like that, can you? Let me tell you something; if that had happened to me, the first thing I'd have done is spend half the day on the phone telling anyone who'd listen. Then I'd have a long hot bath, or two. And then a bottle of wine. Or two. Business as usual? Forget it!"

"That's two attacks in ten days. The yellow Lab . . ."

"I shot the photos, remember? That was

disgusting. You ought to do something about it."

"The cougar? Not my department. Fish and Game. But you're right: They should certainly hear about the attack on Danny."

"What do you think of him?"

"Danny? He's okay."

"Not professionally. I know you busted him. I mean as a person."

"Don't really know him. Kind of difficult to separate the two."

"But first impressions?" she asked.

"He asked you out," Walt stated.

"Yeah. Is that bad?"

Walt knew Danny Cutter as a womanizing playboy who'd had a two-thousand-dollar-a-week cocaine habit prior to the bust. He thought the cocaine part had gone away. He wasn't sure the other part ever changed. He liked the man in spite of his criminal record.

"We got some crime-scene photos from Salt Lake," he told her. "Pretty gruesome stuff. But they're lousy photos. I'd like to en-large some, crop and zoom some others. Above my skill set."

She looked out the top of her eyes at him and said disdainfully, "I see."

"I need them pretty quickly."

"It's a date, is all."

"A guy named Capshaw—TSA down in Salt Lake—thought it important enough to send these. I have a five o'clock with everyone who's anyone connected to C^3 security. But as I said, the photos are pretty heavy. If you'd rather not do them, maybe you could give me a five-minute course in Photoshop for Dummies."

"I'll do them myself." She sounded angry. "Just tell me what you want."

The surprise in the photos, especially under enlargement, was the degree of the horrors. The victim's fingers had been cut off with precision. Teeth had been pulled, shown in the photos with a latex-gloved thumb holding the dead man's upper lip up over the gap. But worst of all: The face was disfigured and both eyes had been carved out of the sockets. Fiona battled her way through the work.

"None of my business," she said, "but why do you even want these? You realize they're far more disgusting as close-ups, right? But evidence is evidence. You can see everything in the originals, so I don't get it."

"Can you load them into PowerPoint and burn a disk for me?"

"Of course I can. But it won't make them any easier to take."

"What is it they say about first impressions?" Walt asked rhetorically.

"You're a diseased individual," she said.

"But you'd watch it?" he tested.

"Of course I would. But I'm sick that way. Like you."

"This goes no further than this office." He paused to make sure he had her attention. "There's been a credible threat on Liz Shaler's life." He watched as the shock registered. "At first I wondered if this killing in Salt Lake might be related. Happened this morning—less than eight hours ago. But once I saw these, once I went through what you just went through, it was no longer *if,* but *how.*"

"Jesus. This guy's *here*?"

He lowered his voice. "Now I need to get several others to make that same jump."

Ten

Cristina's lunch crowd had thinned out an hour earlier, leaving only a few tables occupied on the restaurant's back deck at 3:30. The wait staff, dressed in all black, hurried about servicing the remaining tables.

"A cougar? Are you sure?" Patrick Cutter wore a pink golf shirt with the C^3 logo embroidered on the breast. He focused intently across the table at his brother.

"Of course I'm sure. Give me a break!"

"Did you tell anyone?" Patrick asked.

"I got out of the shower about ten minutes ago. Besides, in case you've missed the news: I'm not overly eager to spend time with Walt Fleming."

"Walt could have been a *lot* harder on you."

"Yeah, yeah."

"What about Liz? She's all right?"

Danny set down his fork, eyed his brother with disbelief. "I almost get mauled by a cougar, and all you can think about is your keynote speaker?"

Patrick pursed his lips.

"Fear not, Paddy: She's all yours. She's going to give her talk, announce her candidacy, and your precious conference will go down in history. Congratulations."

Patrick shook his head but not a hair moved.

"That is what it's all about, right?" Danny asked. "How many millions of your own money do you spend on this thing? And for what? A little respect? You're the Rodney Dangerfield of Wall Street, Paddy. The sad thing is, nobody has the balls to tell you."

"If it was all about my vanity, would Bill Gates attend? Warren Buffett? Ian Cumming? The conference serves its purpose or I wouldn't do it."

"That money could be put to better use."

"Says the man who can't hold on to a dime. You're hardly one to talk. You're off fishing and chasing tail when you're still ten short on your angel round."

"It irks you, doesn't it? My turning you down?" Danny asked, his tone softened.

"The offer still stands," Patrick said.

"And it's an incredibly generous one, but one I can't accept."

"It just seems to me—"

"Don't start! Please." Danny placed his napkin on the table and pushed his plate away, growing more serious.

"Keeping it in the family—"

"And I wish I could, but I can't."

"Of course you can," Patrick said. "You choose not to. There's a big difference."

"I choose not to because you've bailed me out of every one of my screwups for as long as I can remember. Not that this is a screwup. It's not. For once I've got a chance at something that could actually work. And your help with the business plan—"

"Was minimal."

"It was *not* minimal. There you go again. Don't do that. You helped, and I'm grateful, but when it comes to financing it, I've got to do it myself. You're the one with all the right gut instincts. You don't become a billionaire on luck. I've got to do this, Paddy. That's all. You know that feeling when you know you're right."

"Then at least start with Stu Holms. This fits right into his latest round of acquisitions."

Danny joked, "Don't tell that to Liz. She'll slap another antitrust suit on him."

"Heaven help us," Patrick said.

"Any tricks to Stuart Holms? Other than not mentioning Liz Shaler?"

Patrick grinned and stabbed at the slices of chicken in his salad. "He's old school. You won't get a second chance. Practice on Sharples and Jenkins. Save Holms for when you're ready. You've got several strong talking points: Trilogy has done well regionally; the push to national distribution isn't that big a stretch; lean on the fact that the big bottlers filter the water and that your source is two miles deep. Stu likes a good story, so don't be shy. He'll appreciate the evolution and growth. You've done a good job, Danny. That'll mean something to him. You won the trademark on 'organic water.' That's huge. He'll see the value. Save that for last."

"All good stuff," Danny said.

Patrick dripped some dressing onto his shirt.

Danny couldn't help himself. "The pink shirt

doesn't work, Paddy. You look like you're wearing house insulation."

"You think?" Patrick blushed, tugged on his shirt, and then looked around the restaurant self-consciously.

Danny saw surprise register on his brother's face, just before he heard the warm, soothing voice behind him.

"Well, look what the cat dragged in. Hey, you two."

Ailia Holms was strong and fit, like so many of the Sun Valley women. Soon to be middle-aged, with a body that peeled off ten years, she held back a restless playfulness. Her red hair forewarned her personality. She was a comfortable flirt in a bright green top and Oilily stretch pants that cleaved to her backside as she bent to peck Patrick on the cheek.

"Speak of the devil," Patrick said.

She faux-patted the top of her head, taking advantage of the moment to show off the latest augmentation to her breasts. "Devil? Are my horns showing?"

She gave Danny an awkward hug that perhaps intentionally thrust her breasts into his chin. "Long time no see, stranger."

"True story."

"Everything good?" Ailia asked unflinch-ingly.

"For a guy who just spent fourteen months in Club Fed, you mean?"

"I don't care where you've been, Danny. It's good to see you, is all. You look good."

"And you."

"So . . . Ailia . . ." Patrick said. "Tell us about London."

"We didn't go, as it turns out. Stu got hung up with some deal. Surprise."

"You've been here . . . all along?" Patrick asked. Danny was surprised by the obvious disappointment on his brother's face.

"We knew you'd be busy preparing for the conference. Looks like a great one, by the way. Elizabeth Shaler! You waited long enough to announce that!"

Patrick reached for a chair from an empty table. Ailia waved away the offer.

"I'd love to, but I can't stay. Stu's waiting." She leaned into Danny a second time and pecked him on the cheek. "See you tonight, I hope," she whispered.

She gave Patrick an air kiss. "Looking for-ward to tonight," and hurried off.

Both men tracked her through the tables.

"Don't go there," Patrick cautioned. "You're damn lucky Stu never found out about you two the first time."

"Who said he didn't?"

"Stu is many things but charitable is not one of them. Nor is he forgiving."

"I thought the whole town knew."

"Apparently not."

Patrick flagged a busboy. "We'll take the check."

The scrawny kid turned around and clearly recognized him. "Ah . . . yes, sir." He lingered a little longer. "You're Mr. Cutter, right?"

"Yes, I am."

"I'm all over the G-six." He patted his pocket.

"Did you opt for multiplayer?" Patrick asked.

"It's bitchin'."

"Kevin?" Cristina, the proprietor, called from the next table. She'd overheard.

"Check," Kevin said to her, spinning around to tend to the vacated table.

Danny asked his brother, "The G-six?"

"A gaming cell phone. Multiuser over

EVDO—high-speed wireless. Teens are our fastest-growing market."

"You never stop."

Patrick took it as a compliment.

"You really think the pink doesn't work?"

Eleven

With the contact lenses removed, his full vision restored, Milav Trevalian studied the mirrored reflection of Rafe Nagler. The corners of his lips twisted up, stretching the theatrical facial hair glued to his face, a grin of satisfaction for having made it through the loss of the dog.

Ricky was no prop; he needed the dog. He'd also left his backpack behind, a calculated risk necessitated by the incompetence of the airline. The Brasilia's lack of overhead baggage space had required all passengers to gate-check their carry-ons. But either the Salt Lake or Sun Valley ground crews had mixed it in with the checked baggage. When it failed to appear on the pickup cart, Trevalian had lost his temper, quickly changing horses and directing his rage at the baggage handlers. With the unexpected loss of the dog, and the sheriff all over him, he'd feared trying to recover the backpack. This, because he couldn't be sure if he hadn't left an old airline identity tag attached to it. With the opaque contacts in place, making him truly blind (he carried two sets, one translucent), he hadn't been able to see if there was a tag there or not. He couldn't afford close scrutiny so the bag and its contents had been left behind.

Trevalian unpacked Nagler's suitcase, tried on the unfamiliar clothes, and discovered the dead man's shirts fit fine; the pants, though big in the waist, could be made to work with the help of a belt. He noticed small bumps of thread had been sewn into tight knots on the insides of the back pockets of the pants—Braille-like personal codes allowing Nagler to determine color. He found the same hand-sewn bumps on the shirttails, and also on the socks.

He unpacked the man's clothes into the dresser drawers, hung shirts and pants in the closet, and spread items from the toilet kit on the bathroom counter. He even smeared some toothpaste to imitate the man missing his toothbrush.

Still contemplating a way around the death of the dog, he settled down onto the bed and lay back. Waiting came easy for him. Milav Trevalian had the patience of a saint.

Twelve

It felt strange to enter his own vehicle as a guest, but the Secret Service would occupy the Blaine County Sheriff Office's Mobile Command Center—the MCC—for the next four days.

A rock-and-roll tour bus confiscated in a drug bust and remodeled and equipped with every conceivable trick, the MCC was currently parked in front of the post office in the obnoxiously large parking lot that fronted the Sun Valley resort.

Deputy Special Agent in Charge Scott Ramsey sat behind a laptop computer in one of two opposing booths. Behind him hung a seating chart for the inn's ballroom, each seat labeled with a guest name.

Ramsey gave Walt a nod. Three other

agents stood and scattered into the back of the bus, from where Walt could hear a live feed of CNN.

Ramsey had the thick neck and shoulders of a steroid user.

"Dryer's on-site in the hotel but busy at the moment. I told you that over the phone."

"Let's make him unbusy, if we can."

"Not possible. How can I help you?"

Walt laid the stack of photographs, cropped and printed by Fiona, down on the table.

"We have a visitor," Walt said.

Ramsey flipped through the first five or six, his face impassive. "Give me the four-one-one."

"Salt Lake City airport, this morning. The victim was discovered zipped up in a body bag and hidden inside a hung ceiling in a restaurant under construction. We got lucky, I guess you could say: He was still warm. I believe his killer is the same person contracted to do Shaler."

Ramsey continued flipping through the photos. "Glad I ate a while ago."

"I can take these directly to the attorney general, but I thought I owed Special Agent Dryer the courtesy of a conversation. If you say that's not important, then that's not important. Thanks for your time." He scooped up the photos, turned around in the small space, offering Ramsey his back.

Ramsey stood. "Hang on." He squeezed past Walt and led him into the Sun Valley Inn, the resort's conference hotel.

Walt felt color rise as he recognized snippets of conversation flood down the hall from one of the conference rooms. He rounded a corner and was greeted by a parade of familiar faces just leaving a meeting. Some of the men stopped to shake hands with him.

"Better late than never, Sheriff," someone called out.

"Nothing like missing your own meeting," a familiar but unidentified voice said.

Reflexively, Walt double-checked his watch, though he already knew the time. The security orientation meeting wasn't scheduled for another forty-five minutes and here it was breaking up.

Thirteen

Walt entered the stuffy conference room prepared for a turf battle with Adam Dryer. He was entirely unprepared for what he saw: his father.

The two men sat next to each other at a linen-covered table on a dais at the end of the boxy conference room. The dais was raised a foot off the floor facing rows of portable chairs separated by a center aisle, reminding Walt of a courtroom, and he the attorney pleading his case.

Jerry Fleming lifted his head and met his son's surprised stare. "I left a message."

Walt checked his cell phone: There was no message indicator.

"That's bullshit," Walt said.

Jerry Fleming served as director of security for Avicorps out of Seattle, the world's largest aircraft manufacturer. He'd taken the job and its six-figure salary, a detail he loved to mention to Walt.

"Who moved the five o'clock?" Walt asked.

Jerry answered, not Dryer. "The cocktail party at Cutter's tonight put a little hitch in our giddyup. It was in everyone's best interest to advance it an hour."

"The five o'clock was *my* meeting. Mine and O'Brien's. You have no say in this."

"Apparently I do," Jerry said.

"Your father brought us intel that First Rights is planning to protest the conference." Adam Dryer made every attempt to make this sound of the utmost importance. "I left you a message on your cell phone about the meeting being advanced."

Walt gave him a look.

"Careful, son," Jerry Fleming said.

"You stay out of this," Walt said.

"Wish that I could. My company's going to have people at the cocktail party, and the five o'clock didn't give me and my team time to get in place. A conference like this is fluid, son. You know that."

His father was a fount of security clichés.

"You want fluid? Try piss and vinegar."

"The presence of First Rights requires additional planning," Dryer said.

"The WTO in Seattle? *That* First Rights?" Walt asked.

"The same," Dryer said.

Walt now stepped forward and placed the Salt Lake photos in front of Dryer, who gravely flipped through the stack, passing each photograph on to Jerry Fleming.

"Son of a bitch," Jerry said, meeting eyes with his son. "This is Salt Lake?" He scrutinized the photographs. "Organized mind. Experienced with a knife. Late twenties, early thirties. Single."

"It isn't a serial killer, Dad. It's a hit man."

"I've hunted them, son," Jerry said. "All you've done is study them."

"The upside," Dryer said, raising his voice and making a conscious effort to separate father and son, "is that clearly our intel was wrong. When and if this dead guy's ever IDed, what do you want to bet his initials come back AG? We got all worked up over nothing."

"And this 'hit,' " Walt said, drawing the quotes, "just happens to occur a couple hundred miles south of where AG Shaler is giving a speech? Give me a break! The intel's solid. The planning for the body bag is the kicker. That should bother us, because it's an indication of premeditation." He paused, allowing that to sink in. "This kill *confirms* the intel. We need to know the victim's identity—fast—and his role in this, because the man behind that knife is on his way here, or is here already."

"You're entitled to your opinions, Sheriff," Dryer said. "But until we have the identification, until we have *any* kind of evidence connecting this kill to the conference, it would be irresponsible to initiate hysteria over what might be nothing."

" 'Initiate hysteria'?" Walt asked. "You want another look at those photos? This guy is a pro—whoever he is, whatever his purpose—and he's within three hundred miles of here. All I'm saying is we'd better sit up and take notice."

Jerry interrupted the debate, saying, "There's a cocktail party in a little over two hours, and First Rights intends to march on this conference. Where's our focus? On a city three hundred miles south of here, in *another state,* or on the business at hand?"

"I need route clearance and a two-vehicle

escort from the AG's residence to Patrick Cutter's residence, on or about six forty-five P.M.," Dryer informed Walt.

"It's already on the itinerary. You'll have your escort." Walt stepped up onto the dais to collect the photographs. "I want to show these to Liz Shaler."

"Out of the question," Dryer barked out quickly.

"She deserves to understand the degree of the threat."

"The AG is my responsibility," Dryer reminded.

"She's speaking at the conference and that puts her with me. Are we really going to get into this?"

"If you want a few minutes with her, I'll arrange it. But no photographs. No one should see these who doesn't have to."

Walt took this as a minor victory. "Thank you," he said.

Jerry Fleming made a show of checking his watch. "I've got to get moving. Walt, let's do this at the party."

"Cutter doesn't want uniforms present," Walt reminded.

"So lose the uniform," Dryer said. "Meet me at the cocktail party, Sheriff. You and the

AG will step out for a minute. See if you can come up with a game plan for First Rights by then. We've got to hit this proactively."

"See you at seven," Walt said.

Fourteen

A knock came on the hotel room door at 4:44. Before answering, Trevalian unlocked the dead bolt on the door that connected to the adjacent room, knowing he would need this later. He then rechecked his appearance—the face of the man, Rafe Nagler, in the bathroom mirror. Satisfied, he grabbed his cane and answered the door.

"Here to take you to the movie, sir."

Trevalian wore Nagler's wraparound sunglasses, but not the opaque contact lenses. The lenses he now wore provided a horrid sight, if anyone caught a glimpse of his eyes, but allowed him to see, though a little muddier than usual. Karl turned out to be a brute of a man, well over six feet, with wide shoulders, a big brow, and deeply recessed eyes. He led Trevalian by the elbow out into the heat and sunshine, along beautifully landscaped paths and past an outdoor mall of boutiques. To the north, the Pioneer mountain range, tipped with snowfields, rose like the Alps.

Karl bought him a ticket and, at his request, showed him to a seat in the back row of the Opera House theater. A large auditorium that seated four hundred. Its seats faced a production-sized stage, in the middle of which hung a commercial movie screen. Rows of exit doors flanked the seats on both sides. The washrooms were not out in the foyer but instead accessed at the back of the hall, behind where Trevalian now sat. Karl offered to arrange for someone to meet him later, but Nagler politely declined.

As the film started, Trevalian counted seven others in the cavernous theater—two families, both sitting much closer to the distant screen. He casually checked behind himself: The red velvet curtains were pulled across the entrance to the lobby.

Fifteen minutes into the movie, Nagler slipped off to the men's room and locked the door. He removed and pocketed the facial hair and wig. He left the stall to wash the coloring out of his eyebrows and lashes at the sink. Five minutes after entering the men's room, he departed one of the side doors as Milav Trevalian, his white cane collapsed and tucked into his sock.

Sun Valley's pedestrian mall included a bookstore, a minimarket, a gallery, and several ski and apparel shops that in the summer carried mountain biking garb, white rafting paraphernalia, backpacking supplies, as well as T-shirts, sweatshirts, ball caps, and golf goodies. Trevalian paid cash for a small overnight bag, some T-shirts, and two pairs of chinos that would fit him better than Nagler's wardrobe. At the minimarket he bought toothpaste, a toothbrush, some deodorant, and a razor.

He headed back to the lodge.

"Checking in?" asked the young blonde, whose name tag read Hannah, Prague, Czech Republic. Trevalian could have spoken fluent Czech to her, but he resisted showing off.

"Meisner." Trevalian supplied the name the reservation was booked under and slid across a valid credit card also in Meisner's name. "I requested a room that—"

"Yes. I have it right here," she said, running her finger across the screen. "We were able to accommodate your request. Your room communicates with Mr. Nagler's."

"My friend is sight-challenged," Trevalian explained. "When I realized we were both going to be here—"

"Yes, of course." After he filled out the register she handed him a key.

"May I have one of our bellmen—"

"No, thank you."

"Enjoy your stay."

Trevalian thanked her and crossed to the elevator, rode it to the third floor, then let himself into the room rented to Meisner. Less than a minute later, with the hallway door locked and secured, he opened the shared door that connected to Nagler's room. He could come and go now as he pleased, under the guise of either identity.

Trevalian pulled a cold beer from the minibar and cracked it open. He worked the television remote, disappointed the lodge did not offer adult in-room movies, and flipped to CNN.

Both the dog and the missing backpack were problems requiring solutions. But he'd established the two identities; he had the connecting rooms.

Calling from the Meisner room, Trevalian arranged for a rental car through the weekend.

He had errands to run in Ketchum.

He had a bomb to build.

Fifteen

In the middle of arranging for barricades to help control the expected protests from First Rights, Walt was alerted by Tommy Brandon of an unexpected complication.

"You're not going to like this, Sheriff," Brandon began. He'd elected to call Walt on his office phone, rather than relay any message through dispatch, telegraphing that secrecy was an issue. "But I went back onto the Taylor Crabtree surveillance after the airport, and I just followed him to one seventy-two Northridge. That's Myra's place, right?"

Walt relived his sister-in-law's earlier intrusion into his office and her pushing him to do something about her wayward teenage son, Kevin.

"Yeah," Walt said.

"So . . . what do want me to do?" Brandon asked.

Taylor Crabtree was a sixteen-year-old JD suspected of drug trafficking in meth and selling to minors like himself. He'd flunked out of Wood River High, had been given a second chance in the Silver Creek Alternative School, and had been tossed after three strikes on drug use. For the past two weeks Walt's deputies had kept him under nearly round-the-clock surveillance. And now he'd walked in to visit Walt's nephew.

"Take a coffee break," Walt said. "I'll look into it."

"Roger that," Brandon said. "I'm on the cell, if you want me to pick the surveillance back up."

"I'll call. And thanks, Tommy."

"Far as I'm concerned," Brandon said, "I went on the break a half hour ago. None of this goes into my report until and unless you say so."

"Appreciate it." Walt disconnected the call, knowing he wouldn't condone cooking a report to favor his nephew. But if he could get a read on the situation, or break it up ahead of anything illegal, then maybe he'd spare Myra and Kevin another family disaster.

He pulled into Myra's driveway and opened the car door to a blast of dry heat. He shut it loudly, making a point of announcing his arrival, and then used a sliding glass window in the next-door neighbor's house like a mirror to watch the back of Myra's house. He'd been fifteen once himself.

Two kids spilled out the back door like the place was on fire.

Walt took off after them: down the driveway, around the corner, past the vegetable garden and the disused swing set. He vaulted the low post-and-rail fence into a neighbor's backyard just in time to catch one of the two escapees in profile.

"Eric!" he shouted in his best sheriff's voice.

Two women looked up from their flower beds across the street. Walt shouted a second time.

The boy stopped.

Walt was angry with the kid for causing him to sweat through his uniform. "What the hell, Eric?"

"Kevin said we could."

"Could what?"

"Could be there. At the house." The boy was more out of breath than Walt. "Kevin said it was okay."

"Kevin works Thursdays," Walt said, testing.

"He just got back from Cristina's. I swear we've been in there maybe ten minutes."

Walt knew it was more like thirty. Kids. "We?"

The boy hesitated.

"I can check all this out," Walt said. He looked the boy over, considered asking him to turn his pockets out. But he was afraid of what he might find. "Who was the other boy?" he asked instead, already knowing damn well. "And before you answer, remember that lying to a sheriff is a bad idea."

Eric lowered his eyes. "Crab," he said after a moment.

"Taylor Crabtree?" Walt paused. "Eric, the best advice I can give you is to not go places you know you shouldn't go. You're a good kid. You hang around a boy like Taylor Crabtree and it's guaranteed that you'll be seeing more of me."

"Yes, sir."

"Now, go on."

Eric took a step or two, then broke into a run.

A minute later, Kevin greeted his uncle from the far side of the screen door on the back porch. "Hey, Uncle Walt." His lanky frame looked all the thinner with his shirt off. His pants hung below the elastic of his underwear—a fashion statement for some, but not for Kevin. No one in the family had fully processed the loss, nearly a year earlier, of Walt's brother, Bobby. Least of all Kevin. Walt had tried to fill the void; had neglected his own family in the process; and had now paid for it with his own divorce. Walt had never been real good at getting close; perhaps Kevin read that awkwardness as something else. He'd never been receptive to Walt's advances. The one thing that connected them was now dead, and they both reminded the other of him so much that it hurt.

"Hey, yourself," Walt said. "Eric and Taylor Crabtree sure took off in a hurry. What was that about?"

He shrugged. "Dunno."

"Maybe the cop car and the uniform didn't help?"

"Maybe."

"Taylor Crabtree is bad news."

Kevin took a moment to study the places where paint had chipped from the door-jamb. "So you've said. Are you going to tell Mom?"

"You kidding me? You think I want to be on the receiving end of that windstorm?" He won a faint smile. "I'm going to tell her we had a talk about the keggers and that you promised me you wouldn't drink and drive, and that you wouldn't get high. Can you keep that promise?"

"Absolutely."

"You know it's my job to bust those parties, right?"

"Yeah."

"And you're the last person on earth I'd ever want to arrest."

"I got it."

"How's the job at Cristina's going?"

"Good, I guess."

"It's shit work."

"Yeah," Kevin said, cracking another slight smile, "it sucks."

"But if you hang in there, she'll move you into the kitchen or out as a waiter. Both of those are better money, and they're better work."

Kevin's face revealed his internal disconnect. Walt had seen that face before—the "oh, shit, here it comes again" look that any teenager learns to command. Walt wanted to take the kid and hug him, to hold him. He knew Myra; he didn't imagine anyone had done that since the funeral. But something stopped him.

"Grandpa called."

"You understand what I'm saying about Crabtree?" Walt owed it to the boy to get his point across.

"Said he was here for the long weekend, that maybe we'd have dinner or something. You, him, me, and Mom."

"You've got to distance yourself from him, Kev."

"Grandpa?" Kevin asked.

"Don't twist things around on me. Tell me Crabtree being here had nothing to do with drugs."

"Jesus, you're not my father." Kevin paused. "I suppose you want to come in and look around." He swung open the screen door and held it.

"I'm not coming in. Shut the door."

"What about it? Seeing Grandpa?"

"Your grandpa and I are having dinner

later at the Pio. Why don't you and your mom come up around eight for dessert?"

"Seriously?"

"I won't be wearing my uniform."

"That doesn't bother me."

"Sure it does," Walt said.

"Yeah, kinda."

"Eight o'clock, all right?"

"Got it."

"Crabtree."

"I know."

"All right then."

Sixteen

Trevalian worked efficiently in the bathroom of the suite adjacent to Nagler's. One misstep, and he'd be at the center of a fire so hot, so incendiary, that it would easily consume him and a wing of the hotel before help arrived.

The litter of packaging overflowed the wastebasket into a pile on the tile floor.

He finished assembling the Coleman camp stove. He'd removed the vent grate, allowing him to clamp and duct-tape a battery-operated fan into its rectangular hole, allowing the fan to evacuate the soon-to-be-toxin-ridden air more quickly. He lit both of the Coleman's burners and began to hum quietly.

He inspected his various purchases. He'd

bought no more than two items from a single store. Untraceable. Undetectable. Unbelievably easy. To the left of the sink he found the bottle of bleach. He broke its seal and filled a Pyrex bowl, then, with the fan running, brought it to a boil. He weighed out the table salt substitute and added it to the bleach and continued boiling until the battery tester registered full charge. Full charge, indeed. He removed the bowl and set it to cool in the ice-filled sink. He then filtered out the crystals, recovering the bleach to boil it again. An hour later he was heating distilled water with the crystals and filtering this as well. At the end of this process of fractional crystallization, he had relatively pure potassium chlorate, which he ground to the consistency of face powder.

He melted equal parts Vaseline and wax, dissolved it over the camp stove, and then poured it over the potassium chlorate in a large Tupperware bowl. Wearing a pair of rubber gloves, he kneaded this until thoroughly mixed and set the bowl outside, in the corner of the balcony, pulling a potted plant over to conceal it.

He double-checked that the PRIVACY PLEASE tag was on the door and the dead bolt was still engaged. As a finishing touch, he angled the desk chair beneath the inside doorknob. Ensured no one could enter the Meisner room without a battering ram, he then cleaned up the bathroom, grouping the various ingredients in a brown paper bag beneath the sink.

He entered Nagler's room, closed and locked the connecting door, pausing only briefly to once again reconsider each and every step. Lightheaded with excitement— or was it the fumes?—he proceeded to the mirror in Nagler's bathroom and resolved himself to the patient application of the facial hair, the clothing, and finally the milky contact lenses that made him blind.

He had a party to attend.

Seventeen

"What have I gotten myself into?" Liz Shaler asked Jenna, her plain-faced executive secretary who'd worked with her for nearly ten years. Liz was putting the finishing touches on her face, in front of a mirror in what had once been her parents' bedroom.

"You'll be fine," Jenna assured her.

"I'm whoring, and we both know it. I might as well just spread my legs and get it over with."

"Just don't let the tabloids see you."

"I'll bet I've had a half dozen of these very people, or at least their companies, under some form of investigation or inquiry in the past six years. And now I'm asking them for money? How hypocritical is that?"

"You're not asking anyone for money."

"Give me a break."

"You're going to make your positions clear, and if *some* of these people choose to support those positions, then fine."

"It is *so* much more complicated than that, and you know it. We're tricking the system, Patrick Cutter and I, and I should know better. This kind of thing always backfires."

"You're doing nothing wrong, nothing illegal. We've vetted this six ways to Sunday. Your job is to have fun. It's only a couple days."

"You mean it's my last couple of days. Feels like some kind of sentence. Everything changes Sunday morning. Don't kid yourself about that, Jenna: *everything*." She dabbed a cotton ball at the edge of her eyes. "We will not have a moment's rest for the next fifteen months and twelve days. We are going way out on a limb here."

"Since when have we not been out on a limb?"

"I'm comfortable as a whore? Is that what you're saying?"

"Beats working for a living."

The women exchanged smiles in the mirror, though Liz Shaler's sank into a grimace. "I hope I'm not making a mistake."

"Of course you are. But what's the alternative?"

"I could be a ski bum," Liz suggested.

"Or sit, bored, on a dozen boards."

"You made your point," Liz chided. She'd heard this often from her advisers: nowhere to go but up. "How's this?" she asked, turning to show her face.

"A million bucks," Jenna said.

"I hope you're wrong," Liz said, "because we need a hell of a lot more than that just to get out of the starting gate."

Eighteen

Standing on the U-shaped wraparound balcony that overlooked the living room of his nineteen-thousand-square-foot home, Patrick Cutter surveyed the cocktail party he'd thrown for 125 early arrivals to C^3. Below him, the elite of America's communications industry comingled and made merry, fortified by the best champagne, liquor, and wines served in crystal flutes and heavy cut-glass tumblers. The appetizers had been created by a chef from a small Provençal gîte located two kilometers south of Gorde. Many of the guests knew one another, contributing to the lively hum of conversation that hit Patrick Cutter's ears like music.

His wife, Trish, glanced up from a tightly knit group on the floor below. In February, she'd spent thirty thousand dollars on her face, so this was her coming-out party of sorts. She offered him no wink, no nod, no subtle smile. But the sparkle in her laser-corrected eyes said enough: a success. The conference was off to a good start.

He hoped it would shape the direction of the communications industry in the months to come. Still these changes were subtle. Sometimes they reached the front page of the *Wall Street Journal*. This sense of history, and his place in it as a leader, thrilled him. In three days' time, Liz Shaler was to announce her candidacy for president at his conference. How could pride be a sin when it felt so good? Who would not forgive him that little indulgence? This conference was all about indulgence.

His gaze swept the crowd. He caught a voyeuristic glimpse down the dress of the lead violinist in the classical quartet.

Where the hell was Liz Shaler?

He spotted and tracked the unmistakable red plumage of Ailia Holms as she and her husband, Stuart, stopped and chatted to friends. He made a mental note to keep Stu away from Liz Shaler. No need for a scene. A waitress took drink orders. The group erupted in laughter. He watched as Ailia gave Stu a subtle tug, and then led him over to the head of the world's leading manufacturer of fiber optic cable. Ailia never missed a beat.

As Stu engaged in small talk, Ailia rose to her toes seeking out their next obligation. But when she lingered a little too long in one direction, Patrick followed her gaze to its target: Danny. Alarms sounded in his head: If Ailia wanted Danny, it was for only one reason.

Patrick sought out the nearest staircase—there were six in this house—and made his move to intervene.

Nineteen

Walt parked the Sheriff's Office Cherokee at the end of a long line of vehicles hugging the shoulder of Adam's Gulch Road and headed on foot down the curving driveway, adorned with twenty-foot blue spruces and a gorgeous array of flowers, which like so much of residential Ketchum and Sun Valley had been built in the past ten years. That meant each of the towering trees had been purchased mature and transplanted. At a cost of fifteen thousand dollars per tree, it was a most conspicuous display of wealth. But nothing compared to the house itself. Fashioned from five antique New England barns, each dismantled and transported and reassembled into an interconnecting village, the compound looked like a small

New England village. Two well-dressed host-
esses, both wearing C^3 badges, greeted
Walt and offered an Orrefors crystal champagne flute bearing a frosted C^3 logo. The
flute bubbled with a 1990 Krug, judging by
the chilled bottles just inside the front door.

"The glass is compliments of Mr. Cutter,"
the blonde informed Walt.

Walt had worn a freshly pressed button-
down shirt and his best pair of chinos, but
knew how out of place he looked compared
to the linen, poplin, and silk on display.

The front door, cut within the enormous
barn door, opened into a vast space of
weathered wood and glass broken into several smaller rooms. The living room's most
prominent feature was a dry stack fireplace
with a six-foot-high open hearth that currently held an opulent arrangement of cut
flowers and cattails. A balcony surrounded
the second floor looking out onto a massive
chandelier made of interconnecting antlers.

Walt tried not to stare at the women, the
jewelry, the sheer blouses, the tempting
necklines. Tried not to succumb to the swirl
of French perfumes, the gleaming white
teeth of flashing smiles, and the heady rush
from the champagne. He retired the half-

filled glass on a passing tray and spotted a few faces he knew, all of whom were private security, keeping to the walls or behind one of the dozen hand-hewn timber posts, allowing their employers free rein. All told, he counted four, one hovering near Bill Gates, another close to Sumner Redstone. He expected to find most of the guys out back with the rest of the help—the drivers, chefs, and personal assistants.

He looked for Liz Shaler, expecting he'd find Dryer within an arm's length, and caught sight of Patrick Cutter coming down a staircase, looking very much like a man in a hurry attempting to look casual. In less than a minute, Walt declined offerings from four different hors d'oeuvres trays.

He watched as Cutter reached the bottom of the stairs and seemed to change directions, heading straight to the front door. Some faces turned in that direction. The buzz of conversation briefly diminished.

Walt glanced back over his shoulder. New York State Attorney General Elizabeth Shaler had arrived.

Cutter succeeded in reaching her first, though nearly out of breath.

Conversation slowly resumed. Shaler's name echoed around the room.

Flanked by two men in blue jeans and blue blazers, one of whom was Adam Dryer, she looked right past Cutter and spotted Walt and waved. Walt wasn't sure of etiquette. He returned a small wave, feeling the eyes of a hundred envious strangers bearing down on him.

Twenty

Danny Cutter saw Ailia approaching—without Stu. Wanting to avoid any gossip, he excused himself from a group of his brother's friends and headed to the toilet. He passed one of the bars, dodged a few greetings, cut through the library (done sumptuously in suede and African leathers) following discreet signs to the POWDER ROOM taped on doorjambs. He needed a GPS. He passed another of the directional signs, noticing that someone had already crossed out the "d" in Powder.

There had been a time when Danny had been caught up in all this himself: the show, the exaggerated lifestyle, the pretense. There had been a time—prior to the 1990s—when Sun Valley had been about skiing in the winter and hiking, tennis, or golf in the summer. But L.A. riots, earthquakes, and fires had given way to White Flight. The Hollywood set. The arrival of Attitude. The glass and steel replacing the funky log establishments on Main Street. He and his brother were a part of that sea change for the valley, and it wasn't anything to be proud of.

Chasing sobriety was about as terrifying as being chased by a cougar. And though Danny was all for success, especially his own, he had no desire to be any of the people in this room, including his brother. Briefly, he thought he'd keep right on walking—out the back door. If he could find it.

Concerned that Ailia was looking for him, and knowing how easy it was to get caught up in her web, he kept moving. With her husband as a potential investor, he wanted to avoid complication and succeed or fail on his own.

Finding the powder room occupied, he headed up one of the many staircases. The second of the five connected barns contained a hotel kitchen and a similar sized laundry room on the ground floor, and three guest suites upstairs—living room, bedroom, bath—one of which he currently occupied. He bounded up to the top of the stairs and turned quickly toward his room. This hallway connected to the central barn's U-shaped balcony that overlooked the living room where the cocktail party now raged. In taking the corner at the top of the stairs too quickly, he nearly knocked over a guest.

The man, who wore wraparound sunglasses, dropped a cane—a thin, white cane.

He was blind.

Danny made immediate apologies.

Twenty-one

Trevalian had found the perfect view. From the balcony he'd watched Shaler's grand entrance. Hearing someone bounding up the stairs, he'd turned and forced a collision, to win sympathy over suspicion.

Now, on his knees, he patted the floor searching for his cane, even though he could see it to his right.

"Sorry." The man who'd knocked into him was profoundly good-looking, and polite in his supplication.

"No problem," he said, moving tentatively toward the stairs and grasping for the handrail.

"You're a long way from the party," the man observed.

"Bird's-eye view." Trevalian openly smirked

at his own joke. "I was taking the dime tour." He was now halfway down the stairs, and with the man behind him he couldn't risk observing Shaler as he'd intended. But given that he'd counted at least four security escorts around her, it was better not to test their abilities to spot people like him.

"If you give me a minute, I could show you back downstairs. I've got a fifty-cent tour that might beat your dime."

"I can find my way, thank you." He added to his voice the curt edge of a man who was used to and resented being patronized because of his disability. He followed the banister around the turn of the landing and continued down the stairs.

A gorgeous redhead arrived at the base of the stairs. "Hello," she said.

"Hello," Trevalian answered, looking in her general direction and raising his head like a dog sniffing the wind. The air smelled of ambrosia, and something earthy and pungent.

"You didn't happen to see . . . that is, I'm sorry . . . Did anyone pass by you just now?" she asked.

Trevalian knew intuitively to stay out of this. The man who'd run into him had clearly been in a hurry: but to make a love nest or to avoid one?

And then, from above, "Up here, Ailia."

Her cheeks flushed and her eyes sparkled. "Excuse me," she said, hurrying past him, leaving Trevalian awash in her complex scents, and, to his surprise, aroused.

Twenty-two

"You look a little lost," a friendly voice said from behind Walt.

He turned to find Clarence Stillwill, a fixture in the Wood River Valley for the past forty years. He'd been a river guide, a saloon owner, a magazine and book publisher, and was currently an organic farmer on twenty acres outside of Fairfield. And for good measure he and his wife filled in as bartenders for friends who ran the most popular catering company in town.

Clarence was a big man, but well proportioned so it didn't show until you stood right next to him, part cowboy, part college professor. He manned a wine bar between two potted trees.

Walt took a beer.

"Money like this . . ."

"Yeah," Walt said.

"This house . . . he's here, what, three weeks a year?"

"If that."

"Talk about a crime."

"I know."

"Why the civvies?" Clarence asked.

"I'm undercover."

"Yeah, you fit right in here."

"I've got to do the impossible: convince a woman not to talk."

"It really *is* a thankless job."

"Jerry's involved."

"How is it between you two?"

"About the same," Walt said.

"Bobby's death?"

"The great divide."

"It was a real loss. How's the kid?"

"Messed up."

"Yeah," Clarence said. "Kinda figured."

"We all are. Gail and I . . . A lot of that was losing Bobby."

"I figured you two forever."

"You and me, both."

"Can't live with 'em, can't kill 'em."

"Cheers to that," Walt said, hoisting the beer.

"In case you missed it, Tommy Lee Jones keeps checking you out."

Walt looked to see Dryer staring him down.

"Guys like that," Clarence said, indicating Dryer, "they'll put up a fight, but they won't take you to the mat. At the end of the day, it's just a paycheck for them."

"Your lips to God's ears."

A waitress interrupted and placed an order. As Clarence went to work, Walt looked up to see Danny Cutter in profile, clear across the room, up on the balcony. He was chatting up a redhead with quite a profile.

Walt's cell phone buzzed, and he ducked behind a potted tree to answer.

A woman's grating voice cleared the wax from his ears. "Kevin tells me we're invited to dessert with you and Jerry up at the Pio. Is that for real?"

"Hello, Myra."

"Why are you whispering?"

"I'm kind of in the middle of something."

"But it sounds noisy."

"Kevin's right. Dessert is for real. My treat. The Pio, maybe eight-thirty, quarter to nine." He checked his watch, realizing if she hadn't called, he might have forgotten the dinner with his father. The Salt Lake photographs had pushed all else from his mind.

"But Jerry?" she asked. "What if he's drinking?"

"Then you'll be doing me a big favor by coming," Walt said honestly.

"Okay . . . okay. But he starts dumping on Kevin, we're out of there."

"And I'll be right behind you," Walt said.

He hung up the call, wondering what he'd gotten himself into.

Twenty-three

"Tell me you weren't running from me," Ailia said.

Danny took a little too long to say, "Don't be silly."

She gestured to the nearest guest room, marked "Guercino" on the door.

"Indifferent. Or trying to be," Danny said.

"But why?"

"New leafs don't turn over easily."

"Oh, God, don't tell me you bought the whole twelve-step thing."

"I bought it, but it was on credit."

"Five minutes. Don't make me beg." She led him down the hall and into the first guest suite—as it happened, his.

She closed the door with authority.

"I'm going to skip the missing-you part,

and how hard it's been, and get to the point: I can help you, Danny. Want to. With Stu, I'm talking about. Trilogy."

"I beg your pardon?"

"Patrick told me all about it. He's in a snit you won't keep it in the family, but hey, if it's Stu and me, it's almost family anyway, don't you think?"

"I think this is my business and Paddy had no right to—"

"Oh, come on! He's looking after you. We're all looking after you. And at least one of us is looking right at you." She stepped closer, a dozen sweet smells swirling in front of her. "I'm not the enemy, you know?"

If she moved another inch toward him their bodies would touch. Now he felt her body heat. It mixed with her scent and his head swam.

"Allie . . . no."

"Ah, come on. Why deny a girl a little pleasure?" Her breath smelled of red wine. "You know how I am about pleasure."

The longer she stood there, the weaker his will. He inhaled deeply and some hairs danced toward his face.

She whispered, "Let me help. Please." She tentatively placed her hands on his waist, above his hip bones. "I'm not going to beg," she said. "Not until our clothes are off, at least. You know how I get." She smiled, and as much as he wanted to see her as self-serving and shallow, a middle-aged flirt, to be turned off by her, he found himself quite the opposite. He liked aggressive women. She knew this about him and exploited it. "I've been fantasizing about you, Danny, for over a year now. In the shower. Alone at night. That's a lot of fire needs putting out. You know me."

He felt his resistance failing. Her perfumes invaded him and hit like a drug. His skin burned where she touched him.

"Feel where I'm the warmest?" she said, pushing her hips forward and burning through to his thigh.

More scents escaped from her neckline— dark, lusty odors that didn't come from a bottle—scents that were designed to trigger urges and instincts, and he was a fool to think he could prevent it. He drank them down and they fed him, and the addict in him, so barely confined, wanted more. He'd sworn no internal oath against this. He had no battle with her. Physically he needed this, and she knew it and the offer that now came out of her, in an expression of hands and a willingness of her lips parting to kiss him, so overwhelmed him that he didn't simply give in to it, he thrived on it.

He pulled off her clothes, down to that tangle of dark, and devoured her in a flurry of impulse, while she pleasured herself behind guttural coughs as she sped toward climax.

Down in the living room, the quartet played on, their strains heard as muted sentimental nonsense, while in the room, behind a wincing call for more, the real music played to its finale.

Twenty-four

Patrick Cutter couldn't find them. He'd lost track of Ailia and Danny, and while overcome with joy at the arrival of Shaler, he wanted to spare his brother from doing something stupid. Added to his motivation was jealousy, but he kept that in check for the time being. Having left Liz Shaler in capable hands, he now searched more aggressively.

He crossed through the kitchen, briefly sidelined by Heinz, his German chef imported from southern France. Ironically, the complaint involved Stuart Holms's personal chef, who had "taken over" one of the three ovens "without regard" for Heinz. Patrick settled the man down and got out of there in a hurry. Holms's chef traveled with Stuart everywhere, supposedly to provide a special diet to the Wall Street wonder. He was currently preparing finger food for a party of one. Chef Raphael delivered each plate of treats to his boss personally, making a great show of it and convincing some—Patrick was sure—to believe it was Holms's party, not his. The delay heightened his sense of urgency: He had to find Ailia before she re-lit his brother's fuse, and perhaps blew them all up in the process.

Passing his wife's study, he stopped short.

"May I help you?"

The man sitting behind her desk wore dark sunglasses. He had a mustache and beard, and looked vaguely familiar.

"Are you a waiter?" the man asked.

"I'm the owner, actually. Patrick Cutter. May I help you?" Only as the man stood out of the chair did Patrick spot the white cane leaning against the desk.

"It's Rafe Nagler, Mr. Cutter."

Patrick muttered an apology and hurried across the room. After some awkwardness of unknown etiquette on Patrick's part, the two shook hands. "So glad you made it!" he said.

"Stonebrook was honored to be invited."

"You have a marvelous reputation."

"The foundation, you're speaking of. My reputation is, as I'm sure you are aware, that of a loner. A recluse. That's exaggerated, I assure you."

"The Nostradamus of new technologies? You're entitled to your eccentricities, Mr. Nagler. We're happy to have you. You're in my wife's study. Did you know that?"

"Her study?" the man asked. He smiled. "Good God, how embarrassing. I was looking for a place to sit down is all."

"You found one, but maybe you'd prefer something a little closer to the party? Or if you want some solitude, I can send a waiter."

"No, please," Nagler said. "I'll rejoin the party with pleasure."

"I heard about your dog, and I'm gravely sorry for your loss. I can't imagine what you've gone through. We're looking into some possible remedies."

"It's kind of you, but don't trouble yourself. I'm pursuing some options. I'm not bad with a cane, if you excuse mistaking a study for the dining room."

Cutter laughed and then helped the man

to the door, turning him toward the noise of the reception. "If you'll excuse me . . . ," he said.

"Pleased to meet you," Nagler said, heading toward the din.

Patrick headed a few steps toward the north staircase when something pulled at him and he reentered the study. It was narrow and long. Not easily mistaken for a dining room that sat twenty-eight. He couldn't identify what bothered him about Nagler's explanation, but it was enough to draw him to the far side of his wife's desk and next to the chair where Nagler had sat. Now he realized what had called him back: the reflection of the computer screen in the window behind her chair. It should have displayed the screen saver: a photo of Bald Mountain in winter. Instead, it showed the Windows home screen.

The screen saver only left the screen if the keyboard was touched or the mouse moved.

Nagler could have bumped it, he supposed. Gnawed at by lost time, he took one last look before returning to his search for Danny.

But a nagging sensation remained: How had Nagler bumped the keyboard or mouse, given that both were at the far end of the desk?

Twenty-five

As Walt followed Dryer and Shaler out of the living room and into the sumptuous library, he caught a brief glimpse of the blind man, Rafe Nagler, just leaving by the front door. It reminded him to try to find Nagler a loaner sight dog.

"So . . . Walt . . . what is it?" Liz asked, once Dryer had pushed the door shut. She sat down heavily in a leather chair and rubbed her right calf.

Walt glanced over at Dryer, who returned an unsympathetic look. The photos weighed heavily in Walt's back pocket.

"We have evidence, Your Honor, of a horrific killing in Salt Lake City. It makes me wonder if we can provide for your safety."

"Adam?"

"I feel differently but promised the sheriff face time with you."

"Of course," she said. Giving her attention to Walt immediately soured Dryer.

Walt reviewed the discovery of the body at the Salt Lake airport, describing it as a gruesome murder but avoiding anything too graphic per his arrangement with Dryer. He finished by saying, "There's a possibility this ties in to the most recent threat."

"There is *no* evidence connecting the two."

Walt countered, "A possible suspect was followed by a TSA agent to the E concourse, where he subsequently disappeared. The first flight leaving that concourse was bound for Sun Valley, Your Honor."

Her eyes tightened and fell away from Walt to an unfixed stare. "I see." As she regained composure she looked up at Dryer, who wouldn't look directly at her.

"We met that flight," Walt said, "having received this intelligence in advance, and failed to identify a suspect matching the description we'd been given. But I should caution: That doesn't mean he wasn't on that flight."

"It's a lot to process," she said.

Walt said, "Evaluation of an event like this can take weeks. I'm told the FBI has seized security video from the airport that might have helped us. Anticipate a wrestling match with Homeland over those tapes."

"We're heading into a weekend," Dryer reminded, "and that doesn't help us any."

"So there's no way to know who this dead man was, or why he was killed?" she asked.

Walt suggested two possibilities: one, that the intelligence intercept had been a ruse and that the target of the contract was now dead; two, that the dead man was killed because he'd recognized the killer or had seen something he shouldn't have.

"Or," she said, "I can hear it in your voice, Walt. Come on. I'm a big girl."

One of Shaler's handlers knocked on the library door, but Dryer took care of it. He glowered at Walt and tapped his wristwatch, out of sight of Shaler.

"There's always the possibility this murder was a warning," Walt said.

"How so?" She looked horrified.

"A message to you—to us—to let us know how serious they are, how professional, how capable. They're telling you not to run, not to announce your candidacy."

"Speculation!" Dryer interrupted.

"I asked him to speculate," Liz Shaler countered. "Intimidation?" she asked Walt.

"Your Honor," Walt said, "I have no doubt that between Agent Dryer and me we can put a screen around you at the various functions this weekend. But none of us can absolutely guarantee your safety. This person killed inside an airport—about as secure a facility as you can get these days. All I'm saying is, if you're having any reservations about announcing your candidacy, you might want to change things up—hold a press conference sooner rather than later. Move the announcement back to New York. If there is a killer out there, it'll throw him off."

"There you are!" Patrick Cutter announced as he charged through the door. He dismissed Walt and Dryer without so much as a glance. "Been looking for you everywhere."

"A little business to attend to," Liz Shaler said. She looked over at Walt and he saw apology on her face.

Cutter's arrival had slammed her back into the reality of her headlining his coveted conference. He wondered what it felt like to be drawn between power and money and one's personal safety. He got his answer more quickly than he wanted.

"Well," she said, pulling herself up out of the chair, but slowly, as if suddenly more heavy or painful. "I'll count on you to keep me up on any developments, Walt. Day or night, okay?"

"Smoky-backroom deals?" Patrick Cutter said in his obligatory sarcasm.

"There's been a murder in Salt Lake that has all the markings of a professional hit." Walt's voice was filled with frustration.

"Well, good," Cutter said, without missing a beat. "We must have been given bad information. What a relief." With a penetrating look, he challenged first Dryer, then Walt, and finally Shaler to contradict him.

Walt was about to when Liz Shaler caught his eye and silently called him off.

"Who needs a drink?" Cutter asked, ever the jovial host. "I'm buying." He laughed at his own joke, took Liz Shaler by the elbow, and led her to the door before Walt gathered his courage.

As Cutter opened the door, there stood Stuart Holms, about to knock. For a moment tension filled the short space between Holms and Shaler.

"Your Honor," Holms said.

"Mr. Holms," Shaler returned.

"I know we've had our issues," Holms said. "I was just wondering if we might get a minute together? I would hope we could both put the past behind us and keep an open mind toward the future."

"From what I read in the press," Liz Shaler said, "the past is hardly behind us. You've made your opinions of me abundantly clear."

"I'd like to discuss that."

Another palpable silence fell between them. "Let's all get a drink!" Cutter moved her through the door. "Come on, Stu—let's get this worked out."

Liz glanced back at Walt furtively, still outwardly apologetic. With the music and the drone of excited conversation entering the room like a wave, Walt found himself making a parallel to Marie Antoinette's lowering her head into the guillotine.

Three clocks tolled throughout the house within a few seconds of one another: 8 P.M.

He was late for dinner.

Twenty-six

Walt joined his father at a table in the near corner of the Pioneer Saloon's restaurant, just below a wall display of barbed wire. Jerry sat with his back to a pair of rawhide snowshoes. The tabletop was sealed in so many coats of polyurethane that it looked like a piece of amber.

"Sorry I'm late."

"Nothing new."

A bouncy waitress arrived. Walt ordered a house salad and ribs; his father, a bowl of corn chowder, a thick cut of prime rib, and another Scotch.

Jerry, already looking drunk, indicated a copy of *The Express Weekender* he'd been reading—a seasonal supplement to the town's weekly paper. "This just in: You've got birds shitting in your county dog pound and a cougar snacking on yellow Lab mountain dogs. The Wild West certainly offers challenging crimes."

Walt had no desire to mention Salt Lake and start an argument. "Beats working for a living!"

"You should patch it up with Gail for the sake of the kids."

"Gail is where she should be, Dad. Leave it alone."

"She's your wife."

"Was. The truth of the matter is, she was a great wife, a terrific wife, but a lousy mother. She never rose to the job, and knew she never would. Say what you want, but some women aren't cut out for it, just as some guys aren't. And she's one of them. It was never going to work."

"This is you talking."

"She'd tell you the same thing, I promise."

"It's going to wreck the kids," Jerry mumbled, trying to sip Scotch at the same time.

"Believe it or not, they're way better than they were. Now when they see her it's for a few hours, a half day at most, and she can handle that just fine. Thrives. She'd grown gloomy and short-tempered. It was a bad scene."

"She's your wife."

"I know it violates your *Ozzie and Harriet* sensibilities, Dad, but it's working. Leave it alone. If it ain't broke—"

"But it *is* broke."

"No, it's not. And why we go around on this every time we talk, I don't know. What's with that?"

Five minutes passed in silence. Walt didn't hear the nearby conversations, or the music, or the guys behind the grill calling out orders—only a droning whine in his ears that the beer would not quiet. His father's voice saying, *She's your wife.*

"Why the end run this afternoon? Why cut me out like that?" Walt said. "How can that possibly help anything?"

"You took that all personal. It wasn't like that."

"You can't stand the thought of me running this, can you?"

"I never said that."

A second Scotch was delivered, along with the salad and soup. Jerry ignored the soup.

"If she made the announcement early," Walt said, "it might help."

"You've had protection experience?" Jerry found this amusing. "Save your energy for this cougar."

Another silence descended. Their meals were delivered.

"Is it so impossible that we all might actually work together?" Walt suggested.

"Is that your experience talking?"

"Where's this coming from? What did I do to deserve this?"

Jerry made a point of dramatically checking his watch. "We don't have near enough of that kind of time."

"Don't mix me up with Bobby."

Jerry slapped the table. His drink jumped. He won the attention of a few nearby tables. He leveled his bloodshot eyes at Walt, wiped his wet lips with his napkin, and then carefully sawed through his slab of prime rib.

"I asked Myra and Kevin to join us for dessert," Walt said. "If you don't want to see them . . ."

" 'Course I do."

"Kevin needs us, Dad. Needs us as role models, not constantly at battle. Maybe we could declare a truce for a few minutes tonight."

Jerry sought answers in his reflection in the drink. "What battle?"

"And at some point we've got to clear the air on Bobby's death."

The man's eyes flashed darkly.

"Kevin and Myra need closure. Keeping it to yourself—"

"I'm not keeping anything to myself."

"You think you're protecting us. I know your heart's in a good place on this. But it's boomeranging."

"All the king's horses and all the king's men," Jerry said.

"We can't help Bobby, but we can put this family back together, Dad."

"You and Gail are doing your part. Right?" Jerry pulled on the Scotch, rescuing the ice cubes from drowning. He peered out from beneath his brow, cruelly, then set the drink down without a sound.

Walt spotted Myra and Kevin by the grill, scanning tables. "Here they are," Walt said. "Remember, Dad, he's not a little boy anymore."

Jerry drained the drink. "Shut the hell up."

Twenty-seven

Trevalian occupied a high stool in a dark-ened corner near the entrance to the Duchin Lounge. At 11:15, the place was jumping.

Immediately to his left, a Madison Avenue type, remade in three-hundred-dollar jeans and colorfully stitched cowboy boots, made sloppy with a woman twenty years his junior. They drank from martini glasses; she had an annoying habit of reapplying her lipstick between sips and kisses.

Joe Fos—a Filipino in his sixties—animated jazz standards and show tunes with keyboard flourishes. The bass player pulled the drummer along, and the dancers never rested.

At standing room only, the volume of conversation overpowered the attempts of young waitresses taking orders.

Trevalian nursed a Drambuie, not out of any great love for the potent liqueur, but because it promised to color his breath for the next several hours, and that might prove important.

He had yet to find a way to work around the loss of Ricky. The idea had been to establish himself with the dog so that a substitution wouldn't be noticed.

At the set break, he studied the clientele, the clubby, familiar way they moved from table to table saying their hellos with air kisses and firm handshakes. Bits and pieces of conversation reached his corner: golf, film, and some politics. Elizabeth Shaler's name surfaced more than once. He kept an eye on the door in case she happened by. He'd read the *New Yorker* piece—he'd read nearly everything written about her. Knew her better than she knew herself. Old habits died hard.

When the band began again, it did so as a quartet, behind the enchanting voice of a dirty blonde in her mid-thirties. She wore a tight-fitting red cocktail dress with a plunging neckline that tickled her navel. She'd

worked on her face to look young and innocent. But her smoky, emotionally charged
voice added to her years. She won herself
light applause, but deserved better. Another
place, another time, and he might have
been interested.

Shaler never showed. The combo stopped
at 11:45, the snifter on the piano overflow-
ing with twenty-dollar tips. The tables slowly
emptied ahead of the 1 A.M. closing. Trevalian left the lodge, stepping out into the
surprisingly chilly mountain air. He walked
quietly along the beautifully lit paths, past
the shops, the theater, and the pond, reaching the inn. He continued on, out into the
parking lot and beyond, finally reaching a
delivery alley.

Moonlit, gray scattered clouds raced overhead, sliced into pieces by the mountain
peaks. He worked into a slight stagger, for
appearance's sake, and proceeded down
the narrow strip of asphalt toward the loading bays behind the inn.

From the study off Cutter's kitchen, Trevalian had found the wife's Outlook program
up and running, and he'd scanned her cal-
endar for appointments and appearances.
Two entries had mentioned Shaler by name:

the opening luau on Friday night and the luncheon on Sunday at 10 A.M.

Rafe Nagler had an invitation to the luau but not to the luncheon.

His foray tonight was to study the layout of the banquet room ahead of her keynote on Sunday—to pace off exit routes and familiarize himself with the look and feel of the ballroom through eyes not clouded by prosthetic contact lenses.

His skin cool, his heart rate calm, Trevalian casually entered a loading bay and moved through a dark service hallway behind the banquet room. He passed food service trolleys, discarded aprons, and a wall phone with a stretched-out cord. The corridor smelled unpleasant but not unfamiliar— years of spilled salads comingling with the stain of human sweat. He pulled open a fire door marked BANQUET ROOM C.

He stepped inside.

Sand. The entire ballroom floor was covered in it. Three inches deep or more. Trevalian sank into it, both astonished and horrified. Then he recalled the Friday night dinner had been themed a luau, and he marveled at Patrick Cutter's excess. Would it stay the weekend, or would it be removed

by Sunday? If it stayed, it would prove a for-
midable obstacle for him.

His eyes were just beginning to adjust
when he heard voices at the far doors.

Someone was coming inside.

Twenty-eight

Nearly an hour earlier, at 12:30 A.M., Walt had hit a wall of fatigue while attempting to catch up on paperwork. Preparing to call it a night, he'd been organizing the Salt Lake photos when he saw one of the retail space's torn-apart ceiling. Then he checked Shaler's master schedule, grabbed his gun belt, and took off at a run.

Now, at nearly 1:30 A.M., driving north, he called O'Brien's cell phone.

"Did I wake you?" he asked.

"I wish," answered the security man.

Walt asked, "Did your guys check the banquet room after the workers got out of there?"

"You worry too much. I like that about you.

We've got all day tomorrow. The first real event is the luau tomorrow night."

"Shaler's scheduled for a walk-through and sound check at 10 A.M., preregistration."

He could practically hear O'Brien thinking.

"We need to sweep the room," Walt announced. "I'm heading up there. I'm going to do a walk-through tonight."

"Tonight? How 'bout first thing in the morning? We've got to move Patrick back into the residence. He dined in town following the party."

Walt could hear O'Brien's despair. Private security often amounted to little more than babysitting. He'd never envied his father his six-figure salary for this reason.

O'Brien offered to send two of his guys over to help Walt.

"I'm good. I've got patrols doing nothing this time of night."

With O'Brien still making offers, Walt politely signed off and called Tom Brandon. Brandon was off duty. When he failed to reach him, Walt turned off into the Red Top trailer park. With so many of the trailers looking the same, he drove past Brandon's on his first try. It wasn't the trailer, but his wife's car that stopped Walt on the second try: Gail's minivan was parked in Brandon's driveway. He slowed, then continued on, catching sight of the trailer in his rearview mirror. Dark. Locked up for the night.

He pulled to the corner, stopped, and threw his head against the steering wheel. He couldn't catch his breath. His heart was doing a tumbling act. He squeezed out tears before he knew it, then leaned back and wiped his face on his sleeve. He kept checking the rearview mirror, the minivan and the trailer now quite small in the frame, hoping he'd gotten the wrong place, the wrong car. He drove around the block again, and this time checked the plates. Stopped at the same corner. Ached the same way.

He thought back to Brandon's comment about running against him in the primary, and he saw it on a whole new level. His deputy was doing his ex-wife. Stealing the best thing in his life. Never mind that it had to end, it didn't have to end like this, and for a brave moment Walt considered confronting them both.

Then he drove on, in a daze of confusion,

a lump like a piece of coal rammed down his throat.

He did his best to control his voice and summoned his patrols over the radio. But a bear had been reported tearing up trash cans mid-valley and his two available cars had responded. He headed to Sun Valley, alone and afraid in a way he'd not felt. His father's sarcastic sting about the nature of crime in the valley—his job—echoed uncomfortably in his mind. Gail had moved on. It was all but unthinkable—but think about it he did.

He checked in at the inn's front desk, not wanting Sun Valley security mistaking him for a prowler.

The Bavarian woman behind the desk said no one was to enter the banquet rooms until morning.

He touched his sheriff's badge, pinned to his uniform. "I'm not asking. I'm just letting you know I'm here. If you'd like, I'd be happy to wake Larry Raffles." Walt pulled out his cell. Raffles managed the resort.

She declined, though a little frostily, dangled a set of keys, and led Walt down a walnut-paneled corridor. She unlocked a set of doors for him and accompanied him inside.

A geometric shape of light flooded across lavishly decorated tables and . . . sand.

The young woman found some lights. Enough to navigate.

"I'll make sure it's locked when I leave. And I'll stop by the desk, so you know I've left." He thanked her. The door clunked shut behind her.

The room was shaped like a shoebox, with Walt in the center of one of the long sides. He faced the elevated riser from where Liz Shaler would give her talk. It currently held six potted palm trees. Gift boxes sat at each place setting. Envy nibbled at Walt—that Cutter, or anyone, should have this kind of disposable income.

He dragged his feet through the thick sand wishing he could take his boots off. He reached the riser, knee height and rimmed with a navy blue skirt.

Through his grief, frustration, and fatigue, something tugged at him. He'd come to respect such sensations. He stood absolutely still, blood thumping past his ears, his throat dry. Wishing for more light, he spotted a bank of dimmer switches forty feet away. Almost automatically, he unsnapped his holster, felt the cool of its gnarled grip.

Moved silently, sweat breaking out all over him.

The bank of light switches was too far. He felt drawn to his right, and he followed his instinct.

His boots moved absolutely silently in the sand. He passed one table after another, looking left, right, ahead, and behind.

The tablecloths cascaded down to seat height, screening the area beneath the tables, leaving fifty hiding places to search.

His radio, clipped to his waist, spit with static. "Sheriff, what's your twenty?"

A blur to his right. A man's form raced for an exit, slammed a door open, and vanished before Walt got a decent look at him.

Running now, Walt reached for his radio's handset and called out the code for a suspicious person, "Ten-one-oh-seven. In pursuit on foot. Sun Valley Inn. Request backup." His belt snagged a tablecloth and dragged it off to the sound of exploding wineglasses.

He burst into a service hallway that was pitch black. He reached down and silenced his radio.

Took two steps forward. Smashed into a

food dolly, tripped, and went down on one knee. Jumped to his feet, his eyes stinging to pierce the dark. The suspect had disappeared.

Twenty-nine

Trevalian, hidden behind a meal cart, kept his back to the wall. He knew the quickest way out: the service hallway to the loading platform. He knew he'd be exposed for several seconds if he ran. But a moving target, at least. The sheriff was less than ten feet away—unmoving, barely breathing. More professional, more careful than he'd have thought.

With his back literally against the wall, he once again calculated the time and distance to the end of the hall. He walked himself through the sharp left turn to the loading dock. He had no desire for confrontation. Only escape.

He hesitated only briefly. Then he shoved the food cart and ran.

Thirty

Walt drew his weapon as the cart smashed into the wall. He didn't remember grabbing his flashlight, but there it was, held with the gun as if a single piece.

The dark shape of a man juked right and left, zigzagging down the hall, and was gone.

Walt turned left at the end of the hall and broke through hanging ribbons of sheet plastic used as a cold barrier. He jumped off the loading dock, lost his balance, and fell forward. As he came to his feet, the suspect was now twenty yards ahead of him. A very fast runner.

Walt holstered the gun at a full sprint. He wasn't going to shoot only to find it was a high school kid, or the wayward son of a hotel guest. He followed out onto the first fairway of the Sun Valley golf course, and heard the *tick-tick-tick* of lawn sprinklers before he felt the first cold shower. Within seconds he was soaked through, his boots slogging through the spongy grass.

He trailed the suspect by twenty yards as he followed him through a wall of towering evergreens and out into a back parking lot. The man ran well and showed no signs of slowing, having increased the gap between them. Beyond the lot loomed a field of white tents that Walt recognized as the Sun Valley Art Show. Closed for the night, the tents covered two acres and offered the suspect a place to get lost.

He disappeared there, Walt several long seconds behind.

Walt slowed to a walk, catching his breath, listening for the man. He was soaked through, his boots squishing with each step. The vendors had lowered the walls of the tents. He took his weapon back in his hand, aimed the flashlight tent to tent. Yanking back flaps and peering inside, he worked down the row. The man was here.

Walt leaned forward for the next tent, when a sharp snap of fabric turned him around in time to see the darkened figure take off and disappear around a corner. Walt cut through between tents, arriving in the adjacent aisle. He saw a tent jerk and wiggle as his quarry caught a foot on a rope.

Walt crashed through into the next aisle. He spotted the man to his right just rounding a corner. Walt took off at a sprint, hugging the same corner.

The other man jumped out and connected with Walt, shoving him and using his momentum to lift him off his feet. Walt was catapulted into a tent across the aisle, crashed into and through the front wall of canvas, and took out the legs of a portable table. He rolled, came to his feet, tripped over a horse saddle, and went down hard.

A harsh beam of light filled his eyes.

"Sheriff? That you? What the hell?" The voice belonged to a Sun Valley Company security man.

Out of breath, Walt coughed out, "A guy . . . running . . ." He pointed. "After him!"

The security man just stood there, confused. "What guy?"

Walt pushed past the man into the aisle. Empty.

"What guy?" the guard repeated.

"Where'd you come from?" Walt asked. "How could you not have seen him?"

"Didn't see no one. Heard you crashing around over here. Came running."

"Get on the radio. I don't want any cars leaving the main lot. Anyone with wet hair gets detained."

"Wet hair. Yes, sir."

Walt took off toward the lodge. The hit man was here to kill Liz Shaler, he had no doubt now. Given the element of surprise, the man could have done far worse to him. Stabbed him. Broken his neck. Taken his gun. But he'd attempted none of these and instead of making him an amateur it marked him a pro: He'd done the minimum required to get cleanly away. Intentional or not, the man had delivered a message.

And whether Dryer chose to or not, Walt intended to listen.

FRIDAY

One

Over the incessant din of the Weather Channel, Danny Cutter heard the telephone system's unique ring tone that signaled an arrival at the front door of his brother's compound. He continued on the elliptical as he used the television remote to view a fish-eye image of Ailia Holms, dressed in a two-color, gray, zippered shell, white iPod wires in her ears. She stared up toward what was supposed to be a hidden camera. She mouthed, "Hello . . ." Her hair was pulled back into a single ponytail, her cheeks red with the cool morning air.

Danny resentfully disembarked the trainer, punched a button on the phone, and told her, "Be right there."

The gym occupied the upper floor of the

swimming pool barn. He navigated his way back through the series of renovated barns to the front door—a two-minute, brisk walk.

A towel draped around his neck, he answered the door.

"Hey there," Ailia said, stepping inside without invitation.

Danny eased the door shut.

"Sleep well?" She used her vixen voice, the voice of the woman who had seduced him the night before.

"He's not here," Danny said. "He's up at the lodge. The rest of the guests all arrive before noon."

She touched his cheek. "Hot and sweaty. Just how I left you last night."

"You could try his cell."

"I'm taking a run out Adam's Gulch," she explained. "You want to come with?" Patrick's compound abutted state forest land. Aspen- and evergreen-shrouded mountains were braided together with interlocking bike and foot trails.

"I'm just wrapping up," he said, declining. "There's coffee, if you want."

"Staff arrives at eight, isn't that right?" She checked her watch and cozied up to him.

"We could put that twenty minutes to good use."

"Rain check," he said.

She complained, "It doesn't rain much here, Danny. You know that." She stepped away and looked around the room. "You'd never guess there were a hundred people here last night."

She had a sultry walk as she prowled the room. He felt himself stir. He wanted none of that, already resenting the night before. "Can I leave a message or something?"

"Or something," she said.

"Allie . . ."

She turned to face him. "Come on, Danny, I'm just kidding around." They both knew differently. "Why so serious? I've got news for you. Good news for a change. The least you could do is pretend you're glad to see me."

"We talked about this."

"Not really. I don't remember talking all that much."

He fought back an urge to just walk away and leave her before it got out of hand again.

"I've arranged a meeting between you and Stu."

He felt his breath catch. "I expressly asked—"

"You can thank me now, if you like." She checked her watch. "We've still got eighteen minutes." She closed to within an arm's reach. "You know how *hard* it was to set up a meeting given his conference schedule?"

Danny felt his face flush.

"Don't gush with thanks all at once. I can take it in little bits. Or little bites, or whatever."

"I asked you to leave it alone."

"You know me, Danny: I'm impulsive."

He took her by both wrists and backed her up several feet against a couch.

"Shit, Danny, that hurts."

He drove himself against her, pelvis against pelvis. "Is this what you want, Allie? Nice and rough. You want it on the couch? On the kitchen counter? Where?"

"You're hurting me," she gasped.

"You love it."

"Fuck you!"

"You wish."

He let go of her, stepped back.

Panting, she inspected her wrists.

"Shit, Danny. I think you bruised me. How am I going to explain that?"

"I'm sorry!"

"Sorry?" she said, rubbing her forearm. "You obviously don't know Stu very well."

"I told you I have to do this *myself*," he scolded. "I don't want Paddy's help, or yours, or anybody else's."

She was still rubbing her forearm. "Shit! Shit! Shit! Long sleeves in July? Are you kidding me?"

"I didn't mean to hurt you."

"What's happened to you?" she mumbled. "You're fucked up, Danny."

"I was fucked up," he said. "Not anymore."

"Don't be so sure."

She pulled the heavy front door open. Morning sunlight had broken onto the opposing hillside, setting it on fire. She didn't look at him, just walked outside.

She started into a slow jog, turned at the end of the drive, and broke into a full run.

Danny stepped back inside, shaken by what he'd done. He wondered where such anger came from, and worse, where it could lead.

Two

Veterinarian Mark Aker's low voice growled as he walked stiffly and slightly bowlegged toward the Sun Valley Lodge, Walt at his side. "This guy must be charmed. You pulled off a miracle." His dark brown eyes peered out from his tanned, bearded face. In his right hand he held a dark blue nylon leash, leading a fine-looking German shepherd.

"We," Walt corrected. "And I don't even know how we did it."

"He has Maggie to thank. And Patrick Cutter's wallet. This is costing north of five hundred bucks a day."

Walt whistled. "What's amazing is she looks just like his dog—the one that died."

"Animals and commercial aircraft shouldn't mix."

The lodge's portico was crowded with vehicles, valet personnel, and bellmen. One of
the bellmen caught sight of the dog and
moved to intercept Mark Aker. "Service
dog," Walt said. "Being delivered to a hotel
guest."

"Sure thing, Sheriff."

Walt had called ahead. Nagler had tried to
talk him out of the offer.

"We may have to sell him on this," Walt
warned.

"I doubt it," Aker replied. "Toey will sell
herself."

Three

With the opaque contact lenses blocking his vision, and anxiety welling in his chest, Trevalian awaited the arrival of the sheriff—the *sheriff*—yet enjoying the irony that the man was now supplying him with a dog that he desperately needed.

He sat on a couch in the lobby, Karl the bellman as his eyes.

"Here they are," Karl announced. "Oh, sir, she's a fine-looking dog."

Trevalian stood.

"A fine-looking German shepherd. You should see everyone looking at her. Queen of the ball."

"Mr. Nagler." The sheriff.

"Sheriff," Nagler said.

"I believe you may have met Mark Aker yesterday."

He and Aker shook hands.

"In less fortunate circumstances," the vet said. "But allow me to introduce Toey."

"Toey?" Nagler said.

Karl took the cane from Trevalian's hand and Aker put the leash into his grip. Trevalian squatted and Toey immediately licked his face.

"She's service trained," Aker said, "and ready to go."

"Are you now, Toey?" Trevalian said, petting the dog furiously.

"She'll direct you to a handrail on stairs on your signal," Aker said. "She'll move through a doorway and return to working position."

"A smart girl, are you?" Trevalian said.

"Take her for a spin?" Aker asked.

"I couldn't possibly."

"But you've got to!" the sheriff said. "It's all been arranged."

Trevalian looked up in the general direction of that voice. *Play hard to get,* he thought. "Sheriff, do you have dogs?"

"Three."

"Then you know there's a bond of trust that forms between the handler and the animal. Whatever I do with Toey will only corrupt whatever training she's had to this point, will spoil her for her real owner. As much as I'd love her company, and her help, I'd be doing a disservice to her and the people who trained her."

"Three days is not going to undo fourteen months of training."

Trevalian leaned his head far back, smiled and rocked side to side. If anyone happened to catch a look behind his sunglasses, they would see only milky orbs, without pupils or irises. "Toey?" he said excitedly. "You want to take a walk?"

He imagined Aker and the sheriff silently congratulating themselves. He wondered how they'd feel two days from now.

Taking hold of the dog's service harness, he ordered in a crisp voice, "Walk!"

Together they maneuvered around the crowded lobby, Trevalian stifling a grin of satisfaction. The sheriff, of all people.

He had his substitute: His original plan was back on track.

Four

The mountains rose steeply on either side of him, a narrow canyon called Chocolate Gulch with a creek that snaked between two dozen custom homes. The mouth of the canyon intersected Highway 75 to the east while to the west it was covered by vast stands of lodgepole pine and Douglas fir, the rolling green of which was broken only by rock outcroppings, copses of aspens, and patches of deadfall.

With his dog in the lead, the tall, nondescript man held to a game path, a narrow, sometimes aimlessly bending strip of bare dirt and rock cut into the side of the hill by years of use by deer and elk. Below him, the rich green lawns were laid out like quilt squares, connected by stitching of post-and-rail fences.

He shifted the rifle to his opposite shoulder, hunched low, and moved stealthily, his breath shooting staccato puffs of gray fog out in front of him.

The dog pulled eagerly, leading him to a stand of saplings. Hearing voices, he ducked and peered down at the houses below and located the source of that sound: a man and woman in a hot tub.

He wanted to avoid being seen: Men with rifles drew attention. The dog had picked up a fresh scent, and he intended to stay on it. The rifle shot would announce him; but by then the deed would be done and he'd have earned his pay.

Less than a quarter mile later, with the last of the homes behind him, he slowed as the dog slowed. She glanced at him then shivered head to toe in excitement as she lifted her front paw into a curl. On point, she leaned forward.

It took him a second to spot his target. Forty yards below, she sat with her back to the hill.

Quietly, he slipped the rifle off his shoulder. He lowered to one knee and brought the sight to eye level.

A stream of drool fell from the dog's mouth to the dry leaves.

With the target now magnified, he held his breath and gently squeezed the trigger.

The gun recoiled in his grip, and the shot rang out, echoing down the canyon like a beautiful piece of music.

The cougar spun sharply, trying to bite the dart that dangled from its haunch. Then it twitched and its front legs went out from under it. It looked once up the hill at its assailant, collapsed completely, and rolled onto its side.

Five

Walt blew across the top of the coffee mug as Dick O'Brien stabbed a roasted potato, shoveled some scrambled egg on top of it, and stuffed it into his mouth.

"Fuckin' delicious," he said, his teeth yellow with egg.

"Not hungry," Walt said.

The lodge's lobby restaurant hummed with conversation, while waitresses dressed like Heidi, their busts bulging, moved between tables shuttling trays. The room smelled of cinnamon and maple syrup.

Walt sat across from O'Brien at a table near the door.

"So, we'll lock down the banquet hall tighter than a teenager," O'Brien said.

"I have daughters," Walt reminded. "Watch yourself."

"It could have been anybody."

"This guy is already here."

"It could easily have been one of the First Rights kids," O'Brien said. "You know that, Walt."

"This guy was in shape, careful; he knew tactics. Does that fit the profile of your average WTO protester?"

"Listen, you know what kind of headache this is for me? I'd just as soon Shaler head back to New York. But the boss? This is his moment in history. You won't convince him."

Walt looked at him skeptically. The coffee was battery acid—or maybe that was his stomach. "You married?" Walt asked.

"Happily. Listen, we'll lock down the ballroom—this is *after* my guys sniff it—and we'll keep it locked and under guard. Right up until the speech. Agreed?"

O'Brien's demeanor instantly changed and Walt didn't need to look over his own shoulder to see it was Patrick Cutter behind him.

"Sheriff," Cutter said, taking a chair by Walt. "That was a heck of a thing you did for Rafe Nagler."

"*We* did," Walt said, including him. "But, yeah, it was a good moment."

"We're just discussing last night," O'Brien said.

"I heard you had a run-in."

"True story," Walt said.

"And that you were unable to identify the trespasser."

"He was in the banquet room, and he didn't want to be caught." Walt sipped the bitter coffee. "For me, that speaks volumes."

"Just don't speak it too loudly," Cutter said.

Walt lowered his voice. "We have to assume it could have been the contractor."

"I assume no such thing," Cutter said.

"We were just running down a bunch of other possibilities," O'Brien explained, "First Rights chief among them."

"And I was pointing out," Walt said, "that this guy's behavior was totally pro. Never looked back. Was familiar with avoidance tactics. Vanished into thin air when it came time. And if he left the property, he did so on foot. We locked down the parking lots and came up blank."

"So you've got nothing," Cutter said.

"I've got a sore side from where the guy

hit me, and real strong suspicion of the kind of person I was dealing with."

Walt's cell phone rang. He checked the screen and took the call. As he listened, his face tightened. O'Brien signaled for the check as Walt finished the call and hung up.

"Fish and Game took down a cougar out Chocolate Gulch. Darted it."

"The one that went after my brother?" Patrick asked.

"Possibly."

"What the hell do you do with a drugged cougar?" O'Brien asked.

"Kill it, I hope," said Patrick. "Thing's a menace."

"They'll probably cage it down at the pound—the Humane Society, in Hailey," Walt said. "She was wearing a tag, so this is at least her second dose of drugs. Not good."

"Because?" O'Brien asked.

Surprisingly, Patrick interrupted. "They used to use PCP to drug the bears and lions. It was discovered with the bears that the drug made them overly aggressive. Released back into the wild, they presented more of a threat to humans, not less."

"I'm impressed," Walt said.

"I sit on the society's board."

"And the cougar?" O'Brien asked Walt. "She doesn't stay there forever, I'm guessing."

"They have a pen there that can hold her," Walt said. "They won't want to destroy her, but they can't re-release her."

"Tough being a cougar," O'Brien said.

"In captivity, yes," agreed Walt.

Patrick's assistants appeared in the doorway looking for him. He sensed them, turned, and signaled for them to wait a minute. He said to O'Brien, "Keep me up on this."

"Yes, sir, I will."

"And you, too, Sheriff. I want to know what you're thinking."

O'Brien signed for the check. Walt protested, but not too hard. Cutter left with his two assistants. He was immediately approached by conference guests.

Walt walked out with O'Brien. "I wouldn't want that many friends."

"I thought you're elected," O'Brien said.

"Yeah, I am. But that's all rigged," he said, patting O'Brien on the back.

Six

The pavement stopped at a variegated edge where chunks of tar met brown dust, marking the boundary between civilization and wilderness. Walt spotted Fiona's beat-up Subaru among the vehicles parked at the Chocolate Gulch trailhead.

He was calling his location to dispatch when she knocked on the side window, startling him.

He looked at her, noticing for the first time a constellation of freckles under her jaw.

But as he rolled down the window, the freckles moved down her neck: nothing but fly specks on the glass. *Some detective,* he thought.

"You mind if I tag along?" she asked. "Pam wants some shots." Pam Brummell was the publisher of the weekly newspaper, *The Sun Valley Sentinel.*

"No problem." He rolled the window back up and climbed out. "It's actually not my scene. Fish and Game."

They walked together. At 9 A.M. the sun was quickly warming the air, the tree-covered hills alive with sunlight, the sky an indigo blue.

"I hope you're not gloating over the fact they got the cougar before the cougar got anyone else, because that's blind luck if you ask me."

"For one thing," Walt said, "I don't gloat. For another, we have no way of knowing if this is the same cat. It's a very dry summer. A lot of game is coming out of the hills for the river."

"This is where the yellow Lab was killed."

"Yes. But you and Danny Cutter and Liz Shaler were ten miles south of here. Cougars cover a lot of territory, but that's a good hike."

Walt admired her from behind as she mounted the trail. She walked a bit like a cat herself. They reached a backpack on the game trail and looked down through the woods to see the cat lying on her side, a man kneeling next to her. Walt and Fiona scrambled down the slope. The cat lay by a slow trickle of a stream, her black eyes open, giving the impression she was dead. But the steady rise and fall of her rib cage said otherwise. The agent had spread petroleum jelly over her open eyes to protect them from drying out, but the result was a deathly gaze.

"Sedated." The man introduced himself as a Fish and Game agent. He looked vaguely familiar to Walt.

"She's beautiful," Fiona said, already preparing her equipment.

"Hell of a shot," Walt said. "From up on the game trail?"

"Yeah. I got lucky being downwind, or she'd have bolted."

The dart still dangled from her shoulder. There was something sad about seeing so graceful and powerful an animal brought down like this. A collision of man and nature. The pungent decay of soil and the mint of the evergreens comingled.

The agent's dog—a yellow Lab—was tied to an aspen sapling.

Walt asked, "Is that dog trained for explosives, by any chance?"

"No, just a tracker."

Walt thought he knew all the tracking dogs in the valley. This one was new to him.

"What's to become of the cat?" Fiona asked, now taking photographs.

The agent pointed out the ear tag and explained she'd be caged and they'd look for a home for her.

"And if you can't find a home for her?" she asked.

"We usually do. We have a month or more," the agent answered.

"Doesn't seem fair," Fiona said. "Do we even know if she's the one who killed the yellow Lab? I mean, is she guilty of anything?"

"We'll be able to watch her stool for hair and bones. That's one place caging her helps."

"Could she possibly have been down in Starweather yesterday afternoon?" Walt asked.

"A male can travel twenty-five miles at night, while hunting. This one could have been in Hailey last night. Starweather? No problem."

Fiona finished taking shots, packed up her

bag, said goodbye to them both, and trudged back up the hill.

"It would help if we could connect this cat to the yellow Lab," Walt told the agent. "There was an attack on a fisherman. Putting all those to bed would be a good thing."

"We won't be able to confirm any of that. And what I didn't want to say was chances are we won't find her a home."

Walt looked down at the beautiful creature and felt depressed.

"Cougars and humans . . . ," the agent said, pausing, "is not a good mix. Add PCP into it, and it's a nightmare waiting to happen. She's trouble, Sheriff. May not be her fault, but trouble just the same."

"Yeah," Walt said, "but she got here first. We're the interlopers."

The cat's open-eyed stare stayed with him on his return to the trail head. Fiona's car was gone.

He thought about finding Gail's car parked at Brandon's trailer and his chest tightened. He'd spent the night on his own couch, unable to sleep in their bed. Hadn't slept much at all. He realized his marriage had officially ended: It wasn't just talk, and tears, and lawyers anymore, and it left an aching hole in him that even work couldn't fill. He wanted to take the day off, maybe hike up into the Pioneers with the dogs. He wanted change, something to take away all the reminders of his own failure.

He climbed back into the Cherokee and held firmly to the wheel, unable to drive. Unable to move.

Seven

Trevalian had a problem: For his plan to work he had to take possession of the second dog, a dog trained for scent—and then make a switch. The sheriff and the vet had unwittingly provided a dog to get his plan back on track. But the vet, Mark Aker, from whom he'd arranged to purchase a scent dog—a tracker—weeks ago, by phone, had been introduced to Nagler that same morning, when delivering the service dog. Trevalian felt it too great a risk to allow Aker to meet Trevalian and Nagler in the same day, for fear he might make the connection—doctors were, if anything, observant. But this was the day prearranged for him to buy the tracker, so he'd timed his arrival in the lobby of Aker's Veterinarian Services, an expansive log structure a few miles south of Ketchum, at a time he knew Aker to be busy with an emergency surgery.

He hid his impatience from the receptionist, wandering an area crowded with parakeet cages, racks of kitty teasers, and sacks of pet food.

Then his impatience gave way and he approached the counter for the third time.

"I don't mean to be rude but is there anyone else I might talk to about this?" he asked.

"I'm afraid he asked that you wait," she answered.

"But the sale has been in place for several weeks," he protested. "I'm under time constraints."

"Mark thinks of these animals as members of the family. He handles all the sales personally."

"But she's ready?"

"Of course."

"Then could I at least see her?" he asked.

"Of course you can. I'm so sorry it's taking so long." She came around from behind the desk and led Trevalian out of the building, across a courtyard, to a small barn. The moment they entered, a half dozen dogs started barking.

Callie was a three-year-old German shepherd with an energetic face and two black socks on the hind legs. Trevalian knelt and petted and talked to the dog.

"She's trained to track, yes?" he asked the receptionist.

"All the Search and Rescue dogs are," she replied. "All are expert trackers. Yes."

Trevalian asked for a demonstration, and the receptionist humored him. He watched and listened carefully to the specific commands used. He committed them to memory, along with Callie's expressions and reactions. She gave him two full demonstrations—the dog obviously enjoying the game of pursuing a scent and receiving a reward for her success.

Trevalian glanced at his watch, making sure the receptionist saw him do so. "Certainly it can't make any difference who takes my cashier's check."

"Mark would kill me. We've spent over a year training Callie. He's going to want to say goodbye."

Trevalian considered killing her himself.

"And if he loses a twenty-thousand-dollar sale?" Trevalian proposed.

For the first time, he saw a crack in her determination.

He pressed on. "I could call him to make sure we've covered everything. Leave you my cell phone number."

"Well . . ." She didn't sound as convinced as before. "Maybe I can interrupt him," she said. "Why don't we try one more time?"

As Trevalian followed her back to the main building he looked for any security cameras that might be recording him and saw none. The receptionist disappeared into the back of the building, returning a moment later.

"I think you're in luck," she said. "He's at a point in the procedure where he can take a minute or two to come out and meet you."

As his gut twisted, Trevalian attempted to look pleased.

"I'm going to run over to the other building," the woman said. "I won't be but a minute. Mark should be out shortly."

"Thank you."

She hurried through the door, obviously pleased to be rid of him.

When she returned, she found Mark Aker in his scrubs, his gloves removed, standing next to the reception desk with a perplexed look of confusion and irritation.

"So?" Aker asked her, his voice revealing the degree of his annoyance. "Is this some kind of joke?"

"Mr. Meisner was right here a minute ago," she said.

But the reception area stood empty.

Eight

The gargantuan white tent shimmered in the late morning sunlight, an imposing edifice of vinyl-coated canvas supported by a steel superstructure. More than fifty yards long and thirty wide, it occupied most of a field adjacent to the art fair's temporary tent city.

Walt parked across from the First Rights protest where several dozen kids in their twenties were already gathered. They waved posters and shouted, "Global capitalism equals world starvation!" A hundred yards to the west, well-heeled guests converged on the Great White Tent.

Sun Valley police maintained a perimeter around the protesters. Walt moved toward the tent, where four of his deputies were working with O'Brien's team to secure the event.

C³ was ten minutes away from its 10 A.M. opening. For Walt, it felt like horses in a starting gate. The months of planning came down to this moment. He fought a fatigue headache, and the soreness from the chase the night before.

The tent could seat an audience of twelve hundred in folding chairs. The stage could hold a sixty-person symphony orchestra. At present the tent held four hundred folding chairs, a bookstore, and a coffee house with a dozen café tables on Persian rugs. A Dale Chihuly chandelier hung overhead. Robert Kelly oil paintings lined the interior walls. There were potted trees, azaleas in bloom, custom pillows, and a red silk draped ceiling that created the atmosphere of the interior of an Achaemenid tent.

Dryer's agents were clustered at the front row near Liz Shaler, who was seated. Classical music played from speakers on either side of the stage and drowned out the anti-capitalist chant. O'Brien's team swiped arriving attendees with security wands—not enough of an imposition to be bothersome, but enough precaution to imply a sense of security.

Moving past the café and down the center aisle, Walt noticed that the tent's side walls, usually left open, were tied shut with locking plastic cable ties. The only way in and out was the one entrance through which Walt had just come.

It might have been a result of his aborted pursuit the night before; it might have been the sight of the protesters, or the faint sound of their chanting; it might have been his father's presence. It might have been his imagination's unrelenting imagery of Brandon fucking his wife. But whatever the reason, he felt agitated and unsettled—that feeling like he'd forgotten something.

Patrick Cutter, wearing a blue blazer over a peach golf shirt, stood conferring with his assistants to the right of the stage. He looked confident and proud.

When a commotion began at the tent's entrance, it drew Walt's attention. He turned and hurried toward it. A pair of college kids confronting O'Brien's guys.

Walt had taken only a few steps when O'Brien's guys converged from every direction. Most of O'Brien's guys, by the look of it. Eager for action.

As Walt approached, he caught a look in the eyes of one of the protesters, a kid wearing a green First Rights T-shirt—and it was not a look of despair or concern over being caught, but one of satisfaction, almost glee. The kid made the mistake of looking toward the stage with anticipation.

Walt immediately reached up for his radio. "Stage entrance. All units crash it, now!"

The two protesters had been sent as a diversion. O'Brien's men had swarmed, leaving other areas unguarded.

Now running down the center aisle, Walt shouted out, "RED BADGE!" The three agents guarding Liz Shaler pulled her out of her seat, pushed her into a crouch, and formed a circle around her. They rushed her to the side of the tent, cut the plastic bands binding the tent panels, and whisked her outside. It all happened in a matter of seconds.

People jumped out of their seats, blocking the stage. Walt couldn't get to Patrick Cutter, whom he now also identified as a possible target.

He scrambled up onto the stage, dodged

across the set: a coffee table, a standing lamp, and two leather chairs. Ahead of him he saw the far wall of the tent wave, the result of air pressure. The moving wave headed in Cutter's direction. Walt dove face-first across the stage, straight off the edge and into the person creating that wave. Something wet spread down him, and as he pinned the kid's arms, restraining him, he saw the blood. It took him a moment to realize it was neither his nor the kid's. Instead, it was chicken blood, intended as a political statement.

He rolled the kid over to cuff him. The kid shrieked and hollered slogans about capitalism and human rights. Brandon appeared and quickly escorted the boy backstage.

Patrick Cutter hurried along the side of the stage to Walt.

"Sheriff? Oh, my God!" he said, seeing the blood down his front. "How did you . . . ? Where did he come from? Thank you! A thousand times thank you."

"No problem," Walt said. "We're lucky it was just a stunt."

"You saved me a huge embarrassment. Are you all right, Sheriff?" he finally thought to say.

"I'm fine. I'm going to get out of here."

Walt headed backstage.

Cutter called after him, "I suppose that thing last night was probably just a dress rehearsal for this. Right?"

Walt turned, the blood covering him from chest to knees. His face and hands were smeared in it. "It was a different venue," he said, "and that was a man last night, not a college kid. Other than that, yeah, they're pretty much exactly the same."

Nine

At 11 A.M. sharp, fifteen minutes after the conclusion of Patrick's opening address in the tent, an event of unbridled excess that included a gift of a Cutter Communications mobile phone for every guest, and marred only briefly by the disturbance, Stuart Holms sat down with Danny Cutter in the hospitality suite. Stuart's head of security, a balding man in a Hawaiian shirt, who introduced himself as Emil, made a quick sweep of the suite and left. Before he shut the door he gave Danny the eye, as if Danny were trouble, and the first thing that came to Danny's mind was an image of Ailia Holms riding him the night before, her face a grimace of well-earned pleasure.

Stu Holms took the couch, selected a

piece of cheese from a tray, and nibbled on it. "So," he said.

He looked much younger than Danny remembered him. A face job? He wore a pair of cream-colored slacks and a dark green shirt. He had wet eyes, thin hair, and ears like bird wings. He needed more sun, but his teeth were perfect. Dentures? He seemed to be looking right through Danny, not at him.

"So. Trilogy looks pretty damn good on paper, or I wouldn't be here."

"It is good," Danny said, playing to his own strengths. Cheerful optimism came easily for him. "We have significant market penetration, brand loyalty with our customers, and fabulous packaging. What we don't have is a national presence."

"Which is where my ten million comes in. Yes, I get all that. But listen, Danny, I don't love paying for marketing and advertising. Infrastructure, sure. SquawkCom could provide all your communications needs, networking, cabling, phone, and data. The million you have in this budget will be more than enough. We can save you a lot there. Your bottling plant makes sense to me. Securing your source—absolutely necessary.

Imperative, even. But ad dollars? Not me. Not my money. Take that out of the cash flow of your existing business. Move my money into salaries and transportation. Human assets. But I hate advertising. Whoever buys anything because of an ad they see?"

Danny sorted through what he'd just been told. "You're going to invest?"

"That's the idea, isn't it?"

"Well . . . yes." He was stunned it had happened so easily.

"You'll make me part of the angel round— I don't want diluted shares," he said, "and you'll give me a seat on the board."

"Our angel round closed two years ago."

"It just reopened. I'm not taking B shares, Danny. I'm first in line, or I'm stepping out of the line."

"That can be arranged."

"Of course it can. And the seat on the board—I had in mind cochairman."

"Cochairman," Danny repeated, his voice tightly wound. "I would if I could, but I control thirty-one percent of the voting shares, and as such—"

"It's cochair, a partnership, or you take your dog and pony show on down the road.

You want to turn me down, Danny, it's a free country."

"I mean no disrespect, Stuart. It's just that I've always thought of this as my company. You must know that feeling. And—"

"Of course I do."

"Exactly!" Danny said. "And so you can see how—"

"Take it or leave it," Stuart said, interrupting for a second time. "No hard feelings one way or the other, Danny." He checked his watch, a heavy thing with a titanium housing, white gold trim, and a platinum band. "It's ten million dollars. My guys will go over the paperwork, if you agree. Your brother's got us all on a tight leash. I'd like your answer now—I like a man who can think on his feet—but if you need more time . . ."

"It's not a matter of time, it's a matter of—"

"Time and money, Danny. Those are the only things that had better matter. If you're good with the money and don't need more time, then I'd say we have ourselves a deal." He extended his hand. "We have an agreement, if you want it."

Danny willed himself to lift his arm. He understood the opportunity this presented.

He'd be a fool to walk away from such an offer.

He was saved from the handshake by a knock on the door. Danny looked up, expecting Emil.

Instead, Ailia entered, packed into a pair of white tailored pants, a long-sleeved shiny salmon blouse, and wearing a string of pearls the size of mothballs.

"We're going to go in for the full ten," Stuart informed her. He extended his hand again, and this time Danny shook it. Ailia joined her husband on the couch. "Ailia will take my seat on the board."

Danny felt the room spin. "What?" he choked out. She looked over at him as if she'd won the lottery.

"Danny," Stuart said, "meet your new partner."

Ten

"Why the top secret treatment?" Fiona asked. She sat in the passenger seat of Walt's Cherokee, its motor rumbling. He'd parked in the lot of the Hemingway School, on the west side of Ketchum, facing an athletic field and an over-forty intramural soccer game.

Walt had changed out of the blood-soaked uniform shirt and into a black SPECIAL TACTICS T-shirt he kept in the back.

"It's not a favor. You'll be paid," he said.

"I'm scheduled to guide on the river most of the weekend."

"It's not like that. I want you to loan us your camera gear."

"You have your own stuff."

"We don't have telephoto lenses, and I

can't rent them here in town. The soonest Salt Lake can get them up here is Monday, and I need them today."

"Because?"

"There was an incident at the C^3 opening."

"I heard."

"Yeah . . . so . . . I got to thinking that if I was a hit man hired to kill Shaler, the best place I could hide would be out in the open."

"With the protesters."

"Yes. I need photographs—digital close-ups of every face. There's a chance I can run them through national databases—facial recognition. Maybe identify this guy—a suspect—in time."

"I can do that for you."

"You're busy."

"I just made myself unbusy. Randy can guide for me."

"It's risky work. Sometimes people don't like their photograph taken. I'm thinking Brandon."

"So I'm supposed to loan you my gear and train Tommy Brandon?"

"You'll be paid."

"This isn't point-and-shoot. Not exactly."

"You can keep it simple though, right? I've got a guy in Seattle with the Marshal Service. I need to get these e-mailed to him this afternoon."

"Then let me do it. Forget teaching Brandon."

"It could get ugly. I'm not putting you into that."

"I'm touched," she said sarcastically. "So, I'll partner with Brandon."

Just the words "partner with Brandon" turned his stomach.

"Face recognition software requires good pictures, Walt. High-quality, full-frontal shots. You think Brandon is going to get this right?"

He was transported back to his imagination: Gail and Brandon sweating in the tight confines of the trailer's bedroom.

"Earth to Walt," he heard her say.

"Okay . . . okay," he said. "You'll team up with Brandon," he agreed. Anything, he thought, to keep Brandon out of that trailer.

Eleven

Trevalian's trick was to put a liberal amount of Vaseline laced with cayenne pepper up both nostrils. His nose ran like a faucet and gave Nagler the excuse to miss most of the events. The beauty of the Nagler identity was that the former academic was a virtual recluse, rarely seen outside the think tank. He did not travel in these circles, nor was he known by them. He crashed the invitation-only luncheon he'd seen mentioned on Cutter's home computer.

No one would be so impolite as to bounce a blind man, and they did not. A place was set, and he sat through the outdoor luncheon, on the lawn of the Guest House, only three tables away from the woman he'd come to kill. Had he not cared about his own freedom, he might have run a knife through her and been done with it, for the Secret Service agents kept their distance, guarding the perimeter but not the woman. With his semitransparent contacts in place, Trevalian could see well enough to not make a mess of eating.

Prior to dessert he excused himself, having exhausted his Kleenex, and wanting to set the hook. As expected, a Secret Service agent escorted him and Toey to a golf cart that then shuttled him back to the lodge. This planted the dog's existence firmly in the minds of the agents.

Back in Nagler's room, Trevalian moved quickly, with a rehearsed system of changing from one man to the other. He locked the appropriate doors, hung out the PRIVACY tags, and then left the rooms and took the stairs to the ground floor.

Trevalian, as hotel guest Meisner, walked hurriedly into the side lot where he'd parked the rental. He drove out onto Sun Valley Road and parked along the bike path with a tourist map unfolded on the steering wheel. Ten minutes later, two black Escalades driving in tandem pulled up to the traffic light. Shaler's escort.

He followed well back of the Escalades, turned and approached a building marked as the library. The television crews gave away her home. He parked and got out, having not figured on such a scene. There was no way he could get near her house without either being arrested or his face being shown on national television. He studied the suddenly excited reporters and news crews, all swilling Tully's iced coffees from paper cups. Their enthusiasm, manifested as shouting and screaming, waned as Shaler entered the house without comment. These same news crews would likely be covering the brunch on Sunday. They would be in the room. Now he was the one who felt on edge: jumpy and excited.

He passed the next fifteen minutes watching them while trying to find a way inside. The journalists suddenly sprang back to life only to realize it was Shaler's Hispanic housecleaner and not the AG at the side door. But where they cursed with disappointment, Trevalian had to contain his excitement: for the housecleaner carried a bulging white canvas sack in her arms. A laundry bag.

The maid launched the sack into the back

of a beat-up Chevy, slammed the hatch, and climbed behind the driver's wheel.

Trevalian was back in the rental in seconds and had the engine running by the time she pulled out of the drive. He followed, knowing a maid wasn't going to check for tails. She drove six blocks and parked. He couldn't find a parking place. He resorted to double parking in a private parking lot that warned of towing unauthorized vehicles. He hurried from the car and caught the door to the Suds Tub as it swung shut behind the maid.

She thanked him.

"Hello, Maria," a woman with stringy hair said from behind the counter. Even with two fans running, the laundry suffered from high humidity and extreme heat. "Shaler?" she said, tapping on a keyboard and beginning her count, as the laundry bag was inverted. "Be with you in a minute," she called out to Trevalian.

"No problem," he said. The appearance of this maid was a gift. The icing on the cake came as the proprietor apologized to the maid that due to the extremely busy weekend and a broken washer, pickup would be Monday at the earliest, no exceptions.

Maria didn't seem to care. She took a re-
ceipt, offered Trevalian a smile in passing,
and left, carrying her empty laundry sack
with her.

For his purposes, that empty sack would
do. But he couldn't see how to get it without making a scene.

"Can I help you?" the proprietor inquired.

Trevalian asked about the pricing, threw in
a few questions about timing, and watched
as the woman transferred Shaler's dirty
clothes into a blue sack, placed a sticker on
it from the order form, pinned a tag bearing
a second sticker to the bag, and then
wedged the sack onto the second shelf
from the floor with a dozen others—all identical.

"I don't know if you heard," she said over
her shoulder, "but we're a little backlogged
because of a faulty washer."

"I'm good," he said. "You've been very
helpful."

As he left, he made a quick study of the
business's security system.

A challenge—but nothing he couldn't work
with.

Twelve

Walt met Fiona in the parking lot of the golf pro shop. She climbed into the Cherokee and immediately fiddled with the air-conditioning, making it colder.

"Damn, that sun's hot," she complained. She worked with her camera, pushing buttons on the back, and then passed it to Walt, who held it gingerly.

On the small LCD screen, he saw a photo of a man he recognized as Andy Bartholomew, the self-proclaimed leader of First Rights. "Where is this, the chairlift?"

"Yeah. River Run. You toggle this flywheel to move to the next shot."

She leaned in close to demonstrate, and he tensed noticeably. Any proximity to a woman was too close for him right now.

Even a bucket seat across a Jeep made him feel as if she were in his lap. She scorned him for his reaction, but went back to her corner. He toggled to the next shot.

What had been a blob in the first photo now turned out to be a man's shoulder. Also, in this second shot the chairlift as a backdrop became more apparent. The Sun Valley Company operated a chairlift to the top of the mountain for summer sightseeing. Bartholomew, and the man belonging to that shoulder, were clearly in line for the chairlift.

The third photo caused him to gasp. "That's Dick O'Brien."

"That's what Tommy said."

He didn't like her referring to Brandon by his first name, and nearly corrected her.

"What the hell is Cutter's head of security doing with the leader of First Rights?"

"Tommy said that, too."

"I don't *care* about Tommy Brandon, okay?" The words were out of his mouth before he knew it.

Fiona sat up straight.

"Sorry . . . I . . ." He pointed to the camera, unable to make eye contact with her.

"What . . . is going on?" she asked.

After a moment, she obliged him, advancing the images. Another several photos, all taken within a few minutes of one another. Bartholomew and O'Brien boarded and rode a chairlift together. "Oh, shit," Walt mumbled.

"Sheriff?"

"The only reason you ride a twenty-minute chairlift with someone like Bartholomew is so that no one can listen in," he said.

"He threatened him," she said. "That's what Tommy said happened: The big guy told the younger one that if he made any trouble for the conference there'd be hell to pay."

"Thing is . . . ," Walt said, "it only takes about thirty seconds to do that. So why all the cloak-and-dagger involving the chairlift? That's a lot of trouble to go through—a long ride to share with the guy—if all you're going to do is try to scare him."

"So?"

"So I'm going to find out."

Twenty minutes later he and Bartholomew occupied the front seat of Brandon's BCS cruiser, which was parked in a Sinclair gas station across from the employee dormitories a few hundred yards from the site of the First Rights demonstration.

Walt introduced himself and shook hands with Bartholomew, a small man with an erudite face despite a grunge appearance. He emphasized that the man was here of his own free will and was under no legal obligation to cooperate.

"We're cool."

"I heard you took in the view from the top of Baldy this morning," Walt said.

Bartholomew grimaced.

"It's a small town. I also heard Dick O'Brien took that ride with you."

Bartholomew studied the car's ceiling fabric. He released a long exhale.

"I like Dick O'Brien—I've worked with him on the conference for the past four years. I don't want to make accusations against a friend of mine, without a complaint to back it up."

"No complaints," Bartholomew said.

Walt considered leaving it there—he'd done his duty. "If he threatened or extorted you, Mr. Bartholomew, it's my obligation to inform you that we will and can protect you against any such malfeasance."

"Such a big word for an Idaho sheriff. But then again, Sheriff Walter Fleming, you're not your average county sheriff, are you? Quantico trained. Your college degree at Northwestern on a full ride. Former two-term president of the state's Sheriffs' Association. Currently serving on the National Association of Counties. Your father, a former FBI special agent."

"You want a gold star for doing your homework, go back to school," Walt said. "Or do I counter by telling you you're a Berkeley grad who joined the Peace Corps, worked for Nader's election campaign in 2000, and then went off track. You're an angry teen on steroids, Mr. Bartholomew. I'm not interested in you, only whether or not Dick O'Brien threatened you."

"I can handle myself."

"Which is what I'm afraid of. It's my job to handle Dick O'Brien, not yours. Don't mess with him."

"You can relax, Sheriff. His interest was in making a contribution to our cause."

Walt mulled this over. "A contribution?" he said.

"Fifty thousand dollars: twenty-five up front, twenty-five when we cross the Blaine County border. He suggested we park ourselves on the capitol's front lawn in Boise."

"Fifty thousand dollars if you walked."

"That's what the man said."

"And what did you say?" Walt asked.

"I told him to get in line. I turned down a hundred grand yesterday."

"I'm in the wrong business. Who offered you the hundred?"

"No idea," Bartholomew said. "An anonymous phone call. Maybe it was a joke."

"You have no idea who made the offer?"

"Cutter, I can understand," Bartholomew said. "He has his gig to protect. But the first one? Who but Cutter cares about it that much?"

"If you try to do to Sun Valley what you did to Seattle," Walt warned, "you'll be met with a show of overwhelming force."

"Shock and awe?" he said sarcastically. "Let me tell you something, Sheriff. You're limited to tear gas and rubber bullets, and we've seen them both."

"I have National Guard Reserves on call. If you start something, I will finish it."

"And whom do I see if I'm threatened by the sheriff?"

"That would be me," Walt said, trading ironic smiles with the man. He reached for the missing door handle, then knocked loudly on the glass for Brandon to let him out.

Walt stood up out of the car to find himself face-to-face with his deputy. Bartholomew slid across the seat and also got out. He headed across Sun Valley Road back toward the demonstration.

"Sheriff?" Brandon said, when Walt failed to move. Brandon was nearly a head taller.

Walt hesitated, his head spinning, his fists clenched. "You two could have waited for the paperwork to come through."

Brandon's Adam's apple bobbed in his throat. He stiffened his posture, standing at rigid attention.

Walt opened his mouth to say more, but then reconsidered, shook his head, and walked away. He didn't look back to check, as he crossed the road, but he sensed the man was still standing there staring straight ahead, and it gave him a much needed sense of satisfaction.

"Asshole," he mumbled under his breath.

Thirteen

Trevalian worked out hard before an operation, believing it mitigated the adrenaline rushes. Late Friday night he spent forty minutes on a treadmill and an elliptical, and another twenty with light weights—half his typical daily routine. With the edge burned off his nerves, he found his response time was quicker, his thinking clearer.

As he returned from the late night workout, his mind on the Suds Tub laundry and not the hallway's wall of fame—photos of Gary Cooper, Ernest Hemingway, Jamie Lee Curtis, and Clint Eastwood—he spotted a scuffle ahead.

It appeared to be a feud between a husband and wife. The man had hold of her upper arms. He raised his voice drunkenly. The woman wore a clinging formal dress, her bare back to Trevalian. With each step she took to distance herself, the man moved with her—an awkward and dangerous dance.

She broke away from him with a sudden jerk, turning toward Trevalian. It was the jazz singer from the night before. The man was not her husband, but some lech of a hotel guest. Trevalian quickened his step. The singer spotted him, locked onto him. Her eyes cried for help.

He knew better than to get involved in this. But as the elevator bell dinged and the doors drew open, he saw an opportunity. The slobbering fool called out, "Hey, there! You come back here! We're not done!" He looked about sixty, though fit for his age.

Trevalian moved toward her with deliberate speed. Her purse thumped against her flank. Trevalian hooked her elbow with his sweat-soaked arm, spun her around on her high heels, and escorted her into the elevator.

The elevator car lifted past the second floor sounding a bell. They met eyes; hers were bright with appreciation.

"I hope that wasn't your husband," Trevalian said.

She held up her left hand: no ring.

The elevator arrived at the third floor. He held the door and let her pass. She opened her mouth to thank him. He said, "No charge." The elevator doors closed and they turned in opposite directions. Then the violent cursing of a man's angry voice rose up the stairway.

She turned back toward him. "Hide me, please. Just for a minute."

On the job, Trevalian did not get involved; he did not womanize.

"Five minutes," he said. He took her by the elbow and led her down the hallway.

They walked briskly. As the man's voice became clearer, far behind them, Trevalian broke into a light jog. The woman stopped, foisted her purse onto Trevalian, kicked off her heels, squatted down to scoop them up, hoisted her dress, and took off at a run. At the sight of him holding her purse she broke into a nervous laugh.

With the door to Meisner's room locked behind them, and the jamb loop in place, he said, "You know where the phone is." He indicated his own sodden athletic wear and, gathering a fresh change of clothes into his arms from the closet, said, "I'm going to shower. I am not going to spring out naked and attack you," he said. "I'm sure you have someplace to go."

"And if I stay?" she asked in her husky, singer's voice. The lace of her bra showed. She adjusted the low-cut dress. "Could we make it ten minutes instead of five?"

"I'm heading out." He was also about to dress in all black, although that was enough in fashion not to be a problem.

When he came back out of the bathroom fifteen minutes later, he found her sitting at the desk, a hotel bottle of liquor uncapped. She was drinking from a coffee mug. She'd applied some fresh lipstick.

"They probably charge a fortune for these, and I'm sorry, but I needed it."

"Did you call someone?" he asked.

"I didn't."

"Because?"

She shrugged. "Fine line. I'm not sup-posed to offend the guests. But I don't have to put up with that bullshit either. If I bring security into it—especially this, of all week-ends—it'll make it into more than it was . . . is . . . whatever."

"He was hurting you."

"He's an asshole. But on a weekend like this the place is full of them."

"I'm sorry," he said, "but you can't stay."

"No problem." She rose, adjusted her dress again, and slipped on her shoes. "I owe you a drink."

"Rain check?" he said.

"This is Sun Valley. It snows here, but it doesn't rain."

"My loss."

"Can you walk me out?" she asked.

"I can get you down to the lobby."

"That'll do." She extended her hand. "Lilly."

"Peter," he said, providing Meisner's first name.

They reached the lobby without incident.

Scouting the area, she said, "I meant it about the rain check."

She turned. She saw only his back, heading down the same hallway from which he'd first appeared.

Fourteen

Just before midnight, with the summer sky ripped in two by a vivid Milky Way, Walt entered Friedman Memorial Airport, still reeling over his brief encounter with Dick O'Brien.

With O'Brien attending a dessert function at Trail Creek Cabin, where the commissioner of the FCC was giving an informal talk on the Politics of Policy to forty-five special ticket holders, he'd suggested meeting Walt at the Hemingway Memorial. A well-trodden path less than a mile from the cabin. Walt had worked his way down through the dark, flashlight in hand, to Hemingway's bust. The famous writer overheard everything they said.

O'Brien, defensive from the start, lit a cigarette, its red ember traveling up and down like a firefly.

"So?" the big man said. "I heard you spoke to Bartholomew. You might have told me you had him under surveillance."

"I might have, but I didn't."

"Hell of a view from up there," O'Brien said.

"I'm not telling Patrick Cutter his business—"

"Wouldn't be any point," O'Brien said, sounding exasperated.

"Making that kind of offer . . . it wouldn't hurt if I knew about it."

"Damned if I do, damned if I don't."

"Did Bartholomew tell you about the hundred K?" Walt asked.

"He did. It wasn't us."

"Then who?"

"That's the hundred-thousand-dollar question," O'Brien said.

"Let me run this by you: If you've been planning to assassinate Elizabeth Shaler, if you've paid out maybe half a million in fees, and a good chunk in expenses and advance work, wouldn't the arrival of First Rights scare you just a little?"

"The protesters get nasty," O'Brien speculated. "It shuts down the conference, and you lose your shot at her."

"The hundred grand serves as an insurance policy—to make sure nothing upsets the conference."

O'Brien whistled.

"Tell me I'm crazy," Walt said.

"Wish I could," O'Brien said, lighting another cigarette.

It felt as if several minutes passed. O'Brien with the cigarette. The sound of the creek.

O'Brien exhaled a pale cloud. "I can't take this to Cutter as further proof of the hit. If that's what you're asking—"

"The hell you can't."

"Do you trust some guy who let his protesters cause two million dollars' worth of damage in downtown Seattle? Patrick Cutter won't."

"She should cancel that speech."

"He's going to need more."

"That's bullshit," Walt said.

"Patrick will see this as a negotiating stance, nothing more. He eats guys like Bartholomew for lunch. This kid has zero credibility."

O'Brien's words stayed with Walt as he

entered the air terminal. He'd received a message that Pete—the former volunteer fireman who now ran airport security—had to see him immediately. He'd called but reached voice mail. Heading to Hailey any-way, he swung by the airport.

"Hey, Walt," Pete said, greeting him at the automatic doors. He'd been waiting for him. Pete wore extra-extra-large and had hands like an NBA player. He sounded as if he'd smoked from birth.

"What have you got?" Walt asked, releas-ing the handshake before it became a con-test.

"Yesterday. You and Brandon," Pete said. "The dog thing."

"Yes."

"Flight seventeen-forty-six."

"If you say so," Walt said. He followed down a wide corridor to the two small and unattended airline counters, pushed through a door marked AUTHORIZED PERSONNEL ONLY. The back room was crowded with un-claimed luggage.

"Pete, it's been a long day."

"The way it works anymore," Pete said, "is we gotta send back lost items to Salt Lake. They got the full-size X-ray machines down there. But we can't scan 'em because of their size, so we open them up. In this case we could scan it, and we also did a hand search."

"Pete," Walt said again.

"Yesterday you were looking for some guy on flight seventeen-forty-six. Today we got ourselves an unclaimed bag from seventeen-forty-six." He mugged for Walt, letting him stew. "I wouldn't have bothered you, Walt, except for its contents."

"Its contents," Walt repeated.

Pete hoisted the bag onto a table and dumped it upside down. The contents scattered. Pete said, "Suture, bandages. Hypodermic needles. Fuckin' traveling emergency room. Only thing missing is a scalpel, and you got yourself a regular surgical suite."

Walt moved the contents around, using his pen. "You touch any of this?"

"No, sir," Pete said.

"It's good work, Pete," Walt said. "Syringes got through security?"

"Diabetics are allowed syringes. See 'em all the time. More than one or two, you're usually asked to put it in with the checked luggage. Not always."

Walt inventoried the contents. A navy blue sweater. A paperback novel by Leslie Silbert. Three boxes of bandage wrap. A box of butterfly bandages. A pair of forceps. Two pairs of needle holders. Two containers of suture marked Ethicon #3 and Ethicon #0. A box of latex gloves. "Shit," Walt said. "No ID?"

"No. None."

He studied the sweater. "Some hairs, looks like. Maybe some prints on these boxes, or the forceps."

"Who leaves something like this behind? You know? Wouldn't you come back to get it? I would."

Walt returned the contents to the bag. He noted a white loop of stretch string at the bottom of one of the back straps. "This coulda been an ID," he said.

"Could have been tore off years ago."

Walt glanced around the disorganized room and its filthy floor. "Do me a favor and ask these guys to sweep up. Let's run any loose ID tags they find."

"Against passenger manifest," Pete stated. "Done."

Walt wrote down the contents of the bag.

"Listen, Pete . . . could you buy me the

weekend, before sending it down there?"
Walt asked. He knew TSA regulations were
strict. "I'd like to get some of these items to
the Nampa lab. The lab will do weekend
work for the right price."

"Prints . . ." Pete said. "You think?"

"It's possible."

"I got ya covered. It'll miss the morning
flight. Shit happens." Pete sniggered. He
zipped the bag shut and handed it to Walt.
"Monday morning, I need it back by seven."

Walt thanked him. Right or wrong, he connected the bag to the shooter. The medical
contents suggested the preparation for in-
jury. If the man was prepared to doctor himself, he meant business.

And if such a man was so prepared to
treat himself, then what exactly did he have
planned for Liz Shaler?

SATURDAY

1 A.M.

One

At a few minutes before 1 A.M., as the bars were closing, the quiet streets briefly came alive again. Vehicles filled Main Street. The sidewalks were crowded with late night revelers. A young woman bent over and emptied her stomach into the gutter.

This was also the hour that city police and deputy sheriffs set speed traps and watched for erratic driving. Trevalian had a thirty-minute window. By 1:30 A.M. the town would be dead and the cops would respond more quickly to a break-in.

It took him seven minutes to pick the lock on the back door of Suds Tub. He entered to the alarm system's steady beeping—a thirty-second grace period to enter a pass code. He had options open to him if he failed to disarm it in time, but he kept a running count as he located the alarm box. *Five seconds.* Flipped open the panel and keyed in the last four digits of the laundry's phone number. *Ten seconds* . . . the warning beep continued.

He crossed the room to the cash register. *Fifteen seconds* . . . Ran his gloved hand around the shelving and came up with a small key that opened the cash register.

Twenty seconds . . .

Opened the cash register. Removed the empty tray. Cleared away some receipts. There! On the bottom of the drawer was a handwritten number on a small piece of paper covered in layers of Scotch tape: 4376.

Twenty-five . . . twenty-six . . .

He raced back to the alarm box on the back wall.

Twenty-eight . . . twenty-nine . . .

He quickly keyed in 4376.

The beeping stopped. The red flashing LED on the device disappeared. He locked the door from the inside. He carried a Maglite with red tape over the lens, cutting back its brightness. He ran a quick inspection: no motion sensors. He rearmed the alarm, working under the assumption that leaving a commercial building without its alarm engaged might raise suspicions. The box beeped for another thirty seconds and then went silent—the system active.

He had fifty or sixty identical blue bags to search. One of them was Shaler's. He checked the tags and rolled bags out of his way.

Vehicles sped past, out on the street. A group of noisy kids left their shadows on the front window. Trevalian had pulled a balaclava over his head, but he lifted it to get better vision. He worked methodically through the piled sacks.

Ten minutes into it, he located Shaler's. He opened it and, with the Maglite clenched between his teeth, searched the contents. He took out a bra, two pairs of panties, and finally touched the Holy Grail: a Capilene, pull-on, sports top. He sniffed just to make sure: sour. He tucked these items into a pouch on the back of his shirt, pulled the drawstring on the sack, and was in the midst of tying it shut when the back door was kicked in. Simultaneously, the alarm box began its countdown.

Trevalian pulled the balaclava over his face. Police? Two people came through the door. But with them backlit by a streetlamp, he saw they were too small to be adults. They were just kids. He decided to intimidate.

"Who's there?" he shouted, stepping forward.

The kids panicked. One turned, stumbled over a drum of chemicals, rose to his feet, and sprinted to the nearest window, which he promptly dove through. Or tried to. A crash of glass, but he didn't make it all the way. Thrashing and bleeding, he fell back inside the building.

"Eric!" the other kid cried.

Trevalian hurried over to the fallen boy. The kid was in shock, but still tried to move away from Trevalian. He smeared his own blood on the floor with his movement.

Trevalian took the boy's right hand, uncurled his unwilling fingers, and pressed the fingers against the gash on his neck. "Push here as hard as you can."

The alarm sounded. A robotic voice announced, "INTRUDER! INTRUDER! GET OUT OF THE HOUSE NOW!" at a numbing volume.

The second kid screamed, "ERIC!" and took off out the back door. Trevalian went after him. His buddy needed to keep that pressure up. If the boy should pass out . . . But the kid panicked and ran hard toward the street. His attention remained on Trevalian a beat too long. He ran headlong into an eight-foot-tall wooden grizzly bear. He might as well have been hit by a truck. He went down hard and lay still on the sidewalk.

The boy was out cold, bleeding from his ear and nose. It looked as if he'd shattered the bone around his right eye socket. He was breathing.

A siren grew louder.

Trevalian blended into shadow and disappeared. He was well on his way back to the rental before the first cruiser arrived.

Two

Most people, when under the harsh tube lighting of the Sheriff's Office, looked somewhat green and sickly. But not Fiona. She had an intriguing look about her, fan lines at the edges of her eyes, giving her wisdom and her small but pouty mouth something of a distraction.

Walt studied her as she arranged the contents of the lost-and-found carry-on discovered at the airport. She spread them out and began photographing them while maintaining a conversation with him.

"It must strike you as odd," she said, "some guy carrying around all this stuff."

"Atypical is how I'd classify it," he said.

"Yeah, that's *exactly* how I'd put it as well."

He'd shut the door to the room and locked it because he didn't want anyone from his office seeing the bag or its contents. For now, the bag was all his.

"Tell me about your father. He's here for the conference, right?" She ran off a series of shots.

"The usual sordid history," he said.

"Sordid's a strong word."

"And accurate in this case."

"Fathers and sons. Mothers and daughters. As old as the Bible," she said.

"There was . . . an event," he said. "A long time ago." He felt on the verge of sharing something he had shared with no one.

She remained focused on the photography. "An event. That does sound ominous." She took a few more shots. "Are you going to tell me about it?"

"No."

"That hardly seems fair."

"He put me through something. He went from god to demon in an afternoon."

"That doesn't sound pretty."

"It wasn't pretty." He added, "And the funny thing is: I'll bet he doesn't even remember it. Strange how that happens—a kid's world crumbles and the adult doesn't even take notice."

"Change is good. Look at what a strong leader you've become as an adult."

"Me?" Walt didn't think of himself as a strong leader. He felt like a failed husband and father. "If it had been adolescence, it might have made more sense. I was nine at the time. I still worshipped at his feet at that point."

"And you're not going to tell me?"

"It's not you . . . I've never told anyone," he said. "I don't know if—"

His cell phone rang, and he answered it. He caught himself holding his breath as a nurse explained the situation to him. He hung up.

"It's my nephew," he muttered. "He's in the emergency room. I gotta go."

"Is he all right?"

Walt couldn't get a word out. He'd lost his brother, his marriage. He couldn't lose Kevin, too.

He climbed into the Cherokee and sped off, his light rack flashing. She'd started him thinking about the past, and he found himself stuck there.

His father had been drinking; Walt had no trouble remembering that day. The furtive promise had been father to son, filling Walt with great expectancy. He'd labeled it "a secret mission," which further played to Walt's imagination, causing his pulse to race. He would not, for any reason, allow his mother to find out.

He was given the task of retrieving the neighbor's cat, a noisy vandal whose crimes included digging up his mother's rosebushes and crying loudly at all hours of the night. Chippers, as the cat was known, had become the stuff of legend in their house, the subject of many dinner conversations.

"Chippers?" Walt had said—an attempt to clarify his mission.

"He's critical to the assignment," his father said. "Get Chippers into the cage in the back of the car and wait for me."

The lure of the adventure had been intensified for Walt by his father's brandishing a handgun: a six-shot revolver, with a barrel as long as a ruler. They'd been down in the basement together at the time. It was a gray gun wrapped in a damp cloth with the sweet smell of gun oil. His father had loaded and unloaded it, inspecting it with a careful eye.

"What's that for?" Walt asked excitedly.

"Target practice."

"Do I get to shoot?"

"If you're a good boy. If you get Chippers into that car like I said."

"But why Chippers?" Walt asked.

"He's a hunter, isn't he?"

It was true. Chippers delivered a dead mouse or mole to their back door every so often.

With a beer pinched between his father's legs, they were off. The Ford Pinto rattled a lot and smelled of exhaust. They drove with the windows down. Chippers moaned in the back.

"What's the mission?" Walt asked, now that they were alone and driving into the mountains.

"A good soldier learns to never question his senior officer. And he learns to *keep his mouth shut* even after the mission is over. Are we clear, soldier?"

"Yes, sir."

"That's good, because this mission is top secret, and I'd hate to see you lose rank and be prevented from taking future missions."

"No, sir. Won't happen."

"What's a soldier's first duty?"

"To God and Country," the boy answered.

"Damn straight. You're a good kid, you know that?"

"To follow orders and never question authority." Walt repeated anything he could remember his father saying about army service.

"Now you're talking!"

"To boldly go where no man has gone before," Walt said.

His father laughed, sipped the beer, and returned the can to his crotch. "I borrowed that one, son, but that's the spirit. You bet it is." He looked at Walt with a smile: His father never smiled. He put his eyes back on the road. "You remember a lot of the shi— things . . . I tell you."

"I try to remember them all," Walt said proudly.

"You're a good kid. Have I told you that?"

"Yes, sir, you have. About one minute ago, actually."

His father chuckled some more. "Just so

long as we got it straight between us that this mission is top secret. Even your brother's not to hear of it. Is that clear?"

"Yes, sir!" The idea of Walt knowing something Bobby did not was nearly too much for him to contain. He jittered and jumped around in the front seat—having graduated backseat to front on his ninth birthday. Asked to fetch a second beer from the cooler, he did so, a task that required unfastening his seat belt while the *car was moving*. He'd never done that before either. This was a day of firsts. It was only while fetching the beer that he noticed an oil-stained towel lying along the backseat. He thought about asking but decided not to.

They drove up the narrow, curving, dangerously steep and precipitous one-lane track to the top of Trail Creek summit. The road was a composition of packed dirt and scree, with no guardrails and drops of a thousand feet or more. Rock walls on the hillside leached water that streamed across the track, cutting muddy ruts into the road bed. His father handled the car poorly. It jumped and skidded as the tires caught in the ruts. More than once, Walt felt they were going over the edge. He rode white-knuckled, his eyes straight ahead, never questioning his superior officer, not even when his father lost control of the car while juggling the beer.

"Fucking thing is a nuisance," his father muttered under his beer breath.

Walt wondered if this was a comment on road conditions or something else. He nearly spoke up, but his father's mood was sliding, as it often did. He was muttering and talking to himself, and looking up the mountain instead of at the road. For the rest of the ride, Walt kept one hand on the door handle, ready to jump.

Shortly after they crested the summit, the dirt road widened out, crossing an open, flat expanse of gray green prairie, wax weed, sage, and tumblebush. To the east loomed the jagged peaks of the Pioneers, and the barren faces of the White Clouds. They turned right onto a dirt track following signs to Devil's Bedstead. The name stuck in Walt's mind. He would be haunted by it for the rest of his life.

A third beer was gone as they arrived at the trailhead Unnamed Lake. Devil's Bedstead, an oppressive gray granite monster wearing a skirt of boulders, rose from the lake, blotting out the sky. Even in late July it wore a cap of ice and snow.

The car rolled to a noisy stop on the gravel, and his father lumbered out from behind the wheel, grabbing for the door to retain his balance. It was cooler here despite a powerful sun. Walt tugged on a sweatshirt he'd thrown into the backseat.

"Get the cage," his father ordered while pissing only feet from the car. His father zipped up his pants and came around the car, shielding his eyes to survey up the mountain. Then he looked back down the road from where they'd come. He wore the revolver on his belt in a leather holster that carried an insignia. From the backseat he withdrew the stained towel that he now unwrapped to reveal a twelve-gauge, over-under, double-barreled shotgun. Sunlight flickered dimly off its polished barrels, as his old man tucked the gun beneath his left armpit.

Now Walt understood what his father had in mind, why he'd been sworn to secrecy. He knew, too, not to question or go up against his father when he'd been drinking. So he drew the cage from the Pinto, his hands shaking, his knees weak.

"Dad . . . ," He pleaded, breaking his own rules.

"Shut up!" his father snapped. "This is what's called the laws of nature. This, son, is real justice. You ask a person any fucking number of times to get the fucking cat off your property . . . and then you take matters into your own hands. You remember that."

He would, as it turned out.

But it had been Walt's hands, not his father's, that had captured Chippers. Walt's hands that had trapped Chippers in the cage. Walt who had been giddy about joining his father. For this . . .

"Release the prisoner," his father said.

He shook his head, fighting back the tears.

"Do it, son."

"Can't we just let him go?"

"That's all *you're* doing."

"But . . . the shotgun."

"Release the prisoner," he repeated.

Walt hesitated, the first tears escaping.

"OPEN THE FUCKING CAGE!" His father hollered so loudly that his voice echoed off the mountain.

Walt opened the cage, and a bewildered Chippers jumped out. The cat landed on the rocky ground behind the car and walked a tight circle, its nose working furiously. Walt sniffled. The cat sprang away from him and scampered up the scree toward a stand of Douglas fir.

Walt's father trotted after the cat, across to the copse of trees. Walt turned toward the lake, its surface peaceful and still. He covered both ears, pressing hard, and sank to his knees, his nose running.

His whole body jumped with the reports— a cramp from head to foot. Wind riffled the surface of the lake.

They rode back in a sickening silence, his father glancing over at him from time to time but never speaking. His father occasionally broke into a grin and chuckled morbidly to himself. Walt hated him—a hate beyond anything he'd ever experienced, so dark and awful that he even considered turning the shotgun on his father and killing him right there. Killing them both, if it came to that—jerking on the wheel and sending the car over the unguarded edge of Trail Creek pass.

For the next two years his mother tried to negotiate a truce between them, having no idea of the cause of their break. She mentioned Chippers's absence one night at dinner; Walt and his father exchanged glances, but that was all. His father came and went, rarely staying more than a long weekend, the time between those weekends increasing, which didn't bother Walt one bit. He and his brother, Bobby, took over putting out the garbage, fixing the heat tape on the roof ahead of the first snow, shoveling the path and driveway. His father returned like an unnamed planet, and then left as quickly as he'd come. Back to his darkness.

Walt finally broke the silence after waiting for his old man to get in his car, about to leave for another several months. Walt tapped on the window. Jerry rolled down the glass and sat there waiting.

"I'll never forgive you," Walt said.

He turned and walked away, at twelve years old, an orphan.

Three

Walt could enter a dark garage knowing there was an armed man inside, but something about a hospital gave him the creeps.

The semiprivate room had one empty bed. Walt passed under a flickering TV and stopped abruptly. Glowing monitors connected to his nephew with wires and tubes. The boy's head was shaved and bandaged. Purple bruising surrounded his right eye socket. A line of stitches at the edge of his lips extended his mouth into a lopsided snarl.

Myra sat in a chair close to the bed. She directed a sullen, resentful expression at Walt. "You could have prevented this."

"Myra—"

"Mom," Kevin muttered. "Not his fault."

She turned and took his hand gently in hers. "Back to sleep. It's only Walt."

"Hey, Kev."

The boy's eyes, bloodshot and swollen, found Walt.

"Eric?" The boy spoke with difficulty.

"No talking, Kev," Myra said. "Back to sleep."

"Eric's okay," Walt said. He saw relief in the boy's only eye.

"Thank God," Kevin said.

"I'm here as your uncle. First and foremost my concern is with your health and your speedy recovery. But we talked about this before, Kevin: I'm the sheriff, and I've got to talk to you about this."

"But we can do this later," Myra said.

"Ketchum police are going to want to talk to him, Myra. They're going to charge him. I need to hear it first if we're going to help him."

"Doesn't matter to me. It's okay, Mom."

"The boy is doped up."

"It's up to Kevin."

"I'm okay, Mom. Please."

Myra huffed, but sat back in the chair.

The bloody eye blinked. "We wanted clothes," he said, "some nice clothes."

"Go on."

"Me and Eric thought we could lift some clothes from the Suds. So we . . . like . . . scoped the place. Checked it out. You know. Parked around the corner." He paused, worked his mouth side to side and started again. "Eric said he could pick a lock, but he ended up kicking it in."

"Eric kicked the door in," Walt clarified.

"We got inside and the alarm went off. We freaked. Eric went for the window—don't ask me why. I took off and hit a pole, I guess."

"Why the window, if the door's kicked in?"

"I dunno."

"Why Suds Tub over something like the Goldmine?"

Kevin grimaced and then winced with pain. "I don't know."

"Walt?" Myra whined "What's going on?"

"Ketchum police will think this had to do with the dry cleaning chemicals. Chemicals to huff, to cook meth—whatever."

"No way," Kevin said.

"If one of your friends coerced you and Eric into doing this, that's a whole different thing. Legally, I mean."

"No."

"Kevin?" the boy's mother questioned.

"You start making things up, Kev, that's a quagmire. You know what a quagmire is?" Walt saw hesitation on his face.

"My head hurts. I gotta stop now."

"Kevin," his mother said sharply.

"Not now, Mom."

Walt stepped closer to the bed and looked down at the boy. "I'm giving you a chance that the Ketchum officers won't."

"The alarm went off. We panicked," the boy said. "I'm going to sleep now." He closed his eye tightly.

Walt's radio squawked. He listened as the dispatcher called out a series of codes followed by ". . . dba: Aker's Veterinarian Services." He checked his watch: 2 A.M. Two break-ins in one night. He called in. The vet's clinic was outside city limits and less than half a mile south of the hospital. Walt was the closest officer.

"I gotta go," he told her. "But I'll be back."

"I'm not going anywhere," she said. "And neither is he."

Four

A Ketchum Police Department squad car, its rack flashing red, white, and blue, was parked at a hurried angle in front of the clinic's log cabin entrance. The front door had been left open and the lights were on. He saw the uniformed officer inside, using the phone.

Walt parked the Cherokee and took over responsibility from the Ketchum cop. Brandon was the next to arrive, his trailer only a quarter mile down the road. The two men couldn't look at each other. Mark Aker's pickup truck pulled in and, much to Walt's surprise, so did Fiona's Subaru.

Aker hurried into the building. Brandon followed. Fiona collected her camera gear. She wore what could have been pajama bottoms and a faded pink T-shirt under a down vest and a pair of blue Keens.

"I'm right up the hill in the Engls' guesthouse. I heard the siren," she explained.

"If you're here as part of my office," he said, "you're welcome inside. If you're here for the newspaper, I'd ask you to hang back."

"Understood. I'm here for you," she said.

They caught up to Aker in an exam room. Walt spotted the broken cabinet and the busted padlock clasp on a refrigerator.

"Meds?" he said.

"Knew what they were looking for." Aker donned a pair of latex gloves and looked through the cabinet.

Fiona stepped away from them and began photographing.

Aker glanced out the window, shouted, "Oh, shit!" and hurried outside.

Walt followed as he crossed the courtyard. Aker entered the back barn and threw on some exterior lights. Animal eyes—dozens of them—peered from the dark.

"They let them all out!" Aker shouted. Walt followed at a run into the back barn. Empty, the cage doors hanging open.

Aker cursed a blue streak, pacing back and forth. "Most of these are sick animals."

"How many?" Walt asked.

The vet shook his head and shot him a hot look. "They're under my care," he mumbled. He threw open another door, looking across a second small courtyard. "Oh, God . . . My training dogs . . . I can't believe this! Who would do such a thing?"

Walt thought he knew the answer to that. "Brandon!" he shouted. His deputy came running, arriving out of breath. Walt said, "When you followed Bartholomew, did you happen to find out where he was staying?"

Five

Walt rolled down the window to fight off the internal heat that arose from him sitting two feet from Tommy Brandon. The Cherokee passed into Ketchum city limits. "Is she there? Did you leave her there when the on-call came through?"

"I think maybe this is between you and her," Brandon said.

"This is me asking you if my wife was in your trailer when you got the call." Walt waited for Brandon to say something. "If you're going to sleep with my wife, you could at least own up to it."

"She's there," he said, turning to face the passenger window.

Walt gripped the wheel more tightly. "How long?"

"Sheriff . . ."

"A month? Six months? What?"

"Turn right," Brandon instructed. He navigated Walt through back streets to a Trail Creek condominium that he and Fiona had identified while following Bartholomew.

"I didn't even know these condos were here."

"Brand-new," Brandon told him.

Walt shot him a look. Did he mean the condos or his relationship with Gail? He let it go, realizing he'd already gone too far. But the guy was fucking his wife, so he expected a little slack.

To him condos all looked the same.

On his fourth ringing of the doorbell, he heard footsteps. He and Brandon displayed the creds for the benefit of the door's fisheye lens. Bartholomew opened the door, barely awake.

"A few questions," Walt said.

"My attorney," Bartholomew grumbled. He scratched the crotch of his boxer shorts. "I'll write down the number." Before Walt could object he'd shut the door. When he opened it again he had a phone to his ear and his hair had been finger combed into place. "Not answering," he said. He set the phone on the side table. "Why don't we try this again tomorrow morning."

"We can do this in Hailey, if you like," Walt said. "Hailey, as in taking a ride."

"Because?"

"The local vet's was broken into and all the animals liberated. Sound familiar?"

Walt considered himself to be a good judge of character. If that was the case, Bartholomew knew nothing about the break-in.

"It's three in the morning. I'm hungover. And you've got us wrong: First Rights is focused on child labor and every human's right to free speech. I do not condone or support militant animal rights groups. Not now, not ever." He rubbed his head. "It's too late for this."

If not politics, had the animals been released as a ruse to cover the theft of medical supplies?

He thanked Bartholomew and said good night. The bewildered man stood watching as he and Brandon returned to the Cherokee.

"What just happened?" Brandon asked from the passenger seat.

Walt kept his eye on the road as he asked,

"What does she see in you? Or is it all about the sex right now?"

They drove in silence, not a word spoken, for the return to the vet's. As he parked the car Walt said, "We have two kids, you know," and left Brandon in the car thinking about that.

Six

Trevalian heard a woman's voice say, "Isn't that him?" It came from the hotel's registration desk. His instinct was to flee.

He turned and headed up the stairwell, pretending he'd not heard her comment.

At 3 A.M. the hotel lobby was empty. The woman at registration had to have been speaking to someone. The hotel detective?

He cautioned himself to stay calm. They couldn't possibly connect him to the recent events. He'd changed shirts. Donned a jacket. Shaler's clothes were in the knapsack slung over his right shoulder.

"Sir? Mr. Meisner?" A male voice a few feet behind him.

He knows my name.

Trevalian stopped and turned on the stairs.

He was looking at a man in his mid-forties, fit and darkly tanned. A full head of hair. He'd sprung up the stairs like a ballerina.

"Yes?" Trevalian said.

"I wonder if you might have a minute?"

"You are?"

"Neil Parker." He offered a business card. Sun Valley Company. Guest services.

"It's three in the morning."

"There's been an . . . incident," Parker said.

Two things occurred to Trevalian: They'd found the compound he'd cooked, or they had him for the break-ins.

"It's a situation that requires discretion on all our parts," Parker said.

"I'm afraid it's very late, and I'm very tired and I don't understand." Trevalian evaluated his chances of breaking the guy's neck without any noise. Not great.

Parker climbed another step.

Trevalian extended his hand to stop the man. "I don't like tight spaces," he explained. He could knee the man in the face from this position.

Parker lowered his voice. "There's been an incident with one of our staff. A Ms. Cunningham." He answered Trevalian's blank expression. "Lilly Cunningham. Our lounge singer in the Duchin Lounge. I believe you met Lilly."

He said nothing, wondering if he'd been set up. She'd managed to get into his room; she'd drunk his booze. An extortion racket?

"There's been an assault. All I need is five minutes. Really. I'd rather not do this in a stairwell."

"Do what?"

"Lilly remembered your room number. That's how I got your name."

Trevalian said nothing.

"She said you got a look at the man," Parker explained. "A possible suspect. These can be tricky cases to prove. He-said, she-said."

"A matter for the authorities," Trevalian said. "Please leave me out of it."

"She's not pressing charges. The police are not involved. But if we can confirm the man's identity, he will never set foot on company property again."

Trevalian doubted the explanation. "I saw her with a man. But I'm afraid I didn't get a good look at him."

Parker's face fell. "Anything about him would help. We'd like to get rid of this guy."

Trevalian spoke, bringing the man into his

confidence. "Let me put it this way: If you saw Lilly and some guy in the hallway, who would you be looking at?"

"Yeah . . . I hear you."

"I'm sorry," Trevalian said, "but that's how it was."

The man appeared crushed. "Listen, you remember anything, give me a call. The front desk can find me."

"My apologies to Ms. Cunningham."

"The difference is," Parker said, more determined than ever, "you can choose not to be involved. But Lilly's going to climb back up on that stage with that creep out there looking at her."

"I'll sleep on it," Trevalian said. He rounded the landing and hurried up the stairs, thinking there was precious little time for sleep.

His mind had briefly been elsewhere—a mistake he rarely made. He had a switch to make, and, if possible, he wanted to do it now, while it was still dark out.

Seven

Civil twilight was listed as 5:41 A.M., a naval term referring to the first glimpse of a defined horizon. Trevalian didn't want the horizon or himself defined or glimpsed as he made the switch, and so two hours after being stopped by the hotel security man, and an hour before civil twilight, he made his way out of a ground-floor exit as Rafe Nagler. Toey, the German shepherd service dog, pulled at the harness at his side.

The first of these switches was changing Nagler to Meisner, for a blind man could not be seen climbing behind the wheel of a car. At 5 A.M. the Sun Valley grounds stood deserted, nothing but faux gas lamps and vacant sidewalks. He followed sidewalks from the lodge to the indoor ice rink and a dark

open-ended shed that contained a backup
Zamboni. He used the shed as a changing
room, stripping off and pocketing Nagler's
facial hair, wig, and glasses. He dumped the
sport coat there—the only evidence he
would leave behind for the next hour—revealing the black fleece vest that had been
hiding beneath it. He quickly clipped a leash
to Toey's collar and unfastened the harness,
concealing it up his back, inside the fleece
vest. He let the string leash play out, to
where Toey had a twenty-foot lead, and the
two made their way out into the giant parking lot that serviced the resort.

He appreciated the black-hole quality of
both sky and air as he drove north from the
resort into national forest. He kept a close
eye on the odometer as well as the rearview
mirror. He turned east onto a dirt track
marked for Pioneer Cabin, and put a half
mile between him and the asphalt he left
behind, having never seen the twinkle of another set of headlights.

The darkest hour really was just before the
dawn. He double-checked the car's ceiling
light making sure it wouldn't turn on as he
opened the door. He stepped outside. The
cold mountain air stung his lungs and he

coughed, immediately trying to stifle the sound.

He leaned back into the car facing two dogs—both shepherds. Toey remained in the front seat, where he'd put her, the leash still attached to her collar. Callie lay down on the backseat, nothing but a long black shape.

He shut his door, came around the car, and opened the passenger door. Callie jumped to all fours and stuck her nose from behind the front seat. Toey bent around to meet noses. Trevalian yanked on the leash and pulled Toey from the car. He double-checked that the small flashlight worked, and then, returning it to his pocket, he led Toey off into the dense forest of Douglas fir and lodgepole pine. A hundred and fifty yards later he knelt and fed her some cheese-flavored chowder crackers from the minibar. He lavished her with praise and softly thanked her for being a good dog. Then he unclasped the leash, commanded her to stay, and walked away.

Twice he turned back and used the flash-light to ensure she was holding the com-mand, her eyes a hollow luminescence in the dark. But in the short time they'd been together he'd learned that Toey was a particularly kind and obedient dog. She wasn't going anywhere.

His original plan had been to cut her throat and bury her out here, miles from any possibility of being found. But now he walked away, then ran, knowing she would obey his command and "stay" for probably ten or fifteen minutes or more.

He reached the car, fastened the guide harness to Callie, and moved her into the front seat.

The switch was made. And with it, he'd cleared the last of his obstacles.

Eight

Walt awakened in his daughter Emily's bed to the ringing of the phone in his own bedroom. For the second night he'd avoided that mattress.

He dragged himself out of the stupor of two hours' sleep, managing to answer the kitchen phone before voice mail picked up.

"It's Kathy. I'm sorry to call you at home, Walt." Dispatch. Walt pulled himself into focus. "I tried both your cell and pager first."

"Go ahead." He rubbed his face to clear his thought. It didn't work.

"Stuart Holms called at five fifty-six A.M."

Walt checked the kitchen clock: seven minutes had passed. "Go on." Maybe he wouldn't need the coffee. Just mention of that name had jolted him awake.

"He was a little abusive, sir. Bossy. I told him nine-one-one took the emergency calls. He told me to go to hell."

Walt knew Stuart Holms by reputation. This didn't surprise him. "What emergency?"

"He wouldn't tell me. That's what I'm saying. Demanded to speak with you personally."

An alarm sounded in Walt's head: He didn't know Stuart Holms personally.

"He sounded upset," she went on.

Fifteen minutes later, Walt was refueling the Cherokee, wearing a fresh, starched blue uniform shirt and sipping hot coffee from a travel mug. He called the number Stuart Holms had left with dispatch, but had only reached an assistant who said Holms needed to speak with Walt "as soon as was humanly possible."

Yet it was Holms himself who met Walt at the front door to the colossal modern home out the Lake Creek drainage. Nestled at the base of the mountains, it felt to Walt like a museum of contemporary art. Holms led him to a café table with a view of an enclosed garden through a wall of floor-to-ceiling windows. They were waited on by a slim woman in her thirties who had a

French accent. Stuart Holms ordered Walt a sausage omelet, toasted bagel with cream cheese, coffee, and orange juice. He took smoked salmon, capers, and guava juice for himself.

Dressed in blue pajamas, Holms wore a terrycloth bathrobe and sheepskin moccasins. He looked younger than Walt had imagined him. His name had been in the business pages for decades.

He focused intently on Walt and spoke in a croaking voice that needed more coffee.

"I apologize for the secrecy, Sheriff, but there's no such thing as privacy, and I need to keep this private. I called you because this home is in the county, not the city, and I've had it on good authority that you're a hell of a lot more trustworthy than the Ketchum police chief."

"I don't know about that. What's the nature of your complaint?"

"Not exactly a complaint. More like a report. It's Allie—Ailia—my wife. She failed to come home last night." He looked to Walt for some kind of reaction. "This is entirely out of character, and I'm worried. If I raise the alarm it'll be over the wire services before I've had my morning swim. With

Patrick's conference and all . . . No need to spoil his party."

"A guy like you? You've got your own people," Walt said.

"You want my people to handle it, they can, I suppose," Holms said.

"Does she carry a cell phone?" Walt asked.

"Last I saw her, she'd gone for a run. This was a little after five, yesterday evening. She missed the luau."

"You've tried her cell phone?"

"I called it, only to hear it ring down the hall. It's on her dresser. Damn awful feeling, that is."

"Five P.M. yesterday," Walt stated. "How 'bout the staff?"

"Did she sleep somewhere else? That's what you're asking, isn't it? *With someone* else? You think she's going to slip back into her room and come out yawning as if she overslept? I don't think so."

The food arrived.

Walt took down the particulars as he ate. Stuart had expected to see her at the C³ luau. He'd left word with the staff that she was to call him the moment she returned home. Upset with her, he'd headed home, had taken a sleeping pill, and awakened at 5 A.M. to find her room still empty.

Walt polished off the omelet. He thought of his own wife—nearly mentioned it.

"Fabulous omelet," Walt said.

"That's Raphael, my chef."

"An artist."

"I'll tell him. He'll be pleased."

"We usually give it some time before investigating reports of missing persons, but we can act on this if you like. My question is: What kind of press can you tolerate? If we take this, it'll mean some phone calls, questions being asked. It's going to be pretty clear, pretty quickly, what's going on. I wish I could change that, but it's going to get out."

"I want her found." He didn't touch his own plate—an artful display of smoked salmon and a bagel.

Walt ran through what his deputies referred to as her 411. "She drives a pale green Volvo SC-90," Holms told him. Then he reached into his robe's pocket and passed a five-by-four card across the table. It included the vehicle's registration number, her age, weight, and the clothes she'd last been seen in—a gray, zippered shell, a white jogging top, and blue shorts. A recent photo had been digitally printed in the lower corner.

"I have very competent staff."

"What about your own detail?" Walt asked again.

"We use a company for overseas travel. Yes. New York. Washington. L.A. But not up here. Raphael goes with us everywhere. A few assistants. That's all."

Walt studied the photo, remembering where he'd last seen this same woman: on the balcony with Danny Cutter at his brother's cocktail party.

"Yes, there's an age gap, if that's what you're thinking," Holms said. "But I'm only sixty. And a young sixty at that. She's beautiful, and outgoing, and a wonderful conversationalist who likes to talk. Find her, Sheriff."

"Her favorite places to run?"

"The bike path. Adam's Gulch. Hulen Meadows. Lake Creek. Over the saddle and into Elkhorn. She varies it."

Walt wrote these down on the back of the same card.

"It's a lot of ground," Walt said.

"That's why you're involved."

"We'll get started," Walt said. "And we'll keep it under the radar as much as possible."

"If you start asking around, Danny Cutter's name is going to come up. That's not news to me, and it's behind us. Just so you know."

"Okay," Walt said, though his voice belied him.

"Ailia and Danny are to be *partners* in a company I'm helping him finance. Those fences are mended."

Walt faintly nodded, wondering why, if they were mended, Holms felt obligated to mention them.

Nine

An hour past a sunrise lost to an overcast sky, the rain began. The dirt road out Adam's Gulch, where the pavement ended, had turned to pale brown slop. Low, swirling clouds concealed the tops of trees up on the crests of the surrounding mountains. The sky fluctuated between a light mist and a steady drizzle. Mountain weather.

Walt donned a tan, oilskin greatcoat bundled in the back of the Cherokee along with climbing gear, snowshoes, and two backpacks capable of keeping him in the woods overnight—one for summer, one for winter. He offered Brandon a poncho, but his deputy refused the offer, content to play the he-man, macho outdoorsy thing to the limit, even if it meant a head cold. The parking lot bustled with law enforcement and Search and Rescue personnel. Nothing like a missing rich woman to get the adrenaline running. A ribbon of Day-Glo tape was lifted, admitting two pickup trucks, both carrying dog kennels in their beds.

Alone, to the right of the Porta Potti and the trailhead sign, a pale green Volvo, its engine cold, was parked over dry dirt. It could have been there an hour or overnight. But it belonged to Ailia Holms and was empty.

Walt addressed the Search and Rescue team. "Listen up! She may be just injured. Could be out for a morning run and the husband has things confused. So let's not scare her to death. It's possible she's been exposed to the elements overnight. Make sure you're covered for that: space blankets, protein bars, and water. You've got your assignments. We're using channel fifteen. Keep off the radios unless it means something. Okay. Go!"

The group dispersed. Walt turned to Brandon. "You and I will take the Hill Trail. I'll take the first entrance; you'll take the second."

"I'm on it," the man replied.

By the time Walt reached the Hill Trail, muddy clay was sticking to his boots like wet concrete, heavier with each step. Twice he stopped to scrape globs off the treads. He followed the narrow path up into the trees over rocky, rutted ground roped with exposed tree roots. With the low clouds and thick forest, an unsettling darkness overcame him.

Fiona's arrival was announced over the radio. She was photographing the Volvo. In his mind's eye Walt saw Search and Rescue spreading out over the trail and covering ground. He checked in with Brandon. The two were approaching each other from opposite directions.

Discovering a snapped branch—the ripped bark green—Walt knelt and studied the disturbance in the trail's soil. Normally dry and powdery, the ocher-colored dust was skimmed with a layer of rain. If prodded, the crust of darkened soil gave way to the fine dirt beneath. He followed some impressions that told him two things: First, the leg that had snapped the branch had done so prior to the rain falling; second, it was a man's flat-soled shoe, size nine or ten, walking slowly and deliberately, not the long strides associated with exercise, not an athletic shoe.

He kept off the path as best as possible and followed the shoe prints, calling ahead to Brandon to switch frequencies. When he met him again on the radio, Walt instructed his deputy to keep an eye out for the tracks, and not to disturb them.

But Brandon professed to know nothing of any shoe prints. It was then that Walt picked up two other such impressions, both heading back toward the parking lot.

The rain fell heavier now, the shoe prints washing away before his eyes. Walt peeled his coat off and lay it across the trail, attempting to protect the matching shoe prints—both heading in different directions. He didn't dare lift the coat to see if he'd managed to cover them, the rain falling steadily now.

He raced ahead, staying off the trail, dodging trees and stumps and massive rocks. "Tommy," he called ahead on the radio, "how many times have you seen a guy in office shoes out on one of these trails?"

"Sneakers," Brandon called back.

"No. These things have a heel and smooth soles. Keep your eyes peeled. Something's not right."

The cold rain soaked through the shoul-

ders and back of Walt's uniform. He wiped
his face on his sleeve in order to see.

"Fucking cats and dogs," Brandon said
over the radio. The rain had greatly intensified.

Walt was running now, looking left and
right, up the hill and down, the narrow trail
meandering just below him.

"I got a million running shoes and hiking
boots, Sheriff," Brandon reported. "But I got
nothing like what you're talking about. No
office shoes."

"Keep your eyes peeled off-trail," Walt ordered.

"Roger, that."

Walt felt a tension in his chest—a knowing
fear. He relived watching the shoe impressions melt behind the destructive power of
the rain. Though but a few miles from downtown, a half mile from the highway, these
woods were national forest and subject to
the laws of nature, not man. Bears were
commonly spotted. Cougar. Elk. Any number of which could scare a runner off a trail,
pursue the intruder for dinner or out of defense of a calf or cub. The combination of
the discovery of the unexpected shoe prints
and the now torrential, cold rain drove home

an anxiety that peaked with Brandon's next radio transmission.

"Sheriff? What's your twenty? I think I've got something."

A moment later Walt flinched with the sound of a dull gunshot just ahead on the trail: a flare.

Brandon had found her.

Ten

A woman's body, bloody and splayed in a tangle of limbs. The top of her running suit was ripped, baring her chest. Her neck was canted inhumanly to one side.

Walt placed a space blanket over her to keep off the rain. Ailia Holms had been mauled. "Bear?" Brandon asked.

"I'm no expert, but I'm guessing cat. Bite marks on the neck, the narrowness of the claws."

Walt ordered the Hill Trail cordoned off. He and Brandon established a perimeter around the body using dead sticks. With Brandon lifting and replacing the space blanket, Fiona, who had trudged up through the woods, shot dozens of photographs before anyone disturbed the scene. Others arrived

through the forest: deputies, a pair of para-
medics, and a local doctor, Royal McClure.
At Walt's request, he would serve as medical examiner, an assignment certain to piss
off the county coroner, but Walt was intent
on doing this the right way. Electing a mor-
tician as coroner did not make him a medical examiner.

McClure, a wiry man in his mid-fifties, had
tight, green eyes and a high raspy voice. "I'll
be able to tell you more later. Much more.
But for now you've got a body dead twelve
to eighteen hours. Trauma, blood loss. All
the appearance of an animal attack."

Walt asked, "What are the odds that two
cougars attack humans within a day of each
other?"

"Who said anything about two?" McClure
asked. "These cats cover a lot of ground."

"We darted one and locked it up yesterday. Down at the Humane Society, the
pound," Walt said. "She sure as hell didn't
do this. I've lived here, off and on, for most
of my life, and I can only remember one
other cat attack before this—and that one
was provoked. Now we lose a yellow Lab.
Danny Cutter gets run out of the Big Wood
by a cat. We dart one, and that same night,

another kills a woman out running. Are you kidding me?"

In the midst of removing the space blanket for Fiona, Brandon suddenly pulled the Mylar sheet aside and let it fall to the ground, like a magician who'd given up on his trick.

"Keep her covered, Tommy," Walt said, turning from McClure.

"Check it out, Sheriff," Brandon said, kneeling close to the body. "What the fuck is that?" The rain continued to fall in sheets as it had for the past half hour. Brandon dragged the space blanket back over her once again, covering her head and face, to below her waist, leaving only her lacerated legs exposed.

Walt stepped closer, seeing for the first time what Brandon now pointed to: a small circle of white.

"Paint?" Walt guessed.

"It's dissolving, whatever it is," Brandon said. "Dissolving fast. And look there, and there." He pointed. Then he lifted the Mylar and studied her more closely. "It's all over her."

Fiona, of her own volition, scrolled through digital shots while carefully screening her camera from the rain. "I made pictures of those," she said. "I count seven . . . no . . . eight on her chest and torso. Another four on her head and hair."

"It's feces," McClure said, having touched it with his gloved finger and lifted it to his nose. "Bird feces."

"Birdshit?" Brandon asked. "How's that possible? Look around her. Nothing."

None of the leaves, sticks, or plants surrounding the body showed any sign of the white splotches.

"Doc?" Walt asked.

"It's not my place to comment on physical evidence."

Walt looked up into the rain. No coverage here, the tree branches not touching. So where had the birds perched?

"You know that blood-splatter course?" Brandon said. "If birdshit's anything like blood, then the size of these, and the tightness of the rings, means it didn't fall very far. A bird takes a crap from up there, it's going to hit like a bomb."

"Expert testimony if I've ever heard it," Walt cracked.

"Not to mention she rolled all the way down the hill," Brandon said, ignoring Walt's jab. "So it's got to be fresh, right?"

"He's right," McClure interjected. "Or she was out running with dried bird feces all over her."

Walt was still bothered by the smooth-soled shoe prints he'd followed earlier. In the excitement of the discovery, he'd neglected to send anyone to protect his oilskin and the tracks it covered. He did so now by radio, but feared a complete loss.

"And there's a question of blood," McClure pointed out.

Fiona, Brandon, and Walt all turned inquisitively toward him. Their faces ran with rainwater. "Blood?" Walt asked.

"I count a hundred and fifty-six lacerations, and we haven't rolled her yet," McClure said. "So where's all the blood?"

Eleven

On his second visit in a matter of hours, something about the indulgence of the Holms estate left Walt with a sickening feeling in his gut. It was far too big for two people; how would it feel now with only one?

He was informed by a staff member that Stuart Holms had already left for the conference. This kind of thing needed to be done in person. Walt drove over to Sun Valley. It took him twenty minutes of moving between various talks and coffee clutches, meeting rooms and hospitality suites to find Holms on the porch of the Guest House in a private conversation with the head of Disney. Walt asked to speak to Holms in confidence and took the vacated chair.

"There's never an easy way to say this. I'm

sorry to have to tell you that we found your wife out Adam's Gulch. She was pronounced dead at the scene, apparent victim of an animal attack."

The other man's clear blue eyes ticked back and forth, alternately searching the air above Walt's head. His brow knotted, and he nodded slightly, and sighed. Then his eyes fell to the plastic tabletop, and he dragged his trembling hands into his lap. "I've known since last night. I knew in here." He touched his chest. "She's never not come home before. Oh, God. An animal attack?"

"A cougar possibly. Yes."

"Was it her period?" Stuart Holms asked. "I don't even know, I'm sorry to say. That's when they attack women, right?"

"A thorough examination is being conducted," Walt said.

Holms kept his head down. He mumbled, "A cat? She liked cats. Loved cats. Volunteered at the pound. Did you know that?"

"At some point I'm going to take a full statement from you, sir. No hurry, but the sooner we can get to that the better."

Holms lifted his head, revealing teary, bloodshot eyes. "Of course," he said.

Walt waited a moment uncomfortably. "When?" he said. "When might we get to that?"

Holms looked away at a piece of the sky. "When I feel up to it, Sheriff. And not a minute sooner."

Twelve

It was difficult for Walt to think of a meeting as clandestine when the sun shone so brightly and a pair of yellow warblers darted branch to branch in play. The Warm Springs tributary to the Big Wood slipped past beneath the concrete bridge connecting to Sun Valley's River Run high-speed quad-chairlifts and the glorious River Run ski lodge. He watched the river's swirling currents, looking for any kind of repeating pattern, but he saw none. A kingfisher hovered low over the silver brown water, staying there for quite some time before zooming up to a cottonwood branch and taking rest.

Dick O'Brien had no place here. He was dressed like a man heading to lunch at Yale: khakis, blue blazer, white button-down shirt.

Thankfully he'd eschewed the tie. It was the man's shoes that Walt paid the most attention to: office shoes, with heels. His mind filled briefly with an image of the dissolving, muddy impressions he'd followed up the Hill Trail at Adam's Gulch. He swallowed dryly.

O'Brien leaned against the bridge's wide, concrete rail. He placed a manila envelope between them.

"Sorry for making the meet out here," he said. "Just a precaution is all."

"This is?" Walt asked, indicating the envelope.

"A DVD. Cutter's home security. I helped design it. We've got eyes on the gate, exterior doors, the garages. He put half a mil into security on that place. This camera is an interior look at the front door. From yesterday morning . . . Friday morning, in case you've lost track. I have one of my guys assigned to monitoring the cameras twenty-four/seven. He pointed this . . . incident . . . out to me yesterday. We dump anything like this to DVD for safekeeping."

"Anything like *what*?" Walt asked.

"The Escalade's got a DVD player, if you want it sooner than later," O'Brien said.

"And air-conditioning. And an electric cooler in the back. Pop. Bottled water."

"You can't just tell me?"

"Worth a thousand words. Right?"

"If you say so."

A few minutes later O'Brien and Walt occupied the Escalade's two leather captain's chairs that made up the car's middle row of seats. The DVD panel was flipped down and glowing blue. Walt had a cold ginger ale in hand. "What? No popcorn?"

"We got Snickers in the cooler," O'Brien said in all seriousness. "Peanuts. Potato chips."

"I was kidding."

The DVD played. Walt watched as a sweating Danny Cutter, a towel around his neck, opened his brother's front door and welcomed in Ailia Holms. Walt dialed the rear air conditioner down a few degrees—he'd warmed suddenly. A time clock ran in the upper right-hand corner of the screen.

O'Brien narrated. "Once we heard about her out Adam's Gulch, I showed this to the boss. He took her death real hard, I might add. And we had a very short discussion about sharing this with you. Just for the

record, the boss never suggested blocking it."

On the screen the discussion grew heated
between Danny Cutter and Ailia Holms, but
there was no sound to confirm that. Then,
all at once, Danny grabbed her by the fore-
arms and shoved her against a couch. For a
moment Walt feared he was about to see
a rape. Then the two settled down. Ailia
clearly complained about her treatment.
Danny showed her to the door, and she left.

O'Brien stopped the playback. The screen
went blue again.

"Those are the same clothes we found her
in," Walt told O'Brien.

"It's yours to do with whatever."

"It's not that I'm complaining, but would
you turn this over if it was your brother?"

"It's complicated between them—the
brothers. Very competitive." He paused and
said, "In all sorts of things." Then he met
eyes with Walt, clearly wanting to drive home
this last statement.

"It's a big help," Walt said, "and I appreciate it."

"No problem."

"It may be for Danny. And I like Danny."

"We all like Danny," O'Brien said.

"Does that include Patrick?"

"Like I said: It's complicated."

"Yes, it is." As they were climbing out of the car, Walt couldn't resist. "Nice shoes," he said.

Thirteen

The hospital morgue was located down a subterranean hallway, wedged between a door marked DANGER—HIGH VOLTAGE and another unmarked room used for storage.

Ailia Holms lay faceup on a textured stainless steel morgue table with drain slits around its perimeter and hoses coming out the bottom.

McClure pulled off the blue rip-stop nylon dropcloth, exposing her chalk white skin torn by cougar's claws. Lacerations and puncture wounds covered her torso like unfamiliar constellations. Her pubis was shaved into a short, vertical column of red tangled hair. Walt looked away and recomposed himself. McClure had already done some cutting on her.

"You asked about any bruising," McClure said.

"I did."

"You know about lividity: The blood settles into the lowest part of the body an hour or two after death. It fixes, in six to eight hours." He directed Walt's attention to some dark bruises. "You'll recall that we found her partially rolled up on her left side." He pointed. "This area is an example of fixed hypostasis—lividity. Certainly six to eight hours after she was killed she was in this position." He nodded toward the sink. "Grab a set of gloves."

Together, he and Walt lifted and rolled the cadaver just high enough to get a look at her buttocks.

"See that discoloring?" McClure asked. "The right gluteous?"

"Yes."

"No proof. But it suggests early lividity."

"So she rolled and landed partially down the hill, and what . . . a couple hours later a coyote pulled her over, and she rolled some more?"

"Could explain it."

"What's the timing?"

"Eight to twelve hours ahead of discovery. Perhaps coincidental with her death."

"May I?" Walt asked, reaching for Ailia's left arm.

"Of course."

Walt lifted the arm. An obvious bruise, shaped like a mitten.

"This is antemortem?" Walt asked.

"Yes. Well ahead of the attack. Maybe as much as a day or more."

"It was early yesterday morning," Walt told him. "That's consistent."

McClure lifted the cadaver's head. He pulled back a flap of skin, exposing tissue, pink muscle, and white vertebrae. "She has a fracture to cervical number seven, just above the facet for the first rib. Another to cervical three. The tissue at seven reveals edema consistent with an earlier trauma."

"The cat broke her neck," Walt said. "It's what cats do."

"Fractures her neck," McClure said. "She's alive but paralyzed. Toys with her for a while."

"For how long?"

"This trauma to the neck occurred an hour or more before the cat mauled her."

"Good God."

"Most, if not *all,* of the lacerations inflicted by the cat were *post*mortem."

"Excuse me?"

McClure met eyes with Walt and just stared. "Cause of death is heart failure: She bled out. But the timing of all this is speculative."

"My guys are out looking for the original crime scene—the location of the attack. All the blood."

"You may not find it," McClure said. He answered Walt's puzzled expression by explaining, "We luminoled her." He picked up a tube light from a workstation. "Get the lights," he said.

Walt cut the lights. McClure waved a short black light over the body. Beneath the neck, the stainless steel showed a luminous green, indicating blood. The body itself showed very little green.

"You cleaned her?" Walt asked. "I hope you checked for prints first."

"That's just the thing," McClure said. "I haven't washed her. There's very little blood and there's a reason for that: The dead don't bleed."

Walt thought back to the shoe prints in the

mud and Danny Cutter pinning Ailia to the couch.

"The cat still could have killed her and mauled her later."

"I'll measure her blood volume," the doctor said. It meant nothing to Walt.

Walt paused. "She was moved."

"One last point of interest," McClure said, switching off the black light and returning the room to the overhead tube lighting. "She's missing her left contact lens."

"Missing?" Walt blurted out.

"Probably somewhere in the woods. She rolled a long way down that hill. You could try to find it, but we both know the odds of that. Still, it's going into my report."

"Would it show if we luminoled the area?" Walt asked.

"No, the luminol binds to the hemoglobin. If it's out there, it's going to take a hands-and-knees search."

"Who goes running with only one contact?" Walt wondered, not realizing until it was too late that he'd spoken it aloud.

"It was a long fall," McClure repeated.

But Walt barely heard him. He was stuck back on O'Brien's shoes and the impressions that had vanished with the rain.

Fourteen

"It's the fishing lady," came the voice of the guard at Elizabeth Shaler's front door. This was heard over Adam Dryer's cell phone with its two-way walkie-talkie feature. Dryer looked over at Shaler, who was currently reading the Saturday edition of *The New York Times* and enjoying some morning sun in her backyard.

"Yes, of course," Liz Shaler said, answering Dryer's inquisitive expression.

He flipped through pages on a clipboard. "It's not on today's appointment list."

"We were supposed to go fishing together, remember? That was all of a few hours ago."

"But it wasn't rescheduled." To the walkie-talkie he said, "Give her the Mossad, and send her in."

"Roger that."

"The Mossad?" Shaler asked, tugging down her sunglasses for full effect. "Or don't I want to know?"

"She'll be thoroughly searched. That's all."

"He better not touch her improperly."

"No, Your Honor."

Several minutes passed before Fiona was led through by one of Shaler's assistants. She handed a bouquet of stem flowers to Shaler, who drank in a whiff before passing them off to her assistant.

"You didn't need to do that."

Fiona took at seat at the patio table. "I was sorry to cancel."

"Was it Ailia?" Liz Shaler asked. "Was it as awful as everyone's saying?"

"I'm not permitted to say. Sorry about that."

"No, don't be. I respect you all the more for it." She lowered her voice. "I wish some of the people around here were as discreet. I might actually have a life." She grinned. There was a line of white sun cream showing beneath her nose where she'd missed it.

Fiona was tempted to point it out, but didn't.

Dryer stood away from them, but remained in the yard under the shade of a tree. He stared at them from there through his sunglasses.

"Is he just going to hang out there?" Fiona asked.

"Yes. Amazing, isn't it? I would be so bored with a job like that. But what are you going to do?"

"Doesn't it bother you?"

"I detest it. As AG, I don't have protection in New York. The governor does. The mayor of the city. But not the attorney general. All this," she said, indicating Dryer, "is thanks to Herb Millington, who made a big stink to the DNC when it was rumored I would run."

"I shouldn't stay long," Fiona said anxiously, causing Liz Shaler to look over at her thoughtfully.

"What's going on?"

"The flowers . . . Your Honor . . . were a pretext."

"For?"

"To get me inside. Not that I'm not sorry about missing the session with you. I am. I absolutely am!"

Shaler pushed away the *Times*. "Okay," she said, "you've got my attention."

Fiona very carefully reached into her purse, slipped out an envelope, and passed it to Shaler surreptitiously. "I shouldn't be doing this, I know. And I'll probably get into a lot of trouble for it. I mean *a lot*. Depending on you, of course."

"You don't have to worry about me." She squeezed the envelope. "Photos?"

Fiona nodded and smiled falsely because Dryer's dark sunglasses remained fixed on her from the shade of the distant tree.

"Should I look at them now?"

"Your call," Fiona said.

"Is he looking in this direction?" Liz asked.

"Yes. Wait . . . Okay: He's checking around."

Liz slipped the envelope open and gasped. "Oh, God . . ."

"Salt Lake City," Fiona said. "These are the shots Walt—the sheriff," she corrected, "wanted you to see. Agent Dryer wouldn't permit it."

Liz flipped through the stack. Then she gathered them and returned them to the envelope. "God," she repeated. "Did Walt—?"

"No, no!" Fiona said quickly. "Please don't go there. This was *entirely* my initiative.

There was nothing said, nothing implied. Please don't think that of him."

"You like him. Walt," Liz said. "Or you wouldn't have done this." She pushed the envelope back across to Fiona. "Your secret's safe with me."

"It isn't like that," Fiona said. "It's just his work . . . it's everything to him, you know?"

"I like him, too," Liz said. "Very much. He saved my life, you know?"

Fiona leaned away, looking shocked.

"Years ago, but believe me, you don't forget something like that. A person like Walt. Not ever."

"He wanted these photos to scare you into calling off your talk. I know that much. Maybe he's trying to save you a second time."

Fiona couldn't see her eyes through the dark glasses, but she imagined them as scared.

"And he'll pay for it," came the low voice of Adam Dryer.

Liz Shaler jumped and her glasses wiggled down her nose.

Dryer snatched the packet of photos with an arm like a frog's tongue. Fiona hadn't seen him coming. He leafed through the photos and then pocketed them. "The sheriff was on notice not to show you these, Your Honor."

"It wasn't Walt!" Fiona protested. "It was me."

"And I can't see through that?" Dryer said, stripping the glasses off his face and drilling a look into her. "You tell him he lost his Get Out of Jail card with me."

"Leave the photos where they were," Liz Shaler said vehemently, "and leave us alone. Fiona's my guest, which is more than I can say about the rest of you."

Fifteen

As the conference adjourned for lunch, Walt caught Danny Cutter outside a break-out room. Showing no sign of being ill at ease, Danny agreed to speak with him and the two headed down into the subterranean reaches of the hotel.

The lodge's private bowling alleys dated back to the hotel's construction in the 1930s and Averell Harriman's vision of grandeur. The two lanes stood empty at 12:30 P.M. on a Saturday. The alleys had been a playground for Gable, Stanwyck, Cooper, and Hemingway. Walt could almost smell the Cuban cigars and the bourbon on the rocks mingling with Chanel No. 5. Never renovated through the subsequent decades, the lanes had nonetheless been well maintained, while allowing the history to show. Danny and Walt sat across a linoleum-topped table rimmed with cigarette scars.

If this table could talk, Walt thought.

He asked the attendant to give them a few minutes, and the young Swede took off without comment.

"You mind if I run this thing? Record our conversation?" Walt held an iPod in his hand, a small white brick plugged into its top. He placed the device on the table and tried to get comfortable in the chair.

"You do what you have to do," Danny said.

"Tell me about Ailia Holms."

"Yeah. Unbelievable. I thought that's what this was about."

"Because?"

Danny gave Walt a transparent look. "You're here, aren't you? If you didn't know Allie and I had a thing going—this is before I went . . . away—you'd be the only one in this town."

Danny Cutter's good looks got in his way at a time like this. Walt couldn't think of him as normal. A guy that good-looking and that rich.

"Is that past or present tense?" Walt asked. "The thing."

Cutter adjusted himself in the chair. "We had a history. She wanted to update the files, as it turned out. Keep them current. But I discouraged that. Didn't avoid it completely, but discouraged it."

"Physically?"

"Meaning?"

"You don't understand physically discouraging someone?"

"She can be . . . difficult . . . to say no to. Was . . . I guess I should say. Can't get used to that." He moved in the chair once more. Then he lowered his voice, despite the room being empty. "I slept with her the night of Paddy's party. The cocktail party at his place. *During* the party. It just kind of happened."

Walt had seen the two up on the balcony hallway. He maintained his poker face, but inside he was reeling. He'd not anticipated Danny's candor. "That sounds like encouragement to me. I'm talking about discouragement."

Danny's eyes went distant, then focused and found Walt. "You're talking about her arms, aren't you? I bruised her, didn't I? She was pissed at me for that. Steaming mad. Said if Stu saw any bruises . . . She was afraid of Stu. I gather the resentful-old-man thing is not entirely an act."

"What bruises?" This was what Walt asked, but mentally he made a note to check on Stuart Holms's jealousies.

"She came by the house. This is yesterday morning. We had words. Allie liked getting her way, and our ways were a little divergent. I took it a little too far. What can I say? Shit happens. She liked to play the sex card, and sometimes, quite frankly, it got a little old. Scratch my itch and I'll do you favors. But I didn't want any favors." He paused and rubbed the corner of his lips with his knuckle. "Rehab wasn't totally lost on me."

"Who doesn't want the favors of a woman like Ailia Holms?" Walt asked.

"A man who's had Ailia Holms," Danny answered. "It wasn't those kind of favors. It was money stuff. I didn't want her help, that's all."

Walt said nothing.

"The really strange thing?" Danny asked rhetorically. "*I* was attacked by a cougar the day before yesterday. Did you hear about that?" He studied Walt. "I'm sure you did. Thing could have taken me down, taken me out, and instead it turns around and leaves me alone. Just like that. Gets you to thinking, I'll tell you what. You kidding me? You know what I decided? I want to be useful. To make my life useful. To someone, something, other than me. And I want to get there on my own. Break out the frickin' violins—I can see it in your face—but I'm serious, Sheriff." He scratched his lips again. "And now Allie out Adam's Gulch last night. A cougar. Right? Maybe *the same* cougar. How bizarre is that?"

"It's plenty bizarre," Walt said flatly. He noted that Danny Cutter had put Ailia's attack as night. Not even Royal McClure had done so. He struggled with seeing Danny Cutter as guilty. He didn't want to believe it.

"So, when was the last time you saw her?" Walt probed.

"And that's another thing," Danny said, not answering directly. "Who goes on a run twice in the same day? Are you buying that? That's not Allie. That's not right."

"The last time you saw her?"

"Yesterday afternoon. I had a meeting with Stu—a business thing. Allie stopped by." He paused. "I've got to tell you: I didn't love it—her stopping by. And Stu was weird about it. They had it planned—frickin' choreographed—and I was the odd man out. And I hate that."

Walt searched the man's face and decided he was telling the truth.

"I don't know how much of this is relevant, Sheriff, but you're probably going to hear it anyway. . . . Stu agreed to invest some serious money in a thing I've got going. I've got to tell you: That surprised me in the first place. And then he drops this bomb on me that the deal comes with strings attached. The strings were Allie: I take her on as my partner or forget the investment."

"And you didn't like that because . . . ?"

"Because of the strings. Whether you or anyone else believes it, I'm serious about changing my act. But the thing is: Stu must have known about us. What kind of husband sets up his wife like that? What kind of fool sense does that make?"

Walt made notes, wondering at the interconnections and the involvement of the husband. "Maybe later today, maybe Monday, I'll get the preliminary autopsy report. We'll know if it was an accident or not."

"Since when is a cougar attack not an accident?"

"I've got to ask for your passport, Danny."

"What?" The man looked shell-shocked.

"Everything we've discussed here is confidential. I hear it come from someplace else, I'm coming after you, and let me remind you, this conversation was recorded with your consent."

"You're flipping me out. What do you mean 'not an accident'?"

"I need your passport on my desk by five P.M. I don't get it by five, I'll seek a warrant."

"Where are you coming from? Me? I *liked* Allie. Not an accident? Leave me out of this. Please."

"No way to do that. I'm sorry to say this, Danny, but you might want to call Doug." Doug Aanestad had served as Danny's attorney during the drug bust.

"I'm starting over here. I actually have something good going." He was pleading now. He looked a little pitiful. Sounded childish as he mumbled, "I have a business plan. A good one. Ask Paddy. Come on, Walt. You know this town. I'm toast."

"It's messy," Walt said. "I wish I could tell you otherwise."

"Me in a mess?" Danny asked, sarcastic anger boiling out of him. "Now there's something new. Give me a break, Walt. Come on! Please."

As Walt stood, he stopped the iPod from recording and pocketed the device. He placed a hand on Danny's shoulder, tried to think of something to say, then turned for the door.

Sixteen

Fiona was leaning against the Cherokee's front bumper, impatiently tapping a newspaper against her thigh. She wore khaki capris and a lavender shirt with oversized white buttons. Valet parking had left the Cherokee under the lodge's massive portico out of the noonday sun. Walt unlocked it with the remote, and Fiona climbed in without invitation.

As Walt took the wheel she said, "Drive me over to my car, please. It's too hot to walk, and I've been waiting an eternity." She rolled down the window. "I looked for you everywhere."

"You could have called," he pointed out.

"I tried. You weren't picking up."

"Ah . . . I was in the basement. The bowl-ing alley."

She looked at him askance.

"Business," he said. "I'm a sucky bowler. Don't go there."

"It's my fault," she said, as Walt turned into the massive parking lot looking for her car. He hoped she might direct him, but her tone told him to keep his mouth shut. "You know when you've got a name or something right on the tip of your tongue, but you can't for the life of you remember it? It was like that for me." She looked at him, her eyes begging that he make the connection.

Walt stared back blankly.

"The bird droppings," she said, holding the newspaper out in front of him now and blocking his vision.

He took her by the wrist, moved the paper out of his way, and pulled over. "What about them?"

"I made the photos."

"I was there, Fiona. I know that."

"Not those photos," she said dismissively, as if it was the clearest thing in the world. "Read!"

Walt took the paper from her. It was folded open to page five. The article was titled

"Bombs Away: County Pound Goes to the Birds." Walt recalled his father teasing him about the article.

"And there's something else—" she said.

Walt cut her off. "Let me read."

"I blew it."

"Hang on. Swallows at the pound," he said, remembering.

"Hundreds of them leaving bird droppings on all the cats and dogs," she said, caught up in his enthusiasm. "The health department threatened—"

"To close them down. Yes."

"Bird droppings, Walt." She stared at him, once again somewhat condescendingly. "The cougar that was darted was transferred to *the Humane Society* until Fish and Game figures out what to do with her. She was at the pound, Walt."

"Oh, shit."

"Yeah. That's about the size of it."

Seventeen

Walt entered the shed extension of the Humane Society a few minutes behind his deputy, Randy Anderson, and a few minutes ahead of Fiona, who'd headed home to pick up equipment. The garish green steel building sat atop a sagebrush knoll three miles out Croy Canyon, west of Hailey, where coyotes cried in the wee hours of the morning and area snowplows struggled to reach in the dead of winter. The volunteer worker, a middle-aged woman Walt recognized from the softball bleachers, threatened him with a cup of coffee. Walt politely declined. He and Anderson donned latex gloves and slipped their boots into paper covers. Anderson, a lanky guy with a narrow, boyish face and big teeth, was as close as Walt's sheriff's office got to a forensics technician. He'd taken a single course called Death Sciences at a technical school outside of Nampa, just after high school.

"You got everything?" Walt asked him, not sure he wanted the answer.

"Yeah. All set." Anderson hoisted a black duffel bag. "Take me about five minutes to mix the chemicals."

Walt approached the interior door that led to the kennel. From the other side came a chorus of loud barking. He opened it, revealing a central aisle that gave way to shelves of cages of varying sizes on either side. The occasional plywood partition segregated the cat cages from the dogs. Though every effort was made to keep the room smelling clean, it was a losing battle. To Walt's left stood a much larger, heavily reinforced cage. As with others along the left wall, it offered a sliding door to an outside run, currently padlocked shut. Pacing silently wall to wall, the cougar kept a wary eye on him.

All down the center aisle he noticed ghostly white stains that had been vigorously scrubbed off the concrete. He looked up and saw the scars where hundreds of the swallows' mud nests had been plucked off the ridgepole. Dozens more had yet to be removed. A few bold swallows peeked their heads from the remaining nests. Made of dried mud and grass, they looked like tiny caves.

"It's a never-ending battle," the volunteer said from behind him. "And a health issue. Most of the smell is the bird poo, I'm afraid. We're still working on a more permanent solution."

"Can we move the cat?" Walt asked.

"Oh, no, sir. Not us. Have to call Fish and Game to do that."

He shouted, "Anderson, will the luminol hurt the cat?"

"Shouldn't. No, sir. It's basically nothing more than hydrogen peroxide."

"Then hurry it up."

Twenty minutes later, Anderson had sprayed the concrete flooring inside most of the cage. The cougar wisely chose to stay as far away as possible during this, pacing the opposite wall from Anderson.

Fiona arrived. She had donned a hairnet, gloves, and shoe covers and made a point to set up her camera gear quickly.

"Was she alive when he did it?" Fiona asked.

"We don't know anything yet. Let's take it step by step."

Anderson returned from mixing another batch. He backed them away from the cage and sprayed the outside perimeter as well.

"I'm all set," Fiona announced.

"Okay, then." Anderson plugged in a two-foot tube light—a black light like the kind McClure had used in the morgue. "Okay," he said, somewhat nervously. "Anything blue-green is evidence of blood."

Walt asked the volunteer to leave the room. He shut the door, and as he did the dogs barked viciously in a chorus that ran chills down his spine. He switched the long wire of overhead lights off. The room went dark. Mixed in with the dogs was the sound of Fiona gasping.

Then Anderson croaked out in raspy voice, "Mother of God."

Eighteen

The cage floor was stained in ungainly neon green smears and streaks and splatters. It looked like a monochromatic Jackson Pollock painting. Walt maintained his poise as he imagined a semiconscious, paralyzed Ailia Holms being mauled, bitten, clawed, and dragged around the cage.

As Fiona clicked off time exposures, Walt thought he heard her crying. Anderson pointed out the long green tail that tapered from the edge of the cage toward the room's central drain.

"Someone tried to clean it up," Anderson explained. "Hosed it down. Maybe mopped. Spent some time on it. I'll luminol the brooms and mops."

"We'll want to check the drain for tissue,

the brooms for prints." Walt indicated an area in front of the cage. "Get pictures of this as well, please."

Anderson illuminated the area in question. "Interesting," he said, his teeth glowing white and standing out from his blue face.

The green smear indicating spilled blood was interrupted by two columns—representing clean concrete.

"These are blood shadows," Anderson explained.

"I don't want to ask." Fiona sounded frightened.

"Blood splatter traveled out of the cage and was blocked." Anderson hesitated. "Someone stood here and watched her die."

Nineteen

Brandon had rounded up Patrick Cutter's seven-person staff, and two security personnel, and was detaining them on the patio until further notice, ensuring they didn't attempt to manipulate the environment or damage possible evidence.

Doug Aanestad read through the hastily scrawled search warrant. "Must be nice to work in a place where judges can be bent to favor at three o'clock on a Saturday afternoon."

"Small-town living," Walt said. "This may take a while."

"Ginny will make us both a latté, if you'll release her for a minute. Best latté you've ever had. Patrick gets his beans flown in from Colombia."

"Pass. Everyone stays where they are."

"It's a fishing expedition, Walt, and you know it. She got caught in the wrong place at the wrong time. Bad luck is all."

"Don't I wish."

"You have evidence to the contrary?"

"Don't you wish," Walt said. "I don't share intel with the enemy."

"Five minutes, and you can put her back on the patio. I'm telling you: flown in from Colombia. You've never tasted anything like this."

Walt answered with a glare. Aanestad slumped into a living room chair that swallowed him. He continued reading the warrant. Again he mumbled something about Walt's good fortune.

By 3:30 P.M. Walt was following Anderson around the house, as Anderson chased electrical outlets to power his black light. When Anderson moved toward the master bedroom, Aanestad steered him clear, pointing out that the warrant contained Walt to a search for evidence linked to Danny, his client, and not the owner of the house. Phone calls were made, and Aanestad won.

Anderson was going through the guest suite when deputies Tilly and Kaiser showed up, beckoning Walt to the six-car garage. Aanestad followed, the vigilante watchdog.

Several of the garage bays stood empty. Four cars remained: a Hummer, a BMW sports coupe, a gleaming black pickup truck, and a Toyota Land Cruiser. All had their doors open, mats out on the poured concrete; some seats had been removed.

Walt informed Aanestad, "Just FYI, we have two teams searching both Patrick's and Danny's cars over at Sun Valley. It's all covered in the warrant."

"I saw that. I still think it's a stretch to include all the vehicles when my client claims to have driven only the Lexus. But there you have it."

"If you aren't careful, Doug, someone's going to accuse you of being Patrick's lawyer."

"I am Patrick's lawyer—locally," he clarified, even though he thought Walt knew that. "I represent the family."

"We found it over here," Tilly said, eager to show his prize.

Walt approached the back of the Land Cruiser with a quickened pulse. Aanestad was getting on his nerves; and Anderson's failure to find a speck of blood evidence was beginning to make him look as foolish as Aanestad made him out to be.

Tilly pointed into the back of the vehicle, where a small white arrow made of removable tape had been fixed to the caramel-colored carpeting.

Walt's eyes followed the white arrow, and at first he didn't see anything. Then he moved slightly to his left in order to catch the light better.

Aanestad called out, "That's Patrick's car. This has nothing to do with Danny."

At the tip of the white arrow lay a single, clear contact lens.

Twenty

Walt stood to the side and down the hallway from the Picabo Street Room, out of the way of the conference guests departing a talk given by the secretary of the treasury. Having Doug Aanestad by his side won Patrick Cutter's attention. The eye communication was between attorney and client, with only a passing glance at Walt.

Cutter dealt with a few enthusiastic guests, waited to make sure the secretary was properly escorted to the next function, and then lingered long enough to have the hallway to themselves for a moment.

"Is that room clear?" Walt asked as he shook hands with Cutter.

"Yes, certainly." Patrick led them into the room and Walt shut the door. Capable of holding a hundred or more, the conference room smelled of warm bodies and coffee. Two food service personnel entered to refresh the ice water and clear glasses from the dais. Walt asked them to leave, and they did so without question.

"As you know," the attorney told his client, "the sheriff and his men searched your residence this afternoon." He focused intently on Cutter's eyes, attempting to communicate the severity of the situation. "He would like to ask you some questions."

"Of course," Cutter blurted out, looking alarmed.

"I advise you, Patrick, to check with me before answering. Do we understand each other? Each and every question, you will check with me before answering. Given this condition, I'm allowing this conversation to take place. But I must have your understanding on this: The sheriff wanted to run a recording device—I have prohibited that; he wanted to see you alone, by himself, also forbidden; he claims to have reason to suspect you in a possible murder investigation, Patrick. That's right: murder."

"Danny?" Cutter blurted out. Despite the golf tan, he looked suddenly pale.

"He'll get to that," Aanestad said. "But there's a good example: I don't want you speaking until I've nodded my okay. And I want you to think clearly about your answers before giving them."

Cutter nodded.

Walt began by asking some of the same general questions he had asked Danny Cutter earlier. Patrick could not recall with any clarity when he'd last seen Ailia Holms—he pointed out the large number of guests he was now dealing with on an hourly basis. He thought it might have been as far back as the cocktail party at his residence. Walt soon moved into more sensitive territory.

"You directed Dick O'Brien to pass along a DVD to me from your home security cameras—"

"Wait just a minute!" Aanestad conferred with Cutter in the corner by a table with a black skirt piled with copies of a book written by the treasury secretary. They returned and both men sat down facing Walt.

"I did," said Cutter.

"Why would you do that? Implicate your brother like that?"

Cutter checked with Aanestad, who nodded faintly. "It seemed the right thing to do.

It's the cover-up that gets you hanged, Sheriff. We all know that."

"You could have destroyed it. Who would have known?"

He checked with Aanestad each and every time. "Same answer."

"You could have warned your brother."

"He's an adult."

"Who has driven which of your cars this weekend, between you and Danny?"

"I drive the Cayenne. I gave Danny the Lexus. My wife either rides with me or uses the Volvo."

"What about the Land Cruiser?" Walt asked.

Aanestad shook his head, and Patrick Cutter, looking confused, raised his eyebrows at Walt. "I'm advised not to answer that," he said.

Walt thought him either a very good actor, or someone who knew nothing of the possibility of Ailia Holms's contact lens being found in his car.

"The keys?" Walt asked.

"Kept on a rack in the kitchen. All but the Cayenne. I keep those with me. I'm passionate about the Cayenne." He smiled.

It was all wrong. Walt had expected him to

be nervous and agitated. Aanestad sat smugly observing Walt's reactions—Walt's, not his client's. Had some coaching gone on in the corner? Walt wondered. Was Cutter seasoned enough from his business dealings to bluff his way through this? It seemed impossible to Walt that Cutter, if guilty, could maintain such a calm facade.

"You were sleeping with Ailia Holms?"

Cutter tried to hold back any reaction, but he slowly crumbled. Feigned astonishment moved into feigned insult. Walt never took his eyes off the man, as the accusation worked through him like an acid. His weapon was patience. He waited, and the waiting was the man's undoing.

"Nonsense!" Aanestad complained, trying to give Cutter a breath of air. "Where'd you get that? It's garbage, Walt, and you know it. You should be ashamed, trying such a stunt."

Walt had gotten it from a single look Dick O'Brien had given him out on the bridge when mentioning the competition between the brothers, but he wasn't about to reveal his source. "Let your client deny it, counselor."

Patrick's eyes shone wetly as he glowered

at Walt. At least a minute had passed. Maybe two. The air-conditioning wheezed from the ceiling. Again, a food service worker tried to enter the room from the far end. Again, Walt sent him packing.

Patrick said softly, "I'm upset over her loss, Sheriff. We were . . . close."

"Of course you were," Aanestad said. "You and Stu—"

"Shut up, Doug," Cutter said.

"How long?" Walt asked.

"This conversation is over!" Aanestad announced.

"Doug!" Cutter chided. "If you can't keep quiet, I'm going to ask you to leave the room."

Aanestad's face went scarlet, his eyes flashed darkly, and he sat back in his chair.

Patrick continued. "I had Dick share the security footage because if Danny did something . . . if he hurt her in any way . . . then God damn it, for once he's going to pay."

"I'll need you to account for your whereabouts last night, from nine P.M. to past midnight."

Without pause, Cutter replied, "I was hosting a dinner at the lodge dining room followed immediately by a dessert function out at Trail Creek Cabin. The commissioner of the FCC. Believe me, Walt, every second of my time can be accounted for, by me, my people, and probably several dozen, if not a hundred or more, witnesses. Do the legwork."

"The same for Danny?"

Patrick answered only with a saddened face.

"We're done here," Aanestad repeated. This time, he won Patrick's support.

Walt had what he wanted: Patrick had admitted involvement with Ailia Holms, just as O'Brien had inferred. The man could have easily hired her murder.

All three men stood.

Walt asked for Cutter's passport, winning another shocked expression. "Have one of your people run it down to my office before five."

"That's less than an hour."

"That's your problem."

"You are *way* off, if you think I had anything do to with Ailia's death."

"Physical evidence was found in the back of your Land Cruiser possibly connected to the victim. Doug was prohibited from saying anything about that—the only condition of his attendance here."

"What evidence? That's ridiculous. Allie and I used that car all the time. We've even—" Cutter stopped himself.

Walt said nothing. He felt sordid and tired.

"We *cared* for each other," Cutter repeated, as if issuing his defense.

"That's enough, Patrick," Aanestad said, taking Cutter by the arm and leading him from the room.

Twenty-one

A few minutes before 5 P.M., Walt parked in his designated space in front of the Sheriff's Office. The officer on duty told him Myra was waiting in his office. He found her reading the Idaho Sheriffs' Association magazine.

"What's up?" he asked, hurrying over to give her a kiss. "Is Kev all right?"

"Better," she said. "They may release him tomorrow."

He sat down behind his desk and checked his e-mail. Too many to deal with. A stack of phone messages. And yet it felt uncommonly good to be back in the office.

"You look like hell."

"I'm okay," he told her.

"Are you eating?" With Myra it was always food.

"I'm good." He looked up, and she looked down, avoiding eye contact. "Myra?"

"Kev lied to you."

"I know."

She seemed both relieved and surprised. Her face brightened.

"He's in with a bad kid," he said. "This isn't like him. . . . We both know that."

"How much trouble is he in?"

"Enough," he answered honestly.

"I gave him the what-for. Told him we can't keep using his father's death as an excuse for our screwups. I've done it as much as him, Walt."

"We're all guilty of that," Walt said. "Why is it we're so willing to lean back, instead of press forward?"

"Fear. Of the unknown. Of the known. Of tomorrow. Of failure." She worked herself up toward a cry, broken by Walt's tossing her a box of tissues, which brought a laugh.

"So that's a good thing," he said. "To get through that, I mean. I hope it's contagious."

"We had a good cry, the two of us. That hasn't really happened since Bobby."

"Glad to hear it."

"He wants to talk to you." The way she said it, her eyes unflinching, he knew this was the real reason she'd come. She closed the magazine and set it aside.

"Okay."

"No, I mean now, Walt. You need to hear this."

"It can wait. If he's getting out tomorrow—"

"No, I don't think so."

Exasperated, he held himself back from saying something stupid, something he'd regret. But his face belied him.

"I probably should have called you," she said. "Caught you on the way down valley. I know how busy you must be. But I wanted to look you in the eye. I want you to understand how important this is. Not for Kevin— I don't mean that. For you. Your job. He wouldn't tell me what it is, but a mother knows. Right? Something happened in that laundry—that's all I got out of him. Something he won't talk to me about."

"I'll be heading up valley later on. The conference is in full swing."

"You've got to go now, Walt."

"Myra . . ." he pleaded.

"He won't tell me, only you. Please. Please do this. He's your nephew."

He had some choice words on the tip of his tongue. He looked at her and nodded. He said, "But we're stopping by your place on the way and you're making me a banana and mayonnaise sandwich."

"Deal," she said brightly. And with that, tears rolled from her tired eyes.

Twenty-two

Kevin didn't look as if he'd be going home the next day. If anything he looked worse than earlier in the day: the bruising around his shattered eye socket had spread beyond the bandages and was a horrid orange. His one supposedly "good" eye was pooled with blood beneath the cornea, the iris barely discernible.

"You look like shit," Walt said, taking the seat by the side of the bed.

Kevin winced as he stretched the stitches at the edge of his lips into a grin. "Yeah," he said.

"Your mom said—"

"Yeah," he interrupted. "I'm sorry for what happened."

"Me, too. I hear you want to change your story."

"If I can."

"Of course you can, Kev. The truth is always a good place to start. You might want to remember that."

"There was a guy," Kevin said.

"A guy," Walt repeated after a protracted silence.

"In the laundry. When we got there. Up there by the register dressed like a ninja. Scared the hell out of us."

"A ninja?"

"You know, a ski mask. Black clothes. Over in the bags of laundry."

"A worker? A ski mask? Didn't you say the alarm went off when you kicked in the door?"

"It beeped and went off. Yeah."

There'd been no report of a manager or employee being inside the laundry at the time. "What was the guy doing?"

"Scaring the shit out of us."

Walt suppressed a grin, then sobered to what he was hearing. "Eric went for the window because of this guy."

"Yeah." Kevin sounded regretful.

"You were, or were not, trying to steal clothes?" Walt pressed.

"Dry cleaners use a solvent . . . ," Kevin said softly.

"Meth," Walt said, closing his eyes tightly. "For cooking meth."

Kevin let out a slow, ragged breath. "Yeah."

"Who?"

"Crab."

"Taylor Crabtree. He put you up to this?"

"Yeah. Said if we were caught, on account we don't have records, criminal records, we'd get off a lot easier than him."

Walt fought valiantly to control his temper. "And this other guy—your age, or what?"

"Didn't seem like it."

Walt found himself hung up on the alarm having sounded with someone else already inside. "Give me a minute."

He stepped into the hall to use his cell phone and called Trident Security, the valley's only security firm. He identified himself and asked to pull up the entry log for the Suds Tub on the previous night, marveling at how quickly he was provided the information.

"There was a log-on at six-forty P.M.," he

was told. "Log-out at one-oh-seven A.M. Another log-on, one-oh-eight. We received an alarm at one-nineteen; called the establishment at one-nineteen, and passed it on to KPD at one-twenty-one A.M."

Walt clarified that a log-on meant logging on to the security system, an act that would suggest someone leaving the laundry, and that a log-off implied a return.

"Yes, sir. Once we caught that alarm, we called the client in case it was a false. Owner's supposed to pick up and give us a password. That didn't happen. No one picked up, so we dispatched KPD."

Walt asked for a hard copy to be faxed to him. He thanked the guy and hung up, and returned to Kevin. The obvious explanation was an owner or employee—someone who knew the access code. But part of Kevin's story didn't add up.

"A ski mask over his head? You're sure about that? It was dark, right?" This was not the description of an employee hitting the cash register.

"I saw him. He helped Eric. Put Eric's fingers on his neck to stop the bleeding."

"The ninja helped Eric?" Walt felt confused.

"You said he saved his life."

"The doctor said that," Walt corrected.
"He helped Eric?"

"And then, when he turned toward me . . ."
Kevin's face bunched and Walt could see it
was painful. "And I . . . I just ran."

Walt helped him to sit. The boy blew his
nose and sipped some water through a
straw.

"You did the right thing telling me, Kev.
We're going to work this out."

"I fucked up. I'm so sorry."

"Couple of things," Walt said. "One, you've
got to clean up your language. Two, you say
nothing to Eric and, above all, nothing to
Crabtree about any of this. I don't want you
talking to these guys. Not a word. Do we
understand each other?"

"I got it."

A nurse cleared her throat. She stood inside the door. Walt had no idea how long
she'd been there.

"Need to change a dressing, Sheriff," she
said.

Walt nodded. Kevin reached out and
grabbed Walt's arm. "Can you stay while
she does this? It kinda hurts."

"Sure," Walt said. He held Kevin's clenched

fist as the nurse removed the bloodied bandage and replaced it with a new one. That side of his face had taken a beating.

"The doctor's going to come look at this," the nurse informed the patient. "He may want to take one or two more stitches." Among the bandages and disinfectant, Walt noticed the sealed needles and suture.

"That's some small suture," Walt said to the nurse.

"Five-zero. Very small. Used for face, eyes, ears, nose."

"You mind?" Walt said, letting go of Kevin's hand.

She passed him one of the sealed plastic bags. It contained a slightly curved needle and a coil of very fine suture. Walt thought back to the contents of the carry-on bag found at the airport. "This is point-zero-zero-five," he said, just to clarify.

"We call it five-zero, yes," she said, "five one-thousandths of an inch."

"What about three? Plain old three? Just the number three?"

"As suture? Number three suture?" She sounded surprised. "Not in people. Vets, maybe—big-animal work. There's a joke when you're studying this stuff: Number five suture is used for towing cars. That's the joke," she said, when Walt failed to smile.

"I've got to make another call," Walt said.

"I understand," Kevin said.

"Remember what we talked about."

"I've got it."

He left at close to a run. His first call was to Fiona. He asked to see any crime-scene photos of Suds Tub.

"And I was wondering if you could get copies of the contents of that carry-on bag to Mark Aker. I realize it's a Saturday. I could have a deputy—"

"It's no problem, Walt. I'll meet you there."

Twenty-three

Walt didn't bother to call ahead to the vet's to check if Mark was in. Given the break-in and the now countywide effort to retrieve the missing pets, Mark wasn't going anywhere.

Walt entered Aker's vet clinic with his cell phone glued to his ear. Both of the Cutter brothers' passports had been delivered to his office. Dr. McClure was consulting an optometrist to verify the prescription of the contact lens found in Cutter's Land Cruiser.

Fiona entered only minutes behind him. "Got them," she declared, holding up an envelope.

The receptionist indicated a door below the sign marked DOGS.

Mark Aker needed sleep and his beard held cracker crumbs.

Walt spread the photos out on the counter, as he said, "Suture, needles, bandaging, hypodermic needles. What's that add up to?"

Aker studied the photos. "Closing an incision."

"Anesthesia, or some kind of painkiller—is any of that missing from your meds closet?"

"We won't know for at least a couple days," Aker answered. "We're still missing nine dogs, seventeen cats, and a handful of house pets including a pair of Peruvian rabbits, confiscated by Fish and Game. Of those nine dogs, two are my own—Search and Rescue training. Ten, fifteen thousand each. One I'd sold already."

Walt tapped the enlargement of the packaged suture in the photographs. "Number three suture," he said. "Not three-zero. Just plain three." He looked to Aker for some kind of reaction.

"Number three is strictly large animal," Aker said. "Horse, or cow, or sheep. Rarely used, even around here."

"Not people," Walt said. "That's what a nurse told me at the hospital."

"No. Never."

"When I first saw this bag and its contents I was thinking: an assassin's first aid kit. But now, I don't know what to think."

"Maybe some vet lost it," Fiona suggested. "Left it on the flight."

Aker rearranged the photographs.

Walt could feel him trying to make sense of it.

"You still could be right," Aker said. "It's a stretch, but if you take all these collectively, they could be to close a human wound. The large suture simply means it's not going to reopen."

"Exactly."

"And you're right about the anesthesia and/or pain meds. With those this makes a fine kit."

"A mobile emergency room," Walt said.

"I wouldn't go that far, Walt. It's a field kit, not first aid." Again, he studied the photographs. "There is one other possibility . . ." He took a moment to collect the same instruments and he laid them out on the stainless steel along with several packets of suture. They looked like a particularly horrific place setting. He nodded to himself and said, "Throw in a very sharp knife or scalpel . . ." Now he met eyes with Walt. "And you have everything you need for minor surgery."

Twenty-four

Trevalian understood the endgame. These final hours of preparation—much of it mental—were for him like an athlete's last night before the competition. Time slowed, but he didn't fight it. He used what felt like extra hours to double-check the plan and prepare for his escape. Extra clothes, sleeping bag, water bottles, handheld GPS, hunting knife, dry foods. He was ready for the backcountry.

He anticipated the valley's only road—Highway 75—would be roadblocked both south and north. The airport would be closed. For these reasons he had packed for the wilderness, his supplies already in the trunk of the rental.

From Meisner's room he dialed an 800 number and a woman answered. "Steel Birds Excursions. This is Laura. How can I help you?"

"It's Ralph Lewis," Trevalian said, "Mr. Bloggett's assistant."

"Oh, yes. Hello."

"I'm reconfirming Mr. Bloggett's pickup. He'll have been in the backcountry a week, and I know he'll be looking forward to seeing you all."

She recited the time and the coordinates: 8 P.M. Sunday evening. 43° 44′ 27.04″ N by 114° 10′ 18.27″ W. Trevalian had the location memorized and approved it.

"Eight A.M. Monday morning if weather prevents."

"And every twelve hours thereafter," he said.

"That's correct."

He thanked her and hung up the call.

Typically unruffled, Trevalian jolted with surprise at the sound of a knock—not from the door, but from *behind* him. He turned to see a woman's shapely form out on the balcony. Although he'd pulled his privacy drapes, he had no doubt she could identify him as well as he could identify her: Lilly, the jazz singer.

He wanted to hide. He wanted to pull the blackout drapes, and he chastised himself for not having done so earlier. The back balcony was shared by a dozen rooms and overlooked the outdoor skating rink.

She knocked again. "Please?"

He didn't need attention drawn to the room. Who knew how many of the people gathered for an early dinner three stories below might hear her? He could make this quick. He parted the gauze curtains, unlocked the sliding door.

"Hello," she said.

She'd done well with the makeup. He saw no bruises or cuts, and though she looked tired, there was no self-pity in her face.

"I'm sorry, but I'm busy, Lilly."

She did not take this well.

"Sorry to hear about your . . . ordeal."

"Please? May I come in, just for a minute?"

"Tomorrow would be better," he said.

"Checking out, are you?" Sarcastic. Nasty.

"No . . ."

"How could you be so spineless?" She pushed past him.

Sympathy was not in his emotional range. She'd come to the wrong place. He slid the door shut behind her.

"All I needed was a description," she complained, now patrolling the room slowly, her back to him. "And don't tell me you didn't see him," she added accusingly.

"I was looking at you," he lied. "I would have helped if I could have. Now . . . at the moment I'm busy."

"Oh, I can see that," she snapped. "Did he buy you off?"

"What?" he fired back indignantly.

"Anything for the right price?" she asked.

"I helped you," he protested. "I took a chance doing that. I had *no idea* what I was getting into at the time—other than I'd seen you on stage, and I liked your voice." He hoped flattery would calm her long enough to get her out the door.

"I'm singing here again tonight."

"Are you sure that's a good idea?"

She shrugged, and caught his reflection in the desk mirror, making sure he was still watching her. "He hit me," she said. "He touched me inappropriately."

"I'm sorry."

"All I wanted was to make sure he was never coming back. Too much to ask?"

"If we could deal with this tomorrow?"

"What's so damn pressing, Mr. Meisner? That's right: I know your name. So sue me. I want an explanation. You seemed so nice. All they needed was a physical description."

"I think you should go now."

"What? You're going to call security or something?"

"Or something," he said. He wanted to tell her to stop wandering around the room. This, above all else, worked devilishly against his nerves.

"I just don't understand it," she whined. "How difficult is it?" She stopped at the connecting door to Nagler's room.

He focused on the dead bolt: unlocked. The door connecting was ever-so-slightly ajar. He watched as her fingers slipped into the opening and pulled. "You didn't tell me you had a suite," she said.

He moved to shut the door—to cut her off. But she was already in.

"A dog?" she asked. "Whose room is this?" She turned around, looking bewildered. When their eyes met, hers were filled with fright.

"What's going on here? Who are you?"

"Lilly," he said. "Oh, Lilly," the weight of disappointment and betrayal impossible to miss.

Twenty-five

Near closing time, Walt caught up to his father at the Sawtooth Club, a Main Street restaurant and bar in Ketchum that serviced a more subdued clientele than the two rock clubs a few doors down. The ground-floor bar was open to a surround balcony for upstairs dining. A canoe hung where a chandelier belonged. The wait staff was women and men in shorts and T-shirts.

Jerry was at the bar making love to a glass of Scotch. Walt had been summoned here. He told himself to maintain his cool. Seeing his father drunk didn't help matters. He persuaded Jerry onto a couch between two silk ficus trees, where he hoped there was less chance of being overheard.

"You shouldn't have used the split tail,

son." His father sounded quite sober, despite his looks. "When you want something done right, always do it yourself."

"Split tail?"

"This photographer of yours."

"You're drunk."

"Such a detective. You coulda been, you know? A detective. More's the pity."

Walt stood. "I'm in the middle of a lot of things right now. If you're looking for a whipping boy—"

"Sit down."

Walt hesitated. The door was only a few feet away.

"Sit . . . down!"

Walt returned to the couch, regretting his cooperating.

"The trouble with the truth is that some people just don't want to hear it."

"You're drunk and I'm tired. Maybe another time."

"Your girlie girl took the Salt Lake photos to Shaler."

Walt felt himself swallow dryly. "Who? Fiona?"

"Dryer caught her, and is, of course, convinced you were behind it."

"Oh, boy."

"Cutter's told Dryer not to let you any-where near her before the talk."

"You must be thrilled," Walt said.

He glowered.

"No worries. He can't roadblock me."

"I wouldn't be so sure. Dryer can play the federal card. Couple phone calls and the lo-cal guy is out of it. That's you."

Walt mulled over his options. "I don't have much of a role anyway. We secure trans-portation routes. That's about it. It's up to Dryer and Dick O'Brien after that. They're the ones that have to keep her safe once in-side."

"But if you're right about this shooter . . ."

"I *am* right," Walt said. "The guy is here, Dad. No doubt about it. He's here and he means to fulfill that contract."

"So how do I help?"

"What?" He made no attempt to mask his astonishment.

"Let's just say, hypothetically, I was going to help you . . . I have six men with me. That's not insubstantial. My men will be on the inside. You may not be."

"Are you playing me?" Walt asked, bewil-dered. He glanced around the bar and up into the restaurant. "What's going on?"

"Focus, son," his father said, motioning to his own bloodshot eyes. "What can my guys do on the inside tomorrow? What are we looking for?"

"You *do* believe me," Walt nearly said aloud. Instead, he reached over and sucked down some of his father's Scotch. Jerry raised his hand and signaled a waitress for two drinks.

"If she goes down on your watch, son, you not only won't be reelected, you'll lose any shot at corporate work, private work. Any kind of work. You'll be blackballed the rest of your life."

"And it'll be a stain on the family name," Walt said bitterly. "Like Bobby."

Jerry stiffened. "That's not what this is about."

"You did such a good job with that one," Walt said.

"Fuck you. I'm offering to help," Jerry said.

Walt caught sight of the waitress heading back with the two Scotches. It all felt too cozy. He stood before the drinks arrived and threw a five-dollar bill down on the table. It landed in a ring of water left from

the Scotch glass. Jerry went back to consulting his ice.

Walt moved toward the door, reluctantly at
first, wondering if he was making a terrible
mistake.

SUNDAY

One

Trevalian had three hotel towels laid out on
the floor. On the first he'd placed a pair of
his own socks. On the second, Elizabeth
Shaler's jog bra. And on the third, a pair of
Nagler's shoes.

"Find it!" he commanded, releasing Callie's collar.

The dog sprang excitedly into action. She
jumped up and made two circles in the
room, then came across the towels and,
nose to the floor, moved one towel to the
next. She sat down sharply in front of the
jog bra.

Trevalian stepped forward and rewarded
her with a small piece of beef jerky, patted
her affectionately, and praised her. He rearranged the towels, moving them far apart,

and began the process anew. Again, Callie found the jog bra. Again, she won a piece of beef jerky.

"Four out of four," he told her. "Good dog!"

Two

Walt had awakened to an alarm clock at 6 A.M. Sunday morning, having had four hours' sleep. He went for a two-mile run to wake himself up, showered, and changed into a fresh uniform. By 8 A.M. he was overseeing Brandon's leadership in securing Sun Valley Road for the one-mile stretch from Ketchum to the resort, while monitoring the Sun Valley Police Department's attempts to contain the burgeoning number of First Rights protesters who twice had broken through a barricade trying to get closer to the inn and the C³ gathering, only to be pushed back to the area allotted them.

By 9 A.M. things seemed pretty much in control. They intended to briefly shut down traffic on Sun Valley Road, allowing for

Shaler's motorcade. He had placed Deputy Tilly, his team's second best marksman, on top of Penny Hill, working with two spotters. Best of all, his two communications with Adam Dryer, whose agents occupied Walt's Mobile Command Center, had been work-manlike and professional.

Liz Shaler came out her front door, amid camera flashes, surrounded by three of Dryer's men. She met eyes briefly with Walt through the gauntlet, and to his surprise she seemed to apologize to him. Or maybe he'd taken that wrong. They moved her into one of three black Escalades.

Walt's Cherokee led the motorcade. Tommy Brandon, in the black Hummer, took up the rear. To the casual tourist, and to Walt as well, this looked like overkill, but something told Walt otherwise. Inside he was thinking: *This isn't enough.*

His cell phone rang, and his intention was to ignore it, but old habits die hard, and he checked the caller ID anyway. The number came as Mark Aker. Walt took the call.

"Mark? Kinda busy at the moment," Walt said.

"You want to hear this." Walt knew from the man's tone that it wasn't a social call.

"Go ahead."

"We've had thirty volunteers working to find our missing animals. As of this morning, we have eighty percent found and most of those returned to us."

"That's great. But maybe we could do this later?"

"Among those returned were several dogs, and among the dogs were a pair of shepherds—my Search and Rescue trainees. Or so I thought."

Walt decided not to interrupt, but he tuned him out slightly to listen in to the running dialogue pouring over the radio. All seemed well with the motorcade—and for some unknown reason that made Walt all the more queasy.

"We tag our dogs. Electronic chips placed beneath the skin in the shoulder. They both came back without collars, so we wanded them just to make sure. One had been picked up at the hospital. One, clear out Trail Creek. Some hikers found her."

"That's a long way away."

"But not so far from the lodge."

"True enough. Better cut to the chase here, Mark. I'm in the middle of moving Shaler. We're about there."

"The ID provided by the chip surprised me. It wasn't one of mine after all. But I *had* chipped this dog. It's Toey, Walt. The service dog we loaned the blind guy. He must have lost her and been too embarrassed to tell us. But what the hell am I supposed to do? Confront him? Return the dog to Maggie? Or what? What do you want me to do?" He added, "Meanwhile—news flash—I'm still missing my twenty-thousand-dollar tracker."

"The one you planned to sell?" Walt asked. He'd tuned out the police band radio under the dash. He tuned out more than he should have, given that he was leading the motorcade. The Escalade behind him honked, just in time for Walt to cut the wheel sharply and turn into the entrance to the lodge, and avoid the total embarrassment of missing the turn. He felt badly that Nagler hadn't mentioned losing the dog. He wasn't sure how to approach this himself.

In his mind's eye he saw the contents of the unclaimed backpack spread out on the table as Fiona photographed them; he saw the gruesome images of the Salt Lake airport killing: the severed fingers, the pulled teeth, the missing eyes . . .

"Laundry," he said, pulling the Cherokee through the lodge's portico. Shaler's Escalade pulled in front of the doors.

"Laundry? Walt, it's Mark," Aker said, not understanding Walt's change of subject.

"All the search and rescue we ever do," Walt said, "the dogs are given a piece of clothing, right? Or some personal item of the missing person's. A hairbrush. A shoe."

"Of course they are. Walt . . . what are you talking about?"

"S and R! The dogs. Your missing dog is a tracker, a sniffer."

"Yeah? So what?"

"He broke into the laundry," Walt said, seeing it clearly now. "He broke into the laundry," he repeated. "Holy shit."

He was out of the car, the phone already back in his pocket. The phalanx of press, and tourists, agents, and his own deputies jammed the landing outside the hotel's doors as Liz Shaler was squeezed inside. His moment or two of delay had cost him— he was on the outside looking in.

"Stand aside," he hollered, but it did no good. Liz Shaler's celebrity had taken over. Nothing was going to part the crowd. There were too many hotel guests and people from town—faces he recognized—waiting there to be coincidence. Patrick Cutter had arranged a big, splashy welcome for her, and for the sake of the cameras.

He lifted up on his toes to see into the lobby. Liz Shaler and Patrick Cutter were at the center of a knot. A camera flashed. Walt followed its source to a pair of thin arms, and finally, Fiona's profile. Despite the clamor of Liz's admirers, despite the shouting of O'Brien and his men for people to get out of the way, despite the chaos and confusion, Fiona somehow turned and looked right at him.

They met eyes and she immediately understood his problem as he pointed inside. Fiona was jostled to the side. She connected with him once again and waved Walt to his left. Walt backed away from the throng, looked left, and saw the door.

A moment later, the exterior door leading to the hotel offices, locked on a Sunday morning, sprang open. Fiona's eyes sparkled. "What a zoo!"

The door closed, eliminating much of the shouting from the protesters.

"I know who it is," Walt announced. "He's here in the hotel."

Three

Trevalian stood in line in the inn's lobby awaiting his turn at the security checkpoint, just past which were the men's and women's bathrooms—a piece of the logistical planning that was already drawing complaint. At the end of the hall: the doors to the banquet hall.

"That's a beautiful dog you have there," said a woman behind him.

He thanked her, wondering if she or anyone else had spotted that, to a large degree, he was directing the dog, not the other way around. The line moved steadily forward, everyone accustomed to, and comfortable with, the routine: Women removed their heavy jewelry, the men dumped their phones into plastic bins. Only one woman he saw was also wanded after passing through the metal detector. Trevalian's turn came next.

"Hello, Mr. Nagler," said the young, wide-shouldered man feeding the X-ray belt. "I'll take the dog through first."

Trevalian turned his head in that direction, but also aimed his face toward the ceiling. He passed the handle of the guide harness in that general direction, making sure not to appear overly anxious or to put the harness squarely into this man's hands—reminding himself to play the blind man.

The dog was held in check as Trevalian searched his pockets. He came up with a cell phone, some coins, and, in his coat's side pocket, a device about the size of a garage door opener. He made a good act of feeling for the plastic dish and catching its edge, deposited his belongings.

"What's this?" the guard asked curiously.

Trevalian could see the man was holding the other device. "My cell phone?"

"A garage opener?" the man asked.

The dog was led through a metal detector and sounded an alarm.

"Don't push it, please!" Trevalian said a little too sharply. He reached out and found the man's hand and returned the device to the plastic tray. "Shock collar. She's still in training."

"We'll have to X-ray that collar. The harness, too."

"No problem. Of course," Trevalian said. "Just don't lose her, please."

The guards removed both and ran them through the X-ray. Trevalian waited anxiously as the collar and harness were imaged by a third guard behind a TV monitor. Finally, he was waved through the metal detector and passed without incident.

The bulky collar was reattached to the dog, as was the harness. Once through he returned his belongings to his pockets, grabbed hold of the guide handle, and moved forward.

He was inside.

Four

The crowd had thinned, the gawkers following Liz Shaler's procession toward a private reception held in her honor, prior to her talk. Walt spotted Chuck Webb, the hotel's house detective.

"Sheriff?"

"Chuck, I need a room number from you. And I need you to put any of your guys you have left over on radios by all the exits. I needed this to happen about five minutes ago."

Webb didn't question any of this. The urgency in Walt's voice had convinced him. He reached for a handheld radio. "Guest's name?"

"Nagler." He racked his memory. "Strange first name I can't remember."

"The blind guy. I know who you mean."

"Yes."

Chuck spoke into the radio, "Christopher Robin," he announced.

"It's Nagler," Walt repeated.

"That's our internal code to block all doors. Kids missing. That sort of thing. My guys'll lock them down."

Walt spotted one of O'Brien's men approaching fast. Cutter intended to throw him out, which wasn't going to happen—but it would delay him.

"The room number," Walt hissed at Webb. "And your passkey. I need both *right now*!"

Webb fumbled for a small hub clipped to his belt from which hung a retractable string attached to a plain white plastic card. He stuffed it into Walt's hand. He saw O'Brien's man as well, and knew trouble when he saw it.

His radio chirped and Webb put it to his ear. "Three-twenty-seven," he said.

Walt didn't want to initiate a chase with O'Brien's guy. But it seemed either that, or confrontation. That was when someone stepped between them and raised a camera. A pulse of white light exploded in the face of O'Brien's soldier. Fiona.

Walt took off for the stairs.

The security man cleared his eyes and looked around quickly. "Where'd he go?" he asked Webb.

"Who?" answered Webb.

The guard spun around. The sheriff was gone. And so was the photographer.

Five

Danny Cutter was on borrowed time. The police were after him for Ailia Holms's murder—and his brother was acting strange. His fears, along with the financial repercussions of her death, had kept him up all night. He knew he looked beleaguered and beaten down. That wouldn't help him any.

The reception for Elizabeth Shaler was held in a private dining room. Danny looked around for Stuart Holms but knew he wouldn't find him.

Conversation quieted in the direction of Liz Shaler. Patrick escorted her through the room, making introductions. Danny tagged along and listened in. Those in this room had already made campaign contributions. The brush with fame was payback.

He heard someone in the group ahead address the attorney general. "We'd love to give more, if only we could, Your Honor, but as much as we'd like to see you in office, we're not willing to go to jail for it." His bellowing laugh followed.

Patrick piped up, saying, "You might consider her as a speaker for a company event."

Liz looked noticeably uncomfortable.

At that moment, Danny understood his brother's determination to make sure Liz gave her talk. He was overpaying her, setting a market value for others to match. Never mind the tax implications, money was money, and candidates were allowed to spend their personal wealth on the campaign trail. Patrick had found a way around the rules, and by doing so had made himself invaluable to Liz Shaler.

Dick O'Brien appeared out of nowhere. He caught Patrick's eye. As O'Brien shook his head side to side, a ghostly pallor swept across Patrick's face. Danny knew intuitively this had something to do with Walt Fleming and the fact that Doug Aanestad had spent the early morning in private with Patrick.

Something was horribly wrong.

Six

Walt, out of breath, stopped in front of 327, Fiona right behind him. "You can't be here," he told her.

"Yeah? Well, guess what? I am."

A plan formed in his head. "Okay . . . There's a hotel phone back by the elevator. Call room three-twenty-seven. A man's going to answer. Say you're housekeeping or something. But keep him holding that phone."

"Yes, of course. Now?"

"Now."

She ran down the hall. Walt followed her with his eyes.

He waited. And waited.

The phone started ringing on the other side of the door. Walt waited for the ringing to stop, Webb's passkey hovering over the card slot. But it kept ringing.

Walt slipped in the card. The electronic lock's LED showed red, not green. Webb's card should have been the equivalent of a master key. He tried it again: red. The only explanation he could come up with was that the privacy dead bolt was thrown from the inside. He tried the next door over: 325.

Webb's card opened it. The room was pitch-black, the blackout curtains pulled. He called out, "Hello? Minibar." His weapon was drawn and aimed at the carpet in front of him. Switched on the lights. The room was empty. There was a connecting door, locked from this side. He worked through the pulled curtains, headed out onto the balcony, and crossed to 327. Locked, and the blackout curtains drawn there also.

He debated breaking the room's plate glass window, but its tempered glass would explode, and that would bring the cavalry. That, in turn, would mean a confrontation with Dryer or his men, and his father's warning remained forefront in his thought.

He returned to 325. Fiona stood in the doorway.

"You *cannot* be here," he hissed.

"We've been over that."

"Shut the door. Lock it, and stay right there."

She did so.

He unlocked the dead bolt to the connecting door. Connecting doors were paired—each lockable from its respective room—and he'd prepared himself to have to break down the second of the two doors.

But it hung open a crack—unlocked.

He raised his weapon. His chest was tight; his mouth dry. He eased open the door, but his eyes weren't adjusted and he couldn't see a thing in the dark room. He reached down for the Maglite at his belt, and the first thing he saw as the light flooded the room was a dog kennel, its door open.

Empty.

Seven

Trevalian was led by a volunteer to his assigned seat at a table that still had empty
chairs. He introduced himself and awkwardly shook hands with the four already
there, making a point of Nagler's insecurity
and timidity. One of the women stared. It
took a thumping from her husband to break
her trance. There was an attempt at small
talk, but Trevalian put a quick end to that.
The dog lay on the carpet to the right and
slightly behind his chair. From behind his
dark sunglasses he stole a look at the program laid out on his plate. It opened with:

JUICE, COFFEE, TEA, PASTRIES

MELON

THE HONORABLE ELIZABETH SHALER
ATTORNEY GENERAL NEW YORK STATE

THREE EGG OMELET, CAVIAR, AND CRÈME FRAÎCHE
or
MANGO AND STRAWBERRY BELGIAN WAFFLE
AND YOUR CHOICE OF
NORTH SEA SMOKED SALMON, IRISH BACON,
BLOOD SAUSAGE
ROASTED TOMATOES, QUICK-FRIED KELP,
CARAMELIZED APPLES

He was amused by Shaler's listing as part of the menu. She appeared to be the second or third course.

This was not the program he'd been told to expect. Originally, her talk had been scheduled to follow the main course, not precede it. This accelerated schedule affected his planning. He had to arm the explosive now, well ahead of his original plan. He reached down and reassuringly touched the bulge in his coat pocket: the shock collar's remote control.

"Oh my God," the woman two seats away gasped. She moved her chair back. "It's bleeding!"

Trevalian looked. There was indeed blood

beneath the dog. His plan unraveling, right before his own blind eyes, he steadied his voice. "She was just spayed. I'll go check on her."

"Let me be your eyes," the woman offered. "I love dogs."

"I can handle it!" Trevalian said sharply. He excused himself. The dog stood, unbothered by her problem, and Trevalian headed out of the banquet room.

Moving against the crush of incoming guests cost him precious minutes. He worried that the woman was going to spring up behind him. Finally he was in the hall and headed for the men's room.

As he made it inside, two men were just washing up at the sink. Both caught Trevalian's reflection in the mirror and both made a point of saying, "Good morning."

"Morning," Trevalian returned, leading the dog into the tight stall and closing the door with some difficulty.

He sat down on the toilet, pulled Callie to face him, her tail swishing back and forth outside the stall door, and he waited to hear the two men leave. Another man entered and urinated, but Trevalian had no time to wait. He removed his sunglasses and, holding the dog's collar tightly, reached into his outside coat pocket and withdrew a pair of tweezers. With no more metal content than a ballpoint pen, the tweezers had passed through security undetected, and he used them now, lowering himself awkwardly to one knee in the cramped space to where he had a good view of Callie's chest. He spread the dog's hair until the pink incision appeared—a string of fine-looking hook-and-knot stitches running in a straight line ten inches up her abdomen. Blood seeped from the middle, but he dabbed it with tissue and it seemed to stop.

He carefully guided the tweezers between the second and third stitches, whispering, "Good girl," into the dog's ear. She tensed with a quick spark of pain. But it was over quickly as the tweezers bit down onto a length of wire and extracted it from her chest. Eighteen inches in all, extremely thin, aluminum, picture-frame wire. He wiped it clean with a piece of toilet paper. Running it up between her front legs, he opened the shock collar's battery pack and twisted this wire to a second wire inside the shock collar. With this connection made, the remote device in his coat pocket was now live. Callie was a four-legged bomb.

He pulled her to standing. The wire was all but invisible. He dabbed her slight bleeding one more time. It would have to do.

He heard a tremendous burst of applause from out in the hall. Elizabeth Shaler was being introduced.

He reached into the small of his back, pulled out the bag hidden there, and opened it. He slipped the jogging bra out and held it closely to the dog's nose.

"Remember this game?" he said, a wan smile forming on his lips.

As he stood off the toilet, the bomb went off. He barked out a gasp of surprise, heat flooding through him. Then he realized it was only the toilet's automatic flush. And he began laughing. A dry, morbid laugh that resonated and rang out in the small marble stall.

Eight

Fiona came into the room behind Walt as he threw the curtains back.

"I told you to wait," he said.

"And I didn't listen."

He inspected the closet. *Clear.*

"What's going on?"

"It's the dog," he said. "Not now," when he realized he couldn't explain.

He tried the bathroom door. It was locked. He knocked and peered beneath the crack with his flashlight. There was no one standing on the bathroom floor. He stood, reared back, and kicked it open. The door bounced off the stop and came back at him. He blocked its return.

Empty. But there was a bloody towel on the floor next to the toilet, and a mess on the counter: a syringe, meds, suture, a bloody razor blade.

"Walt . . ." She was scared.

"I see it." He caught sight of the trail of blood leading to the tub. He pulled back the shower curtain, revealing a blond woman, her eyes fixed, her limbs twisted and contorted unnaturally. She was covered in blood.

Fiona tried to speak, but stepped back and threw up on the carpet. She apologized immediately, the vomit still coming from her.

On the floor by the trash can he spotted several bloodied bandages and a pair of bloodied latex gloves. He saw the corner of a cardboard box beneath a bloody towel. The box read: ESS FENCE. Another piece of trash caught his attention: EverTyed Surgical Suture 3.0.

"You all right?"

"Yes, I think."

"Call downstairs for Chuck Webb. Tell him what we found. Then tell him I'm on my way over to the inn. There's a shooter at the brunch. A blind guy. He may or may not have a dog. I need backup. *His* backup. Not the feds. Have you got that? Hey! Fiona!"

"Got it," she whispered.

"Keep your cell phone free. I may call back here. I may want details."

"Details . . . ," she mumbled.

"Hey!" he shouted, to break the trance. "Do you have your cell phone?"

She looked up at him and nodded.

"Okay?" he said.

"Okay."

Walt hurried down the long hallway to a set of fire stairs. A minute later he was outside and running.

Light and sounds blurred. The art fair. Kids playing. People shopping. Another day in paradise. He heard nothing but his own quickened pulse.

People turned to watch the red-faced sheriff at an all-out run.

He was passing through the outdoor mall when his cell phone rang. "Fleming," he said.

"Walt." Fiona's voice. "It's not her blood. She's not cut anywhere I can see. Can you hear me? It's not her blood."

"Three-point-oh," Walt said. "Large-animal suture."

"The dog? He hurt the dog?"

He pushed himself faster. A teenage kid went by on Rollerblades.

Bursting through the doors, he alarmed the inn's desk clerk. He turned the corner and ran smack into the security station.

"Sheriff," he spit out breathlessly.

He walked briskly through the metal detector, tripping the alarm. A meaty hand grabbed him by the upper arm, spinning him around. Walt wrestled to break the grip.

"No weapons inside," the man said.

"No time," Walt said, out of breath. "The shooter's in there. Where's Dryer?"

"No weapons." The two men faced each other. Walt knew where this was going. His father had warned him. He removed his gun, held it out, and broke the man's grip. The gun fell. He took off, an agent close behind him.

Nine

Patrick Cutter watched from behind Elizabeth Shaler, savoring the moment. He saw a room of captivated faces and the unblinking eyes of the five television network news cameras given permission to record.

Liz Shaler spoke with authority and passion, animating her talk with her beautiful hands. "There is a growing abyss in this country, a divide between haves and have-nots that must finally be addressed. Those of us here today are fortunate to be in the former category, but that also puts us in a position of responsibility to have a critical impact on this country's future. An obligation for improvement. I see a need for moral certitude, yes, but administered with a compassion promised by the present administration but never delivered. It is time we stand up and say, 'If not me, who? If not now, when?' "

The audience erupted into applause. A good number jumped to their feet. Patrick allowed himself a smile.

Then he spotted a red-faced and out-of-breath Walt Fleming at the back of the room, and he knew he had trouble.

Walt paused only briefly at the door. Dryer's men were likely on orders to keep him out of this room. He searched for Nagler, for the dog, as he walked away from the doors and toward a corner where he could get a look back at the faces. Much of the crowd rose in applause, blocking his view of the room. Then he spotted his father straight ahead. His father spotted him and shook his head as if to say, "You'll never make it."

Ten

"We stand at a threshold," Shaler said from the dais, "a turning point where we can elect to go back or push forward. The choices have never been more clear. . . ."

Cutter watched as some heads turned with the sheriff's quick movement. Here was the very distraction he'd hoped to avoid—Dick O'Brien would hear about this! Shaler, too, took notice of the sheriff, angling her head slightly—looking for a possible sign. Now Dryer's two agents, flanking the stage, picked up on him as well.

Liz Shaler pressed on: "We will find solutions with friends from both sides of the aisle. But find them, we will! The best days still lie ahead."

More applause rippled through an increasingly divided crowd.

"It is no easy task what I propose. But I believe I am up to the challenge. Ladies and gentlemen, citizens of the United States, I come here today to humbly offer you my services, as a fellow, concerned citizen, a former educator, a litigator, and yes: as a woman." She paused and studied the crowd. "I offer you my candidacy for the president of the United States of America."

Walt continued searching the room for sight of Nagler. The crowd jumped to its feet. He saw nothing but frantic waving and excited faces.

He risked a look back: two of O'Brien's men, closing fast.

Walt reached Jerry and raised his voice over the thunderous cheering. "It's the blind guy . . . maybe the dog is concealing a piece. This is for real, Dad. You've got to go with me on this."

Walt met his father's questioning look with absolute conviction and confidence.

"You were right," Walt said. "They're coming to get me. And they took my piece."

"I'm with you," Jerry said.

"Okay. Sorry about this," Walt said. He reached inside his father's sport coat and took his gun.

As he spun around, there were Nagler and the dog, on the opposite end of the cavernous room.

Eleven

As the audience rose to its feet, Trevalian knelt and once again slipped the jogging bra in front of Callie's snout. As he did so, he spotted the sheriff immediately. Both men knew what was going to happen next.

Trevalian let go of the guide harness. He said, "Find it!" The dog took off into the thunderous crowd. Shaler stepped away from the lectern and began a series of bows. It was, for her, a beautiful moment.

He looked behind him: The cameras rolled. He plunged his hand into his coat pocket, his thumb hovering over the remote's button.

Twelve

Liz Shaler waved and bowed, her moment of glory upon her. Cameras flashed brightly. A news cameraman tried to part a seam down the standing crowd to get a better shot of the candidate. O'Brien's men hurried to cut this off.

Then one of the agents shouted, "GUN!" He pointed at Walt.

His counterpart dove to take down Elizabeth Shaler. But she had had her eye on Walt for the past few seconds. When she saw him with a gun in hand, she knew he'd been right all along. "W . . . A . . . L . . . T!" she screamed.

Walt took a step toward Nagler just before he heard someone else cry, "GUN!"

It never occurred to Walt that warning was

in response to *his* gun. Somehow Nagler had sewn a gun *inside* the dog as a means to secret the weapon through security—that was the picture in Walt's head. By now Nagler had removed the gun and intended to use it. Obviously, one of Dryer's men had been alert enough to see Nagler reach for it in his coat pocket.

What threw him off this notion, in those slow split seconds, was Nagler's calm composure, his keeping his hand in his pocket, and his uninterrupted attention out ahead of him—not looking at Shaler, but at something much lower in the room.

The dog . . .

At that moment, his father's profile entered his peripheral vision, coming in front of him. The man was running—a rare enough sight. He shouted, "Nooooo!" as he threw himself in front of Walt, who recoiled to avoid a collision.

A loud report of a gun.

Blood sprayed across Walt's face. His father was spun around by the force of the gunshot. He'd taken a bullet to protect Walt, and the two met eyes briefly as Jerry went down. He coughed out roughly, "Go!"

Screams and cries as the crowd panicked.

Walt checked the stage: Liz Shaler was pinned down by two agents.

As men and women stampeded toward the exits, he caught one last glimpse of Nagler: The man was still as a statue, his attention locked on the dog.

And there was the dog, nose to the carpet, as it roamed in illogical loops.

Sniffing . . .

Another look in Nagler's direction, but he was obscured by the crowd. His father, bleeding at his feet. The dog hot on a scent. And now he knew. . . .

"BOMB!" he shouted.

Thirteen

The dog shied around a fallen chair. Walt danced through a field of people lying on the floor and crawling under the tables. He lunged for the dog, caught a back leg. She snarled, snapped at him, and rolled away. But Walt got a piece of her collar, lost his purchase, and found his fingers wrapped tightly around something firm and thin. The dog yelped and threw Walt off, her legs in the air as she rolled away from him.

Walt saw a hastily stitched incision running up the dog's abdomen. Saw that he'd been holding a piece of lamp wire that ran from the incision to the dog's collar.

An image of the discarded box in Nagler's bathroom: ESS FENCE. He completed the crossword: *Wirel*ess Fence. A shock collar;

a battery carrying enough voltage to trigger a blasting cap.

Trevalian's hand inside his coat pocket . . .

Walt rose and dove again. A woman screamed, and the dog changed directions. Walt fell forward and hooked his fingertips around that wire. He pulled down hard. The dog cried out, twisted its neck, and bit Walt's arm. The wire broke free.

Walt dropped his father's gun and picked it back up.

Pandemonium as the two agents dragged Liz Shaler off the stage. But for Walt there was only Nagler in the room as the man feverishly pressed a remote device that failed to answer.

A group of fleeing guests obscured his view.

He glanced over at his father, balled up in pain on the carpet.

He looked back for Nagler.

Gone.

Fourteen

Trevalian's plan had been to escape out the service corridor, but being so close to the main doors, as the stampede of terrified guests approached, he went with the flow, using it as cover.

He was carried out and past the metal detector. The service corridor would be to his right. He turned in that direction, separating from those headed for the exit. He peeled off the facial hair and ditched the sunglasses, worked his arms out of the sport coat and dropped it into a chair. Now in the bar, he spotted an unmarked door to his right and turned toward it. The bartender shouted, "You can't go there!" But he did go there: through the door and a small room of two sinks and shelving, and from there, directly into the service corridor.

He headed out the first door marked EXIT.

The braying of angry protesters filled the air. They stood in the blinding sunlight behind sawhorse barriers marked SUN VALLEY POLICE DEPARTMENT. If there had once been cops there to support that line, they'd left at the sound of a gunshot.

He caught sight of black vehicles speeding off: Shaler and the Secret Service. The protesters charged forward, knocking down the barriers. Trevalian briefly stayed with the group, then broke away, hurrying across a patch of lawn toward his rental car, parked behind the adjacent dormitory.

He cut across the grass to the shouts of the protesters. "Free trade equals child slaves!"

He glanced back once instinctively. A man jumped from the loading dock. A blue uniform.

The sheriff.

Fifteen

If Nagler reached the art fair, already crowded with shoppers, Walt knew he'd lose him.

He considered taking a shot, but the man had wisely put himself between Walt and the fair.

Lose him to the art fair, or risk hitting an innocent bystander?

Following the man through a crowded parking lot, Walt ran hard to keep up. To his right, a line of trees blocked the parking lot from the inn. To his left: tennis courts. Straight ahead, the art fair.

His only hope was to drop the man ahead of the art fair. He angled to his right, through a line of parked cars, a wall of evergreens, and out onto a wide strip of lawn cloistered between the inn and the parking lot. In doing so, he lost sight of the suspect. Nagler had started out of the blocks at an incredible pace, but that was not sustainable at six thousand feet above sea level. Not without weeks of training. Walt paralleled him.

At the end of the parking lot, also the end of the line of evergreens, was an access road that headed out of the lot to the southeast. It dropped down a hill. A shot taken in that direction presented the least chance of wounding a civilian.

He'd have one shot, maybe two.

Ten trees . . . nine . . . eight . . .

He envisioned each step, each motion.

two . . . one . . .

He turned and slid on the grass. Lowered his right knee. Bent his left knee for support. Braced his left elbow on his left knee. Hunched forward to sight the weapon. He picked up the target, a running blur, led him slightly, and squeezed the trigger.

Sixteen

Trevalian felt a burning in his right knee and then heard the shot. Too late. His right leg collapsed and he tumbled forward in an ungainly and painful somersault. His head dulled. He rolled, pulled himself up toward standing. He went down again. Blood everywhere. His leg on fire. He heard screaming.

Then the sole of a boot stomped down on his blown knee, and the pain darkened his vision.

He found himself looking up into the barrel of a gun. The sheriff was out of breath and looking down on him.

Seventeen

At 2 P.M. Jerry's eyes opened.

Walt sat in a formed fiberglass chair facing his father's hospital bed. Like his nephew before him, Jerry was hooked up to every kind of wire and tube.

"You're in recovery," Walt said, not sure his father heard him. "They operated on you. Got the bullet. Cleaned you up. Your lung's collapsed and your right shoulder's going to need some physical therapy, but all in all you should be pretty happy that those private security boys can't shoot for shit."

He thought he saw the twinge of a smile and he realized Jerry had heard him, had understood. Jerry tried to say something, but it came out as more of a dry wheeze. Walt slipped an ice chip between his father's lips. He'd never seen Jerry sick, had never seen him incapacitated. It felt as if this had to be someone else.

His father croaked out, "The shooter?"

Walt nodded. "Liz Shaler is fine. I'm fine. No guests were killed."

His father shut his eyes. A moment later he was asleep.

"Sheriff?"

Walt turned to see Special Agent in Charge Adam Dryer's acne-scarred face. "Suspect is out of surgery and has been moved to his room."

"Thanks."

"Doc says no visitors for four to six hours. But we'll get a crack at him later tonight. FYI."

"I'll be here," Walt said. "I'm going to stick around."

"Yeah, sure," he said.

"Hell of a thing your father did."

"Yes, it was."

"Maybe saved us all."

"Maybe so."

An apology hung between them, but it didn't come.

"Later," Dryer said. The door hissed shut behind him as he left.

"What a prick," his father said, one eye creeping open and finding his son.

Walt laughed, surprised at how good it felt.

Eighteen

Trevalian opened his eyes to the sound of beeping.

He noted the IV tubing and the finger clip monitoring his vitals. The bedside curtain was pulled back, revealing a private room, its wall-mounted television dark. No phone. Blackout curtains pulled. He wore a hospital gown, white with little blue daisies. They had a catheter in him.

Alive, he thought. This was followed immediately by: *escape.* He knew how this would go down, because he'd done a few of these jobs himself. Eighty thousand patients died unnecessarily in U.S. hospitals each year. Not all of those deaths were the hospitals' fault. His being in federal custody was now somebody's worst nightmare.

Phone calls were being made. Arrangements. He'd be dead by morning.

Escape, he thought for the second time, taking in all the medical equipment, his wrapped leg, the elevated bed, the room. The temporary absence of handcuffs suggested the nurses needed to move or monitor him during this early going; it wouldn't last long. He was no doubt heavily guarded from the outside. With a bum leg and no weapons, he was his own biggest obstacle. A sitting duck. If he didn't make a phone call within a few hours . . .

He looked around the room. So little to work with. Some tubes, a few machines. Too many pillows to count. He had several IV stands to work with, but they weren't going to measure up against Tasers and semi-automatic weapons.

He strained to retrieve the purple plastic tub sealed in stretch film from the adjacent end table. There was a washbowl within the tub. A toothbrush and toothpaste. A comb. No razor.

He wasn't going to win any footraces. For all he knew he couldn't put weight on the knee. He was trapped. They'd caught him.

He couldn't begin to accept that.

If he asked, they would never bring him a razor. He needed for them to bring him one *without* his asking. He spent twenty minutes lying there contemplating this dilemma before spotting the communications jacks in the wall marked EKG.

He reached for and pushed the button clipped to the stainless steel side rail, summoning a nurse. Three minutes later, his room door opened, and a matronly woman in blue scrubs appeared. Behind her, looking in briefly, was one of the sheriff's men.

Trevalian told the woman, "My chest . . . I'm having this pain . . ." He tapped his sternum. "Right in here."

"Okay," she said kindly, though both concerned and afraid of him. "I'll let the doctor know. We'll take care of it."

She knocked to leave the room. This was a twist he hadn't expected: The door locked from the hallway side.

Nineteen

"His name is Milav Trevalian," Agent Dryer said to Walt from the other side of the front booth of the Mobile Command Center, currently parked twenty yards from the emergency room. "We have very little on him at present. U.S. Attorney's office is stalling us, basically because it's a Sunday and everyone in Washington is out on a yacht or a golf course. My guess is nothing much happens until tomorrow morning."

"But we question him later tonight," Walt said. It was pushing eight o'clock.

"With the doctor's permission, yes."

"I've got him on capital murder charges—the singer, the woman we found in his bathtub. Boise is sending up forensics to process that scene."

"That's between you and the AUSA. I have no idea how they'll want to charge him. Listen, I gave you a shout because the AG wants to see you. If you're going to do that, it has to be right now. She's at the house."

"I can't leave," Walt said.

"Understood. I'll pass it along." Dryer pushed some papers aside. "How is he?"

"Going to be okay."

"He saved your life."

Walt lowered his head, the man's words resonating. His uniform shirt was speckled with his father's blood. At one time he'd thought he'd spend his life hating the man. How quickly that had passed. He needed time to decompress.

"Hell of a thing you did, too," Dryer said.

"It came together. It was a group effort."

"The hell it was, but it's good of you to say so."

Walt motioned to the back of the bus. "You mind? I've got some clean shirts back there."

"Help yourself. It's your vehicle, Sheriff." He grabbed hold of Walt's arm as Walt passed. "The dog . . . how the hell's the dog?"

"We're awaiting a bomb squad tech from

Salt Lake." He checked his watch. "Probably here by now. He'll work with our vet."

"A fucking dog . . . ," Dryer said, sounding exasperated. "Right through our checkpoint." Knowing he had failed and that at some point this was coming back onto him, knowing Walt's earlier warnings would come back to haunt him.

"Yeah," Walt said. "How about that?"

Twenty

A different nurse—young and overweight, in loose-fitting blue scrubs—wheeled in the EKG trolley.

She maintained a professional air as she asked some questions, explained the EKG, and then helped him to sit up. She got his arms out of the nightgown and folded it across his lap. Trevalian scanned the contents of the cart.

He had a chest thick with brown hair, but it was his nine scars that caught and held her attention. Her eyes jumped clinically one to the next, and he could imagine her explaining them to herself. Two bullet wounds, three stabbings, and four lacerations. She dispensed some shaving cream from a can and applied it to several areas on his chest.

She then shaved him, rinsing the razor between strokes in the purple tub of warm water that she'd filled in the washroom.

When she was done, she took a towel to him and told him they'd wait a minute for the skin to dry completely.

"Could I trouble you for a refill?" He handed her the plastic pitcher of ice water from his bedside.

"No problem." She headed into the washroom.

Trevalian slipped his hand through the side rail and snatched a disposable razor from a box on the lower shelf of the EKG trolley. He slipped it under the covers, between his legs—let her find it there—and lay back on the pillows. He'd spiked his heart rate and pumped up his adrenaline, wondering if that might skew his EKG.

The nurse returned with the water, poured some, and actually held the cup for him as he sipped from the straw. *Like taking candy from a baby,* he thought.

Twenty-one

Trevalian waited for the dinner tray to be removed and the hospital room door to shut, and the clicking of the dead bolt in the doorjamb. He checked the clock: 8:06 P.M. The nurses had been checking on him every two hours.

He administered one last dose of painkiller from the electronic box attached to his bed and went to work disconnecting the IV tube. They had removed the catheter in the late afternoon and were no longer monitoring his vital signs, so he had little concern of alerting the nurses' station to his activities. He lowered the side rail, unhooked his leg, swung it over the bed, and waited for the rush of blood and pain to his head to subside. Then, one-handing the IV stand, he prodded the ceiling tile, and to his relief, it moved. He was reminded of placing Rafe Nagler's body bag into just such a hiding place at the Salt Lake City airport. How interesting, he thought, that things should come full circle like this.

He moved the panel out of the way and slid it to the side, but only far enough to look vaguely out of place. The key to any ruse was psychology—to push and pull the adversary, allowing him his own discoveries. Trevalian wasn't going to make this too obvious.

He covered the disposable razor with a towel and crushed it against the vinyl tile floor, making sure to pick up every last speck of broken plastic. He then removed a piece of adhesive tape from his arm and taped one of the razor's two narrow blades to the end of a pen that read "St. Jude's Community Hospital." He tested it and added yet another piece of tape for reinforcement. Now it behaved like an X-Acto knife, the blade holding strongly to the end of the pen. A tool. A weapon.

He listened carefully for any indication his

crushing of the razor had been overheard. Silence.

He checked the clock one last time, and then continued his work.

Twenty-two

Tommy Brandon sat across from room 26 at St. Jude's Hospital. "Furnishings compliments of Christopher Guest and Jamie Lee Curtis" read a plaque immediately below the door number.

"You ever see her in that one with Arnold?" Brandon asked the Secret Service agent, who had the chair closer to the hospital room door. This man was technically in charge. He was also unresponsive. Brandon continued, "*True Lies*? Jamie Lee. That little dance she did. Funny. Really funny. And sexy? Come on!"

Still the agent failed to acknowledge him.

"This is what they call the technical integration of law enforcement agencies, right?"

Brandon said sarcastically. "The politicians are fucking brilliant."

"Put a sock in it, will you?" said the agent. "We start out like this, it's going to be a long night."

Both agents saw a nurse approaching. Brandon immediately looked away, keeping his eyes on the exit door at the end of the hallway; the two men had the entire hallway covered.

"He had an EKG not an hour ago," the agent said to the approaching nurse. "How often are you going to check on him?"

"Just doing my rounds, Officer. Doing my job, same as you."

"It's Special Agent," the man corrected. "I was just making conversation."

"And I was just making conversation back."

"We've got to search you," the man advised her.

"I know."

Brandon did not take his eyes off the far door. "He just came on shift. You'll have to forgive him. He doesn't realize you've already been through this three times, Maddie."

"It's all right. Let's get it over with, please." She raised her hands out like wings. She told the agent, "You get fresh with me, and your senior officer will hear about it."

"Special Agent in Charge," the man said, correcting her again.

"He's still going to hear about it."

He patted her down—gently and carefully—and cleared her. "Okay. You can go inside."

"Gee, thanks," she said.

She waited for the agent to unlock the door. She went inside, and he relocked it behind her.

"It's Sunday," Brandon told him. "No one likes getting a call on a Sunday."

"Every day's the same to me," the agent said.

"That's kind of sad, you ask me," Brandon fired back. With the room door shut, Brandon was free to look in whatever direction he wanted. He chose to stare down the agent.

"But no one did ask you," the agent said, determined to have the last word. Brandon could have kept playing, but decided against it. It *was* going to be a long night, and the sheriff seemed determined to keep him here—and away from his trailer—for as long as possible.

Twenty-three

Only seconds after the nurse entered the hospital room there was a pounding on the door—not the casual knock that Brandon had grown used to but a frantic, full-fisted effort. Her voice barely made it through the thick door, but it sounded as if she was in a panic.

Brandon and the agent took positions, both with their weapons drawn, and the agent unlocked the door. He stepped back, prepared for a hostage situation where Trevalian was using the nurse to startle them.

She was red-faced, wide-eyed, and overly excited.

"He's gone!" she said. "The bed . . . I checked the bathroom . . ."

Brandon glanced at the agent, then

punched his radio and rattled off several codes, relaying an emergency. It was quickly worked out that the agent would go in, but without his weapon.

Brandon pulled the nurse out of the doorway. "Get gone," he said.

The agent pulled open the door. The bed was empty. He edged toward the closet and slid the door across. Empty. Glanced under the bed. Nothing. Moved cautiously toward the bathroom, the door standing open. Checked the reflection in the mirror first— the bathroom appeared empty. He yanked the shower curtain back. No one. Then he caught it out of the corner of his eye: a ceiling panel over the bed. Slightly askew. Not like the others.

"Clear!" he shouted. He returned to the hallway, where several more deputies had gathered. He used hand signals to direct Brandon to follow. Together they entered the room. He pointed to the ceiling panel. Brandon climbed onto the end table and popped the ceiling panel out of its frame. He poked his head inside and squeezed a flashlight past his chin.

"Shit!" he exclaimed, his voice dampened. "Looks like a panel over the bathroom goes up into a crawl space or something." He jumped down and repeated the procedure from the countertop in the bathroom. He broke away several of the flimsily hung ceiling tiles, stretched onto his toes. "Affirmative. There's egress here." He ducked out of the ceiling and looked down. "He could be fucking anywhere by now."

Twenty-four

Walt had spent the last hour in the Mobile Command Center writing up a summary of events. His eyes strayed to a seating chart thumbtacked to a corkboard.

It was a large sheet, showing tables and seating arrangements for the Shaler brunch. Of all the seats, one was marked with an X.

Dryer felt his presence. "What?"

"That's the seating plan for Liz Shaler's talk," Walt suggested.

"Yes it is," Dryer agreed.

"Why the X on Stuart Holms?" Walt asked.

"We were reaching. On the off chance the contract on the AG came from someone attending the conference, we looked at who failed to attend. His was the only empty seat."

"And the initials by his name?" Walt asked. "Explain it to me."

"Exactly what it says: meal preference. Do you want a regular meal, vegetarian meal, do you have your own personal chef, are you allergic to wheat . . . You know how these people are."

Walt referred to his notebook and flipped back through the pages. He asked, "And what's that date printed down there by the file name? Bottom of the sheet?"

Dryer leaned closer. "Six-six. June sixth. What is it, Sheriff?"

"Stuart Holms uses a personal chef. Name of Raphael," he said, consulting his notebook. "Won't eat a bite if it's not prepared by Raphael. He's fanatic about it."

"Well, that's Stuart Holms's seat, and he's down for a regular meal. What's it matter? I think you need some rest."

"What it means, I think, is that six weeks ago—on June sixth—Holms already knew he wouldn't be attending Liz Shaler's talk."

"And so, why bother with meal preference if he's not going to be there?"

Walt nodded. "Maybe. Yeah."

Dryer did a double-take, first looking at the seating plan, then back at Walt. His brow creased, tightening his eyes. "Naa . . ." But he didn't sound as convinced as a minute earlier.

A knock on the coach's door was followed by the big head of Dick O'Brien. "Sheriff, you got a minute?"

Twenty-five

Walt climbed out of the Mobile Command Center wearing a fresh black T-shirt that read SEARCH AND RESCUE on the back. O'Brien apparently never stopped sweating.

"Hey there," O'Brien said.

"Hey there, yourself," Walt answered.

"How is he—your dad, I mean?"

"Came through the operation with flying colors."

"Good to hear."

"Yes, it is," Walt said.

"My guy . . . who shot him . . . It was meant for you: the gun and all."

"That's comforting."

"I just mean he was doing his job. If you can go easy on him . . ."

"We could make a trade, you and I," Walt proposed.

"Could we?"

"Must have steamed him, her taking to his brother all over again."

"Don't go there, Walt."

"Jealousy is a powerful motivator. A man like Patrick gets anything he wants, right? But when your rival turns out to be your own brother, what then?"

"This is a big mistake."

"*Was* a big mistake. His mistake," Walt said. "You helped me. On the bridge. Why'd you do that?"

"Don't know what you're talking about."

"Let's say your boss killed her—some kind of accident. Lost his temper. But who took her down there and put her in that cage? Who did that to her? Who was it carried her up the Hill Trail and dumped her?" He studied O'Brien, who seemed to be sweating more profusely. "It was his trying to implicate Danny that pushed you over the top, wasn't it? Danny was a good fit for it, and you knew that's how I'd see it. That Danny would go down for it."

O'Brien remained tight-lipped.

"You must have also known there wouldn't be near enough evidence to prove any of this—it would come down to a jury trial. And if Danny went down for it, he'd go down and that would be that."

"I wish I had the slightest idea of what you're talking about."

"The thing I don't get is the workout clothes. She'd already run that day. She wouldn't have gone running again. So you— or someone else—had to get her into running clothes. It had to be running clothes to sell that she'd been out Adam's Gulch. But where'd they come from, those running clothes? Did she keep some clothes at Patrick's? Was that it? Something she could jump into if his wife came home early? I don't get the clothes."

"I'm glad your dad is doing better." He turned to break off the conversation, then turned back again. "I've been within an arm's reach of Patrick for four solid days, Walt. That's the God's truth."

"You give me Cutter, and any of your guys involved in the cover-up will walk."

Brandon's frantic voice called out a series of codes over the radio.

Walt went running right past O'Brien, clutching his gun belt to keep it from slapping, wishing he'd had more time to see if the man had been ready to make a deal.

Twenty-six

Walt paced Trevalian's empty room, Brandon standing in the doorway, watching. He checked the windows—all fixed glass, none broken. He wandered into and then back out of the bathroom. He approached the closet and slid open the doors. Walt had only glanced in there the first time. Now he returned for a more thorough look. They'd been searching the grounds for the past hour, with no sign of the suspect.

"There's a ceiling hatch leads up into the joists," Brandon said, breaking the silence. "Up over the bathroom. Three of the rooms on this floor have similar access."

"Climbing with that knee of his. You think?" Walt said.

He squatted and looked beneath the

raised bed. He turned over a pillow, then another. He lifted the bedding and peered under the sheets. "This guy is seriously wounded, and he's clever. If we're thinking he climbed out through the roof, then you can bet he didn't."

He touched another pillow, then spun around sharply on his heels, facing the closet again. "You went through all this?" he asked, indicating the closet.

Brandon answered, "There's nothing in there, unless he's hiding in a drawer."

Walt reached up into the closet and pulled out the pillows. As he did so, he said, "Did you happen to notice that three of the pillows on the bed—the ones that were under his knee—were stripped of their pillowcases? Do you pay attention to *anything* other than the nurses?"

Brandon fumed but knew better than to answer.

Walt opened the end of one of the pillowcases taken from the closet, then looked up disapprovingly at Brandon and shook its contents onto the floor, discovering big chunks of foam and fabric. A section of a zipper. He hurried now and shook out the other pillowcase as well, spilling out similar contents. "Help me out," Walt said, spinning back around and lowering the hospital bed's side rail. The two dragged the mattress off the bed and flipped it over, upside down, onto the floor.

The bottom of the mattress had been cut away with something sharp into a human form—head, shoulders, legs, arms. Three sections of clear tubing had fallen to the floor.

"He was in the room all along," Walt said, "faceup, under the mattress. Breathing tubes," he said, picking them up. "In here the whole time we were *out there* looking for him." Furious at him now, Walt shouted, "One officer *always* protects the crime scene! Jesus Christ, Tommy."

He stormed out of the room, already putting himself into the contrarian mind of Trevalian. Where would he go? How could he hope to escape the valley? Was there someone helping him?

Then it came to him: Dryer's men and most of his deputies had been deployed to search the hospital, top to bottom.

He hoped he wasn't too late.

Twenty-seven

Trevalian had found his way into town on the most direct route available, and one he was quite certain the cops wouldn't think to search or roadblock: the bike path. He'd stoved in the head of a deputy who stood guard outside the bottom of the hospital fire stairs, and had left him unconscious and stripped of his clothes, a sock down his throat, his hands cuffed behind him. He had the man's cell phone and now wore his uniform, though the shoes were a size small and his feet were killing him. A wheelchair had gotten him most of the way into town along the bike path, while fifty yards to his right cop cars raced up and down the highway. He'd ditched the chair at the turn to the ski slopes. When the painkillers wore off, he was going to be in serious trouble.

From somewhere near the center of town, he called the memorized number and left a page when the recorded message told him to do so. He hoped he wasn't too late. If a contract had gone out on him, it might not be rescinded.

He waited. Five minutes passed. Ten.

Finally the phone rang and he answered the call.

"Go ahead," a male voice said.

"The engagement was broken off," he said.

"So I heard. Most disappointing."

"I had a little problem getting away from the church, but that's behind me now. I'm free."

"Free?"

"Yes. But my in-laws are never going to let me out of this town. I could use a place to stay."

"That's the problem with being single," the man said. "You'll think of something."

"I need your help with this."

"I'm afraid not. You failed to consummate the marriage."

At that moment, a helicopter passed overhead. At first Trevalian had trouble hearing, and hoped the contact hadn't hung up. But then, much to his surprise, the *same* sound of the helicopter was in his other ear: the ear pressed to the phone.

He scanned the sky and spotted the flashing red and white lights as it flew to the far end of town. It hovered and then landed halfway up Knob Hill. It looked to be a private home the size of a country club.

In the phone he heard nothing. The call had disconnected.

A moment later it rang again and he answered. There was no sound of the helicopter in the receiver, and he wondered if he'd actually heard it coming from the phone, or not.

"The bride is still in town," the voice said. "Her father's place. Try to work things out with her. If you're successful, contact me again. I'll see what I can do to assist you."

Trevalian hung up wondering if he could walk any farther.

Twenty-eight

Walt reached the emergency room at a run. A Secret Service agent guarded the door.

"Dryer?" Walt asked, not slowing.

"Special Agent in Charge Dryer is in the Command Center."

"Tell him it's Shaler. He's going for Shaler."

"I'm not your message boy!" the agent shouted after him.

Walt jumped into the Cherokee—and sped away. Five minutes later he was negotiating the streets of Ketchum. He parked uphill a block from Shaler's house, pulled the shotgun from the dashboard, and double-checked its load. He realized too late that his protective vest had come back from cleaning and was still in his office.

The crickets chimed. A dog barked in the

distance. The smell of wood smoke lingered in the air. He moved stealthily in shadow, avoiding the streetlight, quickly closing the distance to Shaler's house. This was the identical route he'd ridden as a pedal patrolman eight years earlier, and for some reason he thought of his brother and how much he missed him. He snuck down a driveway and past a neighbor's house. He slipped over a rail fence that bordered Shaler's driveway, his heart tight, his breath short.

Procedures called for him to wait for backup: Dryer's men couldn't be far behind. His earpiece carried the monotonous prattle of his dispatcher's voice. He needed silence. So he called in his location and went off-air.

He approached Shaler's kitchen door stealthily but not wanting Dryer's sentries to mistake him for an intruder. He paused and studied the layout, looking carefully for signs of the agent guarding the back door.

No one.

Adding to his confusion, the interior lights were out. This went against protocol. The place should have been lit like a Christmas tree. He carefully made his way to the back door. His shoe hit something slippery right as his nose picked up the metallic smell of blood.

He one-handed the shotgun and checked the shrubbery with his Maglite. Twin soles faced him. The agent had been clobbered. His head was bleeding—a good sign. He was out cold.

Walt moved quietly through the door and into the kitchen. The all too familiar hallway stretched before him.

Trevalian would have taken the agent's gun. *No vest,* he reminded himself.

He crept down the hallway, the flashlight off but held beneath the shotgun.

The first door hung open: a small bedroom. Empty. The study door, to the right, also open. The room empty.

His eye caught a glint on the carpet. He reached down and touched it: sticky. Blood. It could have been an agent's, or Shaler's, but something told him Trevalian's stitches had popped. He worked down the hallway, passed a bathroom and a linen closet.

One door remained: Shaler's bedroom. Consumed by his memory of eight years earlier, his courage waned as his scar pulsed with pain.

He twisted the head of the flashlight,

kicked open the door, and stood to the side, expecting a shot.

Then, an enormous crash of glass. Someone—something—going out a window. He dove into the bedroom, the shotgun pressed tightly against his shoulder. Looked left . . . right. *Clear.* Belly-crawled to the louvered doors of the closet. *Clear.*

Walt got to his knees. Shaler lay in the bed, absolutely still. But then the flashlight caught her: It wasn't Shaler but a mannequin.

A safe room? A panic room?

He kicked some errant glass from the broken window and climbed outside.

A man in uniform—a sheriff's deputy—was well up the hill, keeping to shadow. He dragged a leg behind him.

Walt heard sirens approaching.

"Halt!" Walt yelled out at the top of his lungs.

Trevalian ducked into shadow.

Police cruisers and sheriff's vehicles slid around both street corners nearly simultaneously—behind Walt and in front of him. They stood off, aware of the limited range of the shotgun. Their overhead racks threw off colors as two searchlights were aimed onto

Walt from opposite directions—each blinding the other car and leaving Walt a fuzzy, glowing image between them.

Walt was no longer wearing his uniform shirt, and the word was out that a sheriff's uniform had been stolen.

"Hands in the air!" a megaphone voice called out.

Walt dropped the shotgun, shouting, "It's me!" He turned to face his own sheriff's vehicle.

"Stand down!" Brandon's voice called out to the Ketchum police car. "It's Sheriff Fleming!"

Amplified shouting back and forth, with Walt caught in the middle. He knew the quickest way to resolve this was to lie down on the asphalt until the Ketchum cop got it right.

Doing so now, Walt peered into the shadows, wondering if they'd lost Trevalian. Again.

Twenty-nine

Trevalian arrived at the mansion's front door sweating, bleeding, and out of breath. A man on the run. He pounded hard on the twin doors, pushed the intercom button repeatedly, and then pounded on the door again. He looked behind him, back toward the gate, then returned to pounding on the door.

A man came from the side of the house. He wore a blue blazer and a scowl. He held a gun and was backed up by a second man behind him. Who now appeared to Trevalian's left.

"Hands on your head. Step away from the door. Good. Hands where I can see them. Okay . . . on your knees—"

"I can't. My knee . . . Listen," Trevalian said

frantically, "you gotta get me out of here. We've got to do this someplace else. You know who I am? I'm being pursued." He lay down on the driveway. "We have to hurry, fellas. The owner of this house . . . Ask him. But make it quick."

Less than a minute later he was loaded into a golf cart and driven around back— through a gate in a ten-foot-high fence— and escorted into what appeared to be a guesthouse. It was all hardwood floors and Stickley furniture. Indirect lighting and lots of glass. The city of Ketchum spread out below, just past the silhouette of the helicopter sitting on its concrete pad on the edge of a vast lawn. Four security guards kept their distance. The man to speak to him wore a Tommy Bahama floral shirt and pale trousers. He offered Trevalian a bottle of water. Trevalian gulped it down.

"So talk," this man said.

"Not to you," Trevalian said. "With all due respect. Him, or nobody. And if you kill me, then the three letters that are in a mailbox in town get picked up in the morning and go to the sheriff, the newspaper, and CNN. They contain all the details about this job—the e-mails, the payments. You think anything is totally untraceable? You want to take that chance? I get what I want out of this, and I give you the location of the mailbox and you put a little lighter fluid down it, and no one's the wiser. And if you think you'll beat the mailbox's location out of me—give it your best shot."

He chugged some more water, draining the bottle.

Tommy Bahama left the building. He returned more than ten minutes later with yet another security guard—that made five—and a man in his sixties wearing a white terrycloth robe and leather slippers.

"Mr. Holms," Trevalian said. "I'd stand, but the knee's a little worse for wear."

"I believe you've made a mistake," Stuart Holms said, waiting as Tommy Bahama helped him into a seat.

"The mistake was yours—or whoever called me back. The package was not at home. You had bad intel. There was a mannequin in her bed."

"You've got the wrong man," Holms said.

"I'm a little short on time, Mr. Holms. The sheriff is out there looking for me. Secret Service. Police. We haven't got long. Elizabeth Shaler cost you. Payback is payback. I understand that. If I've made a mistake, then turn me over to them. If, on the other hand, I've not, then we should be talking about me spending a few days in your panic room, or catching a ride in your helicopter."

Stuart Holms regarded him with contempt. "Then we wait for the police."

"Hide me until they drop the roadblocks," Trevalian said. "Use your position, your power, your attorneys—whatever you've got—to keep me well hidden. Get me to someplace like Reno or Portland. That's it. No money. No extortion. I have a reputation to protect. We both do."

Holms exchanged a look with Tommy Bahama—impossible to read.

"The location of the mailbox," Tommy Bahama said.

"Not yet," Trevalian said.

"How do you know we won't kill you once you've given us the location of the mailbox?" Holms asked.

"How do you know I'll give you the right mailbox? What if it's a UPS drop box that doesn't get picked up until six P.M. tomorrow night? They can't keep roadblocks up indefinitely. I don't intend to be here past six P.M. tomorrow."

"You didn't post any letter," Holms said.

"You can play that card if you want."

"Thought it all through, have you?" Holms could no longer sit still. He came out of his chair and paced.

"That's what you hired me for. Tell me otherwise."

He stopped in front of Trevalian, glaring.

"It was the helicopter that got you," Trevalian explained. "I heard the helicopter over the phone. How many guys have their own helicopter in this town?"

"More than you'd think."

"Six P.M. tomorrow, and then you're gone," Holms stated. "And I'll want those letters."

The security guys all touched their ears at once.

"Perimeter alarms," one of them said.

With his finger to his ear, Tommy Bahama nodded. "It's a fucking army."

Stuart Holms growled at Tommy Bahama. "Tell me you searched him for a wire."

Bahama grimaced and looked over at the lead security guard, who stared back vacantly, dumbstruck.

Trevalian casually unbuttoned the top two buttons of his shirt, revealing the tiny microphone taped to his shaved chest. "I was a little slow on this bum leg. Business is business. Am I right, Mr. Holms?"

"Shoot him!" Holms shouted to the paralyzed Tommy Bahama.

The door crashed open and in charged a SWAT team, all shouting at once for hands in the air.

The third man through the door was Sheriff Walt Fleming. He was grinning.

MONDAY

1 A.M.

One

They separated the suspects. Stuart Holms was confined to the Situation Room, the small conference room down the hall from Walt's office. Emil Guyot, Holms's director of security, a man outfitted in Tommy Bahama casual wear, was given the coffee room, a closet-sized kitchen that held a beat-up aluminum-legged table for two in the corner.

Adam Dryer had no jurisdictional authority to question anyone, and with the general consensus being that Stuart Holms and his attorneys would find some way to get him out of lockup within the next few hours, and certainly by morning, for Walt it all came down to these two interviews.

He sucked down what remained of lukewarm coffee. Dryer nursed a milk tea, but kept looking into the cup, his acne-scoured face snarled in disapproval. They occupied Walt's small office, overcrowded with stacks of journals piled on the floor and some backcountry gear crammed into the far corner. Dryer sat facing Walt's desk.

"Brandon!" Walt called out, his voice echoing down the hall.

His deputy arrived promptly, the only person in the office who didn't look completely exhausted at 1 A.M. "Sheriff?"

"Shut the door," Walt said.

Brandon closed the office door and stepped inside. Walt did not offer him the only remaining chair. He lowered his voice, despite the fact that both Holms and Guyot were down the hall behind closed doors, each being guarded by a deputy. "I want you to find me a plaster cast, a boot impression, in the evidence room. I'm thinking the Thompson case, or maybe the Ramone arson. Adult shoe size, no matter what. I want it in an evidence bag marked 'Hill Trail, Adams Gulch.' Date it yesterday: Saturday."

"Got it," Brandon said.

"And I need a contact lens. Find someone out there who doesn't mind making a sacrifice for the cause. The office will buy 'em a new one. Now here's the important part: Julie has a whole rainbow of highlighters in her desk. I want to use the blue highlighter to make a small dot on the side of the contact lens. Not too small, not too big. You got all that?"

"Shoe impression. Contact lens," Brandon repeated.

"Go on. And close the door behind you."

Brandon left them alone.

"I don't follow," Dryer said, once they were in privacy.

"The AUSA out of Boise isn't going to get up here until tomorrow around noon," Walt said, referring to the assistant United States attorney. "You and I both know that Stuart Holms will have four or five attorneys around him by that time—most from out of state—and that what we caught on Trevalian's wire, while incriminating, and enough to give us probable cause, may not carry the day in court."

"I'm no legal scholar," Dryer said.

"We have Trevalian's use of one of my deputies' cell phone—he stole it at the hospital—that may be able to be connected to an incoming call he received. If we can confirm that call was from Guyot, then we have a substantially stronger case against them, and we took a cell phone off Guyot. Cloned or not, that could be the smoking gun we need."

"I can hear in your voice that you're doubting all this," Dryer said.

"Holms is a shrewd businessman. You hear words like 'tenacious' and 'ruthless.' I have to think that if Guyot's involved, and I believe he is, that Holms has promised him the moon if anything ever went wrong. Now it has. You can bet the two of them have coached each other, rehearsed, and worked through all possibilities, including this one: arrest. They're following a plan that's been in place for at least six weeks—we know that from the Shaler seating plan. Maybe six months. They're too well prepared on the Shaler front. They know what to expect, what's coming. My one hope is to end-run them before the attorneys get involved."

"Fucking attorneys."

"How are your acting skills?" Walt asked.

"With a baby face like this?" Dryer asked. Even a weary smile did nothing to improve his gangster looks.

Two

"I'm not speaking until I have representation," Stuart Holms announced from the far side of the conference table. He looked at home, as if this were another of his boardrooms.

"You just spoke," Dryer said, "but I get what you mean." He sat across from Holms, who'd been given time back at the estate to lose the terrycloth robe and don a pair of slacks and a plaid shirt. He wore loafers with no socks. He looked old.

Dryer's chair fronted a corkboard where Walt had had the Shaler seating plan hung prior to Holms's arrival. The man had been facing it now for the past ten minutes.

"The thing about businessmen like you:

They're always trying to save money, conserve resources."

A tape recorder ran on the corner of the table. Stuart Holms could barely take his eyes off it. He said nothing. He seemed to be working hard to keep contempt off his face, but it was a losing battle.

"The sheriff has an interesting theory. You want to hear it? I'll take that as a yes. It's a little far-out for me—his theory. But he's convinced Mr. Guyot has a lot more to lose than you, and so he's starting there. With Mr. Guyot. Down the hall. The point being that one of you will deal. You think you won't, but of course you will. Everyone goes into this thinking they won't deal. And whoever deals first rolls on the other guy, and then that other guy is . . . pardon my French . . . fucked."

Dryer sipped from his tea, and gave it that same look of disgust. "If you spend the night here, don't ask for the tea."

"I'll be home within the hour," Holms said.

"A Sunday night, early Monday actually, in July? You think? You could be right, I suppose." He sampled the tea again; same result. He said, "So here's the thing. Have you

had a chance to look at this seating plan behind me?"

Holms looked up and gave the impression
this was the first time he'd paid any attention to it.

"You know why we got that out to take a
look at it? Because we wondered if any of
Cutter's invited guests had missed the
Shaler brunch. Because there could be two
reasons for that: Someone was sick, or had
a scheduling conflict; or someone wanted
to avoid being present when the bomb
they'd arranged to kill Shaler went off. And,
as you can see by the X's, only two people
missed the talk: you and your late wife."

"You should be ashamed of yourself."

"This is the sheriff we're talking about,
but your point is taken. Anyway . . . the
sheriff said something about a guy named
Raphael. Your chef, I believe?"

Holms did a very good imitation of being
bored by all this. Dryer knew differently—he
had his eye on a vein in the man's neck. His
pulse was elevated, his eyes dilated, and he
was growing increasingly restless. Walt's
emphasis had been on taking away the
man's sense of control. It seemed to be
working, Dryer thought.

"He said how you don't eat anything that isn't prepared by this guy Raphael. And I suppose that's a personal thing, and I've got no comment, although my personal chef is a guy named McDonald, but I doubt the two know each other. So, anyway, the problem for the sheriff is this seating chart, prepared back in June, that has you down for the regular meal. No Raphael. And I've got to admit, he has a point: It seems to suggest you knew back in June that you wouldn't be attending the Shaler brunch."

Holms glanced up at the seating chart. Then his eyes darted to meet Dryer's before once more landing on the chart. Wisely, he chose not to comment. The blue bead on his neck was growing, and beating wildly. His Adam's apple jumped as he tried to swallow.

"I figure—or rather the sheriff does—that you wanted to save Raphael in case the bomb took out the kitchen help. So you didn't book him. Why lose a good chef? Here's where it gets a little extreme, even for me," Dryer continued. "The sheriff believes not only that you killed your wife—or had her killed—but that you planned it far enough in advance to make sure it gave you the ultimate excuse not to attend the Shaler brunch. Who was going to question a grieving widower? But that's where the irony comes in: because here I am questioning you. So maybe that part didn't work so well."

Holms blinked rapidly but still managed to say nothing. Dryer smiled openly, well aware that when contrasted with his acne-scarred cheeks, he looked menacing when doing so.

"Here's what may interest you, Mr. Holms. It did me. The sheriff has no intention of pursuing Trevalian and you for the attempted assassination of Elizabeth Shaler. That's why I'm here—I'm federal, he's state. He's leaving all that to my office and the AUSA to sort out. He's focused on one thing and one thing only: the murder of your wife. That was done on his turf. He says you're good for it—something about a fingerprint developed on a contact lens—and who am I to argue? It's his show. If he wants to make an ass out of himself, who am I to interfere?"

Holms endeavored to stay calm, but it was a battle he was quickly losing.

Three

Emil Guyot, in his Tommy Bahama Hawaiian shirt and what had once been cream-colored trousers, looked like he belonged on South Beach. Walt perused a copy of the man's California handgun registration, learning what little he could from it.

"So, Emil, you understand that possession of an automatic weapon carries a minimum sentence. Idaho has very liberal gun laws, but on that one we're kinda strict." He added, "Be advised that I'm running a recording device"—pointing to his iPod—"just so we don't get into who said what."

Emil mugged for Walt but didn't speak. He was, no doubt, on orders to wait for Holms's attorneys.

"The only hope for you on the gun charge

is to have it dropped altogether. There's no such thing as a lesser charge when it comes to customizing a weapon. Not in this state."

"I've got nothing to say to you. I'm waiting for my attorney."

"We're all waiting for something," Walt said, pleased that the man had started talking. "For one thing, I can't drop the charges without an attorney present."

"You're not dropping any charges."

"No, you're right. I'm adding to them," Walt said. "How's capital murder suit you?" He had to give it to the guy: He wouldn't want to play poker against Emil Guyot. "A guy like Stuart Holms? Amazing businessman. A legend, I hear. Probably a pretty lousy husband. His love is for money and power, and since women love both of those, too, it comes down to control, and that can get nasty. I'm recently divorced—or about to be. Something of an expert. He's probably a good guy to work for though, right? You must make five, six times what I do—"

"Ten."

"Ouch," Walt said. He leaned down and set the plaster cast on the table with a thump. It was enclosed in a large plastic evidence bag marked as he'd instructed Brandon. Then he pulled out the small evidence bag containing the blue contact lens. He spread Fiona's crime-scene photographs out like fanning a deck of cards, where the handcuffed Guyot couldn't help but look at them. "You strike me as a gambling man— a man who knows his way around a deck of cards or a gaming table. I've got some odds for you. In case you're wondering why we collected your shoes a few minutes ago, it's because of this." He patted the plaster cast. "Thankfully my job doesn't require too much thinking. It all comes down to the evidence. Juries just love evidence. The TV show *CSI*? That's helped us prosecute cases in ways you wouldn't believe. Juries eat this stuff up. They understand it better. They *believe* it."

"Fuck you."

"Me? What'd I do? You're the one who killed her."

"Fuck that."

"We're taking plaster casts of your shoes right as we speak. By the time they dry and are compared to this," he said, patting the bag again, "any opportunity to plea-bargain is gone. Tell that to Holms's attorney. Gamble all you like."

"I'm not talking to you," Guyot said.

"Then what do you call it?"

Guyot stared back with a stoic face.

"He promised you a ton of money, didn't he? Promised you he'd get you out on appeal if anything went wrong and that you'd be rich as Croesus when you got out. The thing is, he was talking about the Shaler thing. Trevalian. And maybe he's right. Maybe he could get you out of that at some point. He's a powerful man, as I understand it."

"You have no idea. He'll have you chasing traffic tickets before this is through."

"No. It's through already. It's over, Emil." He held up the blue contact lens. "You know what that is? The lab uses fumes to develop prints on certain surfaces. They can develop prints on human skin, on fabric—on things you wouldn't believe. Contact lenses, for instance."

Walt pushed back his chair, poured himself some more coffee, and sat back down, making a point of his fatigue.

"You guys heard about us going into the pound, didn't you? Word got out—it's a damn small valley and people can't keep their mouths shut, and that doesn't help me any, I'll tell you what. Once we made that connection, I imagine Mr. Holms became a bit concerned. The idea had been to blame it on a cougar, right? But you L.A. guys don't spend enough time here: two separate cougar attacks in two days? Are you kidding me? Not in ten years. Twenty. Forty. Not ever. And when Holms realized we'd figured out you dumped her in the cage, when he knew we'd be looking at murder, he overreacted. You both did. He let his jealous-husband side take over. You should have been looking for that."

"You been smoking contraband from the evidence room, Sheriff? You better watch out for that."

Walt went absolutely still. He let a minute pass. Then another. To both men it seemed much, much longer.

Then he took a deep breath, let out a long sigh, and let his true emotions color his voice. "You picked the wrong car, asshole." He waved the bag containing the contact lens in the man's face. "Danny Cutter wasn't driving the Toyota, *Patrick* was. Danny's the one Mr. Holms wanted framed for this. Not Patrick. We were all over Danny until we found the contact lens. This contact lens.

The one on which they developed a latent print. The blue stuff: That's what the fuming does—turns any oils from fingerprints blue. But Patrick didn't kill her—we can account for every second of his existence. And Danny never drove the Toyota. Duh! You should never have gone along with trying to frame Danny. You've got to learn when to say no to the boss."

Guyot had lost all his color and found it impossible to sit still. His upper lip held a sheen of nervous sweat, and his eyes could no longer risk finding Walt's.

"He's in the other room, right now, hearing about this same evidence. He's being offered a deal, a plea bargain. Now, who do you think is the better deal maker, you or Stuart Holms? Who do you think is going to come out on the short side of this one? When you found that contact lens, you should have just thrown it out. Those are your prints on it, right? We'll be comparing them in the morning. They sure as hell aren't his. Hers, if you're lucky—but I don't think you're all that lucky, Emil. And forget about him ever springing you for this. You go down in this state for capital murder, they throw away the key. Welcome to the Wild West."

The man was breathing hard. Like a runner at the end of a race. All that pent-up anger and frustration straining at the edges of his eyes and pursing his lips to where they'd gone white.

"Never follow the wishes of a jealous husband," Walt said. He thought of Brandon and Gail.

He waved in one of his deputies to keep an eye on the man, but stopped at the door and jiggled the bag holding the contact lens and the other one holding the plaster cast. "You think either of these is going to implicate Stuart Holms? No. And he knows that. He was counting on that. That, and the power of your greed. He knows all about greed, Stuart Holms. All he needs is for your greed to buy your silence through the trial. Then he's home free, and you're the one in the orange suit."

Four

Fiona ran off a series of photographs as Stuart Holms, Emil Guyot, and Milav Trevalian were walked out of the Sheriff's Office in orange jumpsuits and wearing manacles. Some stragglers from the First Rights gathering, including Bartholomew, were contained across the street by the new city hall, chanting and waving their fists. Walt couldn't make out their slogan.

Several of the national reporters had remained in town for the 3 P.M. news conference conducted by the assistant United States attorney. There would likely be even more press by the time the convoy reached Boise, a good two-hour drive.

"He confessed about two minutes after Holms's attorneys arrived," Walt told Fiona.

"This was around three A.M. They walked right past him and went in to talk to Holms, and Guyot had a total meltdown. Lousy customer service, it'll get you every time."

"But you said Holms will get off?"

"I said guys like him always get off. Who knows?"

"His poor wife."

Walt had a couple of things to say to that, but he kept them to himself. Tommy Brandon was one of the deputies helping to get the two into the waiting vehicles—the suspects were being driven down separately in their own Suburbans. The feds had bigger budgets. Dryer and his men were part of the escort. None of the three would have any further contact with one another until the various trials. If there were trials.

"And Trevalian?" she asked.

"A lot of this is still up in the air. We caught Trevalian shortly after my own people tried to arrest me outside of Liz Shaler's. He's no newcomer to this. He thought he knew the location of the person who'd hired him, and he parlayed that into a quick deal with the AUSA." He answered her bewildered look, "Assistant U.S. attorney—and was promised a maximum of eight years if he cooperated, which he then did. He led us to Stuart Holms.

"He and Guyot," he continued, "will both do time. Either one could benefit from further plea-bargaining. There are a lot of stories to tell."

"I'd like to hear your story. The one you wouldn't tell me," she said.

He wondered about asking her out for dinner. Not a kiss-at-the-door kind of dinner, just food shared across the same table. The spark was there for a minute, but then it faded behind an aching fatigue that warned he might not wake up for days.

Brandon caught them standing together, maybe caught a glint of the spark Walt had felt, because he looked quickly away when Walt busted him for staring.

As he walked past them, he spoke to Fiona. "He tell you about the contact lens? Frickin' piece of genius." And he continued into the office.

"Genius, huh?" Fiona said, trying to make Walt look at her.

"At some point I'm likely to wake up," Walt said, watching the Suburbans pull out, one by one. "And when I do, I'm going to be dying for a cup of coffee." *Start small,* he was thinking. *Work your way up to lunch.*

"So call me," she said.

"I will."

"I hope you will, but fear you won't."

He drove home alone. Took a shower alone. Sat down on the bed alone with plans to call Mark Aker about the dog's condition, and wanting to follow up on Kevin's legal status. He looked forward to the girls being home and getting back some semblance of life. The phone rang, and he nearly didn't answer it, but something compelled him to—he had a hell of a time saying no.

"Walt?" Liz Shaler's distinctive New England voice.

"Your Honor?"

"You weren't going to call me that, remember? Forgive me for taking so long to call."

"Hardly necessary."

"You did it again, Walt. Saved me. I hope this isn't becoming a habit. I'm going to have to knight you, or something."

He could only think of clichés, and he didn't want to use one. While he tried to come up with just the right choice of words, she interrupted.

"I attended that conference for all the wrong reasons. Welcome to politics. And I listened to the wrong people. Most importantly, I ignored the few warnings you gave me, and I feel like a complete ass for doing so. I told you I was going to put my faith in you, and then I did the opposite, didn't I? The good news is, maybe I learned something here, and if I did, it's thanks to you, and that's all I really called to say: thank you."

He was too tired to play games with her. "I could say something like 'Just doing my job, Your Honor,' but it sounds so ridiculous that I'm trying not to. But that is the truth, more or less. I was just doing what I do. I like doing it. And I like you, Your Honor— Liz—so I'm especially glad it worked out. That sounds equally stupid, doesn't it? Sorry about that."

"No. Not at all. It's touching. Listen, I know a little bit about the differences between your father and you—it's a small valley—but if you ever have anything like an inkling to take your work to the federal level, I could pave the way, make the transition both smooth and rewarding for you. And if I happen to win this election . . . Let's not lose touch in any case."

"If you win this election and make Sun Valley your winter White House, you're going to give me a whole bunch of problems. Maybe I'll vote for the other guy."

"Don't you dare."

Walt thanked her for the call and sat on the edge of his bed reflecting on the past few days. He considered taking an hour or two to start his report before he forgot the details. But he fell asleep still sitting up, slumped down onto the bed with his head nowhere near a pillow, his feet touching the floor. Woke up twice from nightmares, the first involving Trevalian and his thumb on a white button; in the second, he was being mauled by a cougar. He never found his way under the covers. He slept, buck naked, on the bedspread, through the rest of Monday and into Tuesday.

And when he woke up, he made a phone call and headed for a cup of coffee.

ACKNOWLEDGMENTS

A special thanks to Walt Femling and the many outstanding officers of the Blaine County Sheriff's Office. Walt has allowed me to fictionalize his character, and just for the record, he and his father, Jerry, and he and his wife, Jenny, enjoy wonderful relationships—nothing like what is depicted here. Being sheriff in an Idaho county the size of New Jersey is no easy task. Walt has worn that badge many years, and the citizens of Blaine County owe him a huge debt, as do I.

Thanks to the colorful personalities of the Sun Valley area where I've lived, at least part-time, for the past twenty-six years. I've fictionalized many friends in these pages, and I beg their forgiveness.

Thanks too, to Dan Conaway, my editor at Putnam. I owe him for hours of work and guidance put into *Killer Weekend.*

Thanks, too, to Nancy Litzinger, who runs the business side of my life; to dear friends David and Laurel Walters, who put in copy-edit hours on the manuscript; to Joey Lambert for all her enthusiasm and energy in the office.

Thank you, Mark and Randy Aker and the Sun Valley Animal Clinic, for allowing me to sit in on canine surgery, and to Barb for her help with the dog training.

Though I fictionalized it, I did my best to represent the business conference as a compilation of many of the (sometimes unbelievable) events (and excesses) that occur in the Ketchum/Sun Valley area. No reference was intended to any one single conference.

ABOUT THE AUTHOR

Ridley Pearson is the author of more than twenty crime novels and several books for younger readers. He and Dave Barry co-wrote the award-winning children's novels *Peter and the Starcatchers* and *Peter and the Shadow Thieves*. In 1990, he was the first American to be awarded the Raymond Chandler Fulbright Fellowship at Oxford University. He lives with wife, Marcelle, and their two daughters, dividing his time between St. Louis and Hailey, Idaho.